HARVEST AMERICAN
Writing

The Book
of Mercy

KATHLEEN CAMBOR

The Book
of Mercy

A HARVEST BOOK

HARCOURT BRACE & COMPANY

San Diego   New York   London

For Glenn

Requests for permission to make copies of any page of this book must be sent to:
Farrar, Straus & Giroux, 19 Union Square West, New York, NY 10003.

Library of Congress Cataloging-in-Publication Data
Cambor, Kathleen.
The book of mercy/Kathleen Cambor.—1st Harvest ed.
p.   cm.
ISBN 0-15-600519-0
1. Middle aged men—Psychology—Fiction.
2. Obsession (Psychology)—Fiction. 3. Alchemy—Fiction.
I. Title.
[PS3553.A4277B66   1997]
813'.54—dc21   97-24442

Text set in Garamond No. 3
Designed by Fritz Metsch and Linda Lockowitz

Printed in the United States of America
First Harvest edition 1997

A C E F D B

ACKNOWLEDGMENTS

THE AUTHOR WISHES to acknowledge the Cultural Arts Council of Houston for its generous assistance during the preparation of this manuscript. For help, inspiration, and support, thanks go to Jack Thornton, Beverly Lowry, Cynthia Macdonald, Rosellen Brown, Donald Barthelme; and to Roger, Carolyn, Stephen, and Glenn Cambor—especially Glenn, who was, for a long time, my only reader. I feel a particular gratitude to Laura Furman, who first published me; Heather Schroder, who "found" me; and John Glusman, whose vision and careful attention to detail helped so much in giving the book its final shape. And for their love and understanding, for all they've taught me, great thanks are owed to Kate and Peter. In many ways, this book is theirs.

Sorrow concealed, like an oven stopp'd,
Doth burn the heart to cinders where it is.

WILLIAM SHAKESPEARE, *Titus Andronicus*

Ash on an old man's sleeve
Is all the ash the burnt roses leave.
Dust in the air suspended
Marks the place where a story ended.
Dust inbreathed was a house—
The wall, the wainscot and the mouse.
The death of hope and despair,
    This is the death of air.

T. S. ELIOT, *Four Quartets*, "Little Gidding"

The Book
of Mercy

Prologue

O N   T H E   F I R S T Sunday of every month he sits at his
window waiting for her. He is Edmund Mueller, eighty-
three years old, weak in the knees, his vision failing. But
handsome still, with formidable arched cheekbones, a shelf of
wiry brows, dark eyes, the wrinkled skin of a seaman or ad-
venturer. And tall; even in his chair; he sits erect, his back is
straight, his chin is raised.

When he was young he was a fireman, sure-footed, quick.
But now it takes him a long time to do even simple things.
So on these Sundays he gets up at 4 a.m. to wash his face and
brush his teeth and comb his ragged white, intemperate hair.
He dresses up for her: faded khaki pants, a plaid flannel shirt,
a bright red cardigan, Adidas running shoes—everything a
gift from Anne, she is always bringing gifts. He refuses breakfast on these Sundays, won't leave the window to go to the
cafeteria. The aides are stubborn, won't bring him a dough-
nut, or a piece of toast, rules are rules, give in to one stubborn
old man, they'll all get ornery, just want more and more. So
he goes hungry on these mornings. His stomach rumbles.
Lightheaded, weak, he doesn't care. He has his cane propped
against the wall beside him, a loose-leaf binder in his lap. The
room is small and institutional—a single bed, a worn pine
chest of drawers, a little metal desk. Bookshelves that he built
himself in O.T., then filled with his books, photos, and formulas. He can cross the room in three steps, but he keeps
what he needs right beside him, he wants everything close at
hand. When Anne gets there he doesn't want to lose a second,

he wants to walk with her, to talk. So quiet all these years, he has a million things to say.

His room is on the eighth floor, a corner room. He has the pleasure of two windows. One has a western view across a broad expanse of lawn, and from there he can watch the light show of the setting sun. The other window looks out onto the parking lot, the trees that line the drive. It is his view of life outside, and he spends long hours in his wing chair looking out. Delivery trucks and gardeners, milkmen, young men and women, supplicants, dressed up, nervous, applying for a job. This wing of the building is called the Tower, and it makes him think of young Thomas Aquinas in another tower, the one at Monte San Giovanni, kept prisoner by his mother, who wished to keep him from his priestly life. On this morning Edmund wonders what Aquinas saw from his tower window, what dreams of escape he dreamed. Edmund knows he'll never leave this place, doesn't even want to anymore; he has his books, he has made friends. Escape, his great preoccupation when he first came, is not the issue anymore. Talking is the issue now, getting all things said. Two months ago, he dreamed that he was sick, he dreamed he died with all his secrets in his heart. And for the first time since he came here, since the accident, he yearns for a confessor.

He hears her car speeding down the highway before he sees it. She's made this monthly trip for six years, but never slows down in time to make the turn. She hits the brakes fifteen feet past the driveway. He hears the squeal of rubber, the whining of the engine as she reverses and backs up fast, makes the wide swing into the parking lot. The area marked "Visitors" is just beneath his window. She has barely stopped, the car engine is still put-putting when her door flies open and she jumps out. Everything she does is fast. She has a doctor's impatient step and style, and also a doctor's somewhat arrogant, brusque look, a certain set of chin and lips, a not-so-ready smile. Hers is a reserved, aloof, and self-protective stance, and Edmund is glad for her, glad because he believes her toughness saved her.

The sight of her moves him. She is forty-two years old, nobody's baby, but he loves her more now than he ever has before. She has his mother's voluptuous full mouth, his straight back and broad-palmed hands. But her Irish mother's freckles cut a swatch across her cheeks and nose; she has her mother's soft, come-hither violet eyes. And even though her hair is wisped with gray, she still looks young to Edmund, like a freckled schoolgirl posing for a photograph, sitting on a fire truck with her father.

She has his grandson Max with her today. He's thirteen, in love with basketball. Even as he walks, he pantomimes dribbling—three quick steps, a sudden turn. He pauses with his hands above his head, pushes off with one foot, makes a long imaginary shot. His T-shirt is an extra-large; it comes down to his knees. His gait is as loose and easy as hers is purposeful and sure. His light hair curls uncontrollably; that and his glasses give him the look of a slightly wacky genius. His wit is sharp, his mind is quick and analytical. There's nothing he can't do on a computer, he has told his grandpa with a stunning lack of modesty, but his real love is making music on a complicated electronic synthesizer with a four-volume instruction manual. He gave Edmund a Walkman for his birthday. Every time he visits he brings another tape of music he's composed himself, and Edmund takes it, and even though it sounds like so much noise to him, he listens to it. He gives it his attention.

There is a long flight of faux-marble steps leading up to the front door. Anne, hair flying, takes them at a run. Max bends to tie his shoe. Edmund rises slowly from his chair, takes up his cane. Max looks up, sees his granddad at the window, waves, and grins. For Edmund, his smile is a flash of light.

Anne

I PRACTICED LEAVING HIM for years.
Even on the night he made me promise I'd stay, he knew the time would come when I would leave him. I stayed out all night for the sake of pure defiance a dozen times in high school, drove with a boy I barely knew to Niagara Falls to see the sun rise in the spring of the year I turned seventeen. Called my dad from a phone beside the road at 5 a.m. to say, Surprise, I'm gone, the sun in Pittsburgh never looked so fine. Kid stuff, what kids do. But I knew every time I left he thought of Fanny, and those thoughts brought a tight sick feeling to his gut. I left anyway.

"I am not my mother," I said every time he tried to talk to me about it. I looked coldly at him, flipped my straight hair back defiantly. "Nor am I Paul. I always come back home. I'm almost a grown woman, seventeen. I do my part." Then softer. "It's O.K. You shouldn't worry."

But when I started talking college in my senior year in high school, he balked, dug his heels in. "What need is there of that?" he asked. But even when he frowned and cursed and banged around the house, I knew he'd give in finally, that for me, the baby, he had what he always called a soft and stupid heart.

There were many things I didn't know about my father when I was young. I know him better now. I go to see him once a month. I carry his loose-leaf binder for him, and he holds onto my arm when we leave his room to walk the grounds. His bent fingers press into my flesh.

"I'm thinking about getting married," I said the last time
I was there.

"Hmph," Edmund offered. He had gotten the rubber tip
of his cane stuck between two of the flagstones in the path.
There are eight miles of flagstone sidewalk winding through
the grounds, and he knows every inch by heart. The nurses
say he walks alone; every time I come he walks with me.
When his cane got stuck he cursed, and let go of my arm so
that he had both hands free to struggle with it.

"Did you hear me?" I asked.

He twisted the cane. No luck with that. Then he bent over
to try to pry it loose. No luck again. Finally, impatient, he
stood straight, wrapped both hands around the handle, and
gave it an upward yank with all his strength. It popped free
so suddenly that it sent him stumbling backward, into the
blossom-laden branches of a lilac bush.

"Careful." I reached out to him, but he's proud, not used
to help. He shook his head no to my offered hand, righted
himself, and with great dignity brushed the feathering of lilac
petals from his sweater sleeve. Then he became courtly;
courtly is his favorite thing. He made a slight gentlemanly
bow, then offered me his arm so we could continue on.

The flagstone path forked at a cluster of forsythia bushes.
The right arm of it trailed behind a row of blue spruce. After
a quick glance over his shoulder to be sure we weren't being
followed, he disappeared into the trees, signaling for me to
follow.

He sped up once he was hidden by the blue spruce. We
were heading toward a row of benches near the wrought-iron
fence that surrounds the property. There was a stand of flow-
ering pear trees, an as-yet-unplanted stretch of dirt beside
them. He motioned for me to sit on a bench, then dropped
carefully onto his knees in the grass beside me. He removed
his rubber cane tip to reveal a sharpened point, which he could
use for drawing in the dirt.

I'd sent Max back to the car to get my sweater because I wanted to talk to Edmund alone. "I said I'm thinking of getting married," I offered again.

"Why?" He licked his finger, paged through the sheets of his loose-leaf binder, searching for a diagram.

I laughed. "Why not would be a better question, don't you think? I've never been, it's way past time."

He shrugged, adjusted his bifocals on his nose, and began to draw. It was the athanor again.

"I thought things were fine for you and Max," he said, but without real interest; he was focused on the task at hand.

"We *are* fine, but . . ."

"Then what's the point?" he interrupted. The body of the athanor was broad and wide.

I fought the urge to chew a tendril of my hair, a childhood habit. "Maybe I'm in love," I said.

His head snapped up. "Are you?"

"Maybe." I shrugged.

He shook his head. "Not good enough."

"Not good enough for what?"

"For getting married. You should be desperate. You should be . . ."

"What?"

He turned away from me. The motion of his hand was sweeping as he drew the athanor's tall fuel-containing tower.

"What?" I asked again.

"You should be crazy in love." He took a handkerchief out of his pocket. Blew his nose.

There was dirt under his fingernails. I could see what looked like a small skin cancer on his cheek.

"It should be as if you can't breathe without it. It should feel . . . essential."

"Sounds dangerous." I pushed my hair back from my face.

"That's why there's magic," he said patiently.

On my April visit he taught me a spell that would enable

me to see what others cannot see. In May he tried to give Max his swallow's heart, preserved in formaldehyde in a Heinz mustard jar. A talisman against forgetfulness.

Edmund Mueller is an alchemist. I am a psychiatrist. There was also Fanny his wife, and Paul my brother. An old house in a grimy city. Now there are just the two of us, and Max, my son, and what Edmund draws in the dirt between us.

He's been in this place for six long years, and all that time his doctors have been waiting for him to talk, to tell his story. They're young and eager, they believe in the healing power of telling. So we're talking. To them, to one another.

We lived in Pittsburgh, and he was a city fireman. He drove the back of a hook-and-ladder truck. The tiller, it was called. They don't make them anymore. The streets are wider now, no need for maneuvering through alleyways that were meant for carts and horses. But it was a big deal when he was a young fireman, an important job, and he loved it. When I was growing up, each June on the day that school let out for summer, he took my brother Paul and me to the fire station and let us sit on the tiller, behind the wheel, while another fireman took a picture of us posing in the sun. He had a real thing about that fire truck. He carried a tin of Turtle Wax in his hip pocket, went after any spot or smudge he saw. The tiller's flank was mirror-bright. Edmund held me up so I could see my reflection in it. "See how beautiful you are?" he'd say.

For years when I was growing up I thought I remembered that he took me for a ride one day, that I sat next to him behind the wheel. So real was that memory that I could feel the sting of rain against my cheek, could feel the steering wheel rub a welt across my leg as my father veered around the corners. I could see the fire dog, Eugene, running in the street beside us, keeping up despite our speed, panting, going faster, until his black spots blurred into the whiteness of his skin as he became a thin pure streak of gray light flying at our side.

Once I became old enough to know that such a thing couldn't have happened, that fire trucks never carry children, I began to doubt all my memories, of what it was like in our house, of how my parents were to me and each other. Yet, even today, I can close my eyes and see the buildings passing, that fierce look in Edmund's eyes. And there is still a slight trace, just a shadow of a brush-burn scar in the soft flesh of my thigh, where the steering wheel would have rubbed against me as it turned.

What is real and what is just imagined? What does any of it mean?

From the beginning of medical school and on into my residency, I was struck by the lives people lead, the stories they tell. I live in Philadelphia now, I have a private practice, do some research, teach. "Stories?" my students challenge. "What about the truth?" And I say, Forget truth, what matters is the way it felt, the tale you tell about it.

My specialty is infants and mothers. How they come together, how they fit. "Tell me," I say to the women I interview. "What's it like for you?" I have pages of history on hundreds of women, hundreds of feet of videotape of their babies. I go over the tapes again and again, frame by frame, with colleagues, students, alone in the video room. In the bowels of the hospital, the basement in the dark. Chewing the eraser of my pencil, smoking. Curling strands of hair around my middle finger, like a kid in second grade. Max calls me Marie Curie, he wonders what I think I'm going to find. I can be as flip as he can. The secret of the universe, I say, and I'm only half kidding. What is it about mother love that makes so much of life revolve around it? The need for

Fanny fueled Edmund, Paul, and me. No matter how we all pretended, missing her was at the center of everything we did. When ordinary living couldn't satisfy our hunger for her, we all turned to magic, nothing less would do. Alchemy, God, psychiatry. Extreme attempts to fill the void, but I guess that's how big the void was. In many ways we hardly knew her, rarely talked about her. One day we just went our separate ways and took up magic. We are Edmund the father, Anne the daughter, Paul the priestly son. This is our story.

"Tell us." His doctors are insistent.

Edmund

CURRIE ARRIVES early on the morning he's to begin the interviews. His starched white coat slaps rhythmically and stiffly at his leg as he takes the stairs by two. The hallway lights are on, the sky outside is darkening quickly, the clouds he sees from the windows on each landing are black roiling masses, heavy with approaching rain. A roll of thunder sounds in the distance.

At the sixth-floor landing Currie pauses, winded. He checks his pockets one more time for pen and pencil. Checks his dim reflection in the window, adjusts the tie knot at his neck. There is a long scar down the length of his left cheek, like a pale thread, barely visible, the result of an accident that occurred the summer after second grade, just after his parents were divorced. There had been ugly fights between them, vindictive efforts on his father's part to keep Currie's mother from him. A bitter time, and the scar, the just perceptible tug he feels whenever he speaks or smiles or yawns, is a constant reminder of it.

As he continues up the stairs he wonders, is his hair too long? The Wizard, as the nurses call him, is old. He probably won't like the ponytail. "Mr. Mueller," he says aloud, practicing the patient's name, the tone he'll use. Authoritative. Calm. He is a very self-contained young man. He'll be poised and reassuring, interested without seeming overeager.

At the door of Edmund's tower room he raises his hand to smooth his hair, and takes one long deep breath before he knocks.

Edmund, at his desk, looks up from the ellipse of light pooled on his open notebook, clears his throat, and bids him enter.

So young, Edmund thinks. He looks like Paul did at his ordination. Angular and lean like Paul as well. The bones on his wrist are protruding, almost sharp when Edmund reaches out to shake his hand. All the young doctors have been thin. Don't these young men eat? Don't they understand the meaning of that gnawing aching pain that hunger brings?

Edmund reads his name tag, then gestures toward the armchair. Sit down, Dr. Currie, he says. Be comfortable. By all means yes, take notes.

He has his swallow's heart in a tiny jar beside him, an aid to memory. Shimmering in the lamplight like a tiny silver fish in its miniature formaldehyde sea. Not on his person as St. Albert's book of spells suggests, because it stank, they said when he first came here. The formaldehyde bath had been a compromise. But, in spite of that, the power of the swallow's heart stays with him. His memory is sharp, his mind is clear. Could we go back to the beginning, the young man wonders, and Edmund nods. He's ready. He closes his eyes and lays his hand across his heart and he is there, in Pittsburgh . . .

Born the year that pictures moved, his mother used to say. The Nickelodeon, the first all-motion-picture house in the country, opened on Smithfield Street in 1905. She took the trolley. They showed *Poor but Honest* and *The Baffled Burglar*. She was Botticelli-beautiful, with rounded hips and breasts, a sweet broad mouth, a full, expectant upper lip the color of crushed grapes. "I waited in line in the summer heat for hours, heavy with you, feeling with my hand the way you shifted in my belly. I had heard these motion pictures were like magic, and when I saw . . ." He can almost hear her, see her in the kitchen of his boyhood, peeling apples at the sink, bloodying her finger with one small careless move. She shook her head and closed her eyes and sucked her wound. "Pictures moving, brought to life before my eyes, you kicking back and forth inside me." She turned to look at him, used the back of her hand to brush a stray hair from her alabaster cheek. "Anything seemed possible. I thought those moving pictures were an act of God. A miracle," she said. "Like you."

And he *was* a miracle.

He survived rheumatic fever in the flood of 1912. What his mother thought was a head cold moved overnight to hot red swollen joints and fever, and a merciless delirium. She said she slept there on the floor beside his bed, never left him that whole week, because every movement pained him and he whimpered for her. The more it rained, the more she feared for him, remembering the way the rivers rose when he was two, and turned the North Side streets into canals. If the rivers rose again there would be no way to get a doctor. His mother's eyes filled every time she thought of that long week.

He remembers none of those details. All he remembers is the way his skin burned, the hotness of his own short breaths, and the sound of blowing rain on window glass, then rushing water as the rivers rose up suddenly to fill the streets outside his window.

After eight long days his fever broke. His mother crossed herself, and took it as a sign from God.

Pittsburgh in those days was as black a place as there could be. The mills spewed filth into the air, then a west wind blew black clouds of it into the city, where it hovered before settling down and becoming part of everything it touched. Sometimes in the middle of the day the sun was hidden, the skies were black. Streetlights were on. In the photograph of him taken on the morning of his First Communion, May 12, 1913, it was so dark the details of his face, his folded hands cannot be seen. Only his white suit is dully visible. Like a photographic negative. Edmund, the boy, the First Communicant, is missing.

Steel *was* Pittsburgh then, it's what brought so many people to the city, what made them stay. Italian, Serbian, Irish. German like his father. They were all called Hunkies, and thirty thousand of them worked in the Homestead mill alone. The boys he went to school with all had fathers who were mill hunks or miners. For school field trips, they went on steel-mill tours; they had a guide who gave a lecture, then showed them grainy photographs of a man posed next to a blast furnace, for scale, for contrast, to show how insignificant man was, compared to fire. The chimneys of the mills shone like bright flares through the smog; you could see them when you couldn't see another thing for miles. Their number doubled by their reflections in the Allegheny and Monongahela Rivers. If you had the money and the time, you could take a boat trip downriver on an old-fashioned steamboat called the *Homer Smith*. It was the thing to do when he was in his twenties. You'd stand on the upper deck with your girl as if there was a view. You'd try to touch her in the dark, as you churned downstream through the watery reflections of the mills, pretending you were someplace beautiful, pretending you were in love.

Sometimes there would be an accident in a mill. A news flash on the radio. A steel worker would get careless, lose his footing and fall into a blast furnace. When Edmund heard about it, he stopped what he was doing, sat and listened. Then he tried to imagine the moment—the surprise, the pain, the blinding light. He tried to imagine it, in the blackened afternoons, carving in the woodshop with his father.

He was required to call his father Sir, and always thought of him as such. Never Father, certainly not Dad. Sir was a serious religious man, trained to be a carpenter. He thought he'd be a priest when he was growing up in Bremen, he had nurtured in himself a priestly haughtiness and pride. His woodwork was without compare; his prayers, profound and pure. In his dreams he was an aesthete, a monk, a celibate. Until he saw the Botticelli beauty at an early-morning Mass, until he saw her vulnerable expectant lip, and fell into a fever of wanting. Until, finally, wanting ruled him. He waited for her at the statue of the knight Roland, pride of that coastal city, then followed her—to church, to school, to market. He knew by some pure instinct every route she took, the pattern of her days, her habits; that she loved peaches, that her favorite color was cerulean blue. And because God allowed him this complete, almost instinctive knowledge of her, he let himself believe that God *wanted* him to have her. He spoke to her, and she thought him handsome, if a bit severe. He wrote long poems for her, odes and sonnets, in praise of God and love and maiden virtue. He was twenty-five, she was only seventeen; her parents disapproved. So he simply took her, stole her, slipped into her house and fled with her into the night, onto a boat where he'd booked passage. He left Germany behind and came with her to Pittsburgh, where he never for one single moment felt at home. He hated it, the mills, the trolleys, the ill-bred foreigners who swarmed the streets. Only *she* was home. Sometimes at night Edmund would lie awake and listen to his parents through the thin shared wall between his room and theirs. He heard Sir moan and call her name—at night he lost himself in her. Edmund saw his marks on her in daylight, the way he'd bruised her with desire. Then Sir spent his days repenting for his lust. He worked long hours for contrition: chairs, claw-footed tables, ornate stair rails for the Pittsburgh rich. Desks for bankers, high chairs for bankers' babies. In what little extra time he had, he carved figures of saints. Fifty, then sixty, then a hundred wooden statues, each a perfect replica. Chiseled wrinkles in thin, chiseled faces, deep folds in chiseled robes. St. Agnes, Martyr, with a sword sliced halfway through her arched, extended throat; St. Edmund, for whom his son was named, the young Angle king, pinned to a tree by arrows in preparation for his pickax torture by invading Danes. St. Luke, St. Bernadette, St. Oengus, the abbot-bishop. He gave them to Catholic churches, Catholic schools, then filled their house with them. He put these statuettes on kitchen cabinets, on dressers. They adorned the mantel, the sideboard in the dining room. There was one poised in the shadow in the right-hand corner of each stair.

A lonely life. Their North Side neighborhood was filled with Irish immigrants, whom his father treated with disdain. Young Edmund had no siblings. His parents never wanted company, never needed friends. For a weekly family outing they'd go to Mass on Sunday morning, sit in the back of the church, then come home to a lunch of sauerkraut and sausage. Grace led by Sir, the meal eaten in silence, the sigh and nod directed at his mother when the meal was ended. "It was good," he'd say, while the boy Edmund watched and listened. Such meager praise, but it made his mother flush with pleasure. It was all Sir had for her and it seemed that it was all she needed.

Under Sir's tutelage, he learned to handle a saw and carving tools before he was old enough for school. It was all his father ever wanted for him. To be like him. To *be* him. He took Edmund with him for some part of each day to the wooden dirt-floored shack he rented just off Chateau Street and sat him on a high stool he'd made especially so that the boy could reach the workbench. Even now, in his day and night dreams, Edmund sees them sitting in that workshop. Formal, separate, silent. When Sir did talk, it was always about Bremen. The old days, old country. How fine a thing it was to work with wood. Cutting, sanding, shaping wood, wood shavings in their hair and lungs, like grit between their teeth. Sir shaped his boyish hands around a saw, a chisel, he learned to make a level edge by sight, by feel. So great was his gift that he did not need to think or calculate or measure. And for this, and only this, Sir noticed him. There were days Edmund even thought Sir might have loved him. His father made him his apprentice. He planned the life they'd have together. Sir's given name was Joseph. Edmund was to be the savior son.

Sir read *Lives of the Saints* to the boy instead of fairy tales. The tales of passion, courage, their lavish spirits filled Edmund's dreams. The martyr Polycarp was burned alive, and when they pierced his charred body with a spear, a dove came forth. It made young Edmund wonder, did some winged spirit live inside of him? What luck or fate or miracle would take him out of his small world? He thought of young St. Edmund when he dreamed of leaving home, of making some new life.

"Fire. Go ahead," says Edmund. "Ask me anything."

Thomas Currie looks up from his legal pad. "Excuse me?" he says, flushing slightly. "I'm sorry. I don't think I understand."

"I said, ask me anything." Edmund gestures to the books on the shelf behind him, then recites from memory.

A frame of adamant, a soul of fire,
No dangers fright him, and no labors tire
or
I am bound upon a wheel of fire, that my own tears do scald like
molten lead
or
Double, double toil and trouble;
Fire burn and cauldron bubble
or
Ladybug, ladybug, fly away home,
Your house is on fire, and your children will burn.

He knows more. He has a notebook full of them, he says. Fire phrases, fire poems. After he became interested in magic, it seemed that everywhere he looked, there was fire. He dreamed about it, even after he was retired, even when his fire life seemed years away. He thought he smelled smoke in the house at night, he feared spontaneous combustion. He put a hook into the wall above his bed at home, got his old hat out of the attic, put his boots beside his bed.

Fire, fire, burning bright . . .

Fire in the books he reads, fire in his dreams. A flash of lightning ripped the darkened afternoon outside his window, cut a fiery trail across the sky.

Bring me my bow of burning gold:
Bring me my arrows of desire:
Bring me my spear: O clouds, unfold!
Bring me my chariot of fire!

After high school, Edmund went to work for Sir. School friends took jobs in steel mills and factories, and, being newly hired, worked mostly nights. Because of this they drifted from him and he spent more time alone with Sir. Claw feet, newel posts, and pie-crust tables. At night he went out with girls he knew, or stayed home in his room, where he listened to the radio, and read the paper. The Great War and news of it had filled his boyhood. It seemed to have brought the whole world closer, and places he had never heard of were pictured in the *Pittsburgh Post* and *Post Gazette*. In elementary school he had clipped those pictures, saved them. Isonzo, Gallipoli, Le Havre. At the war's end he read interviews with young men just a few years older than he who had seen, had battled for these places. In photographs they posed with arms thrown around one another's shoulders, and glasses raised, and to Edmund they looked wise and seasoned, proud of what they'd faced. Enlarged by their membership in the fraternity of man.

For four years after high school he tried to be satisfied with what he had. He spent time with his few friends, had several casual but satisfying love affairs. In his work, he took pride in his competence and craftsmanship. Reeded bedposts, rosettes, acanthus leaves—he was a much-sought-after master carver, and he was aware of and moved by the beauty of the things he fashioned out of wood. But even with all that, he found himself yearning for another life, a life where luck and risk came into play, with comrades by his side and powers to be defeated.

He liked everything about the idea of being a fireman. The excitement, the danger, the chance to be a hero or a prince. The dress-blue uniform, dark serge, a knife-like crease down the center of each pants leg, patent-leather visor on the cap, in which a man could see himself reflected. "Very fancy," said his mother. His father's eyes were wells of rage and disappointment. He spit onto the floor.

Job security, pension, opportunity for advancement. Edmund knew what to say. His mother raised her eyebrows, nodded, begrudging her approval, but he could see that it was there. That she was proud to see him become so much of a man so suddenly. He was twenty-three, he'd even found his own place, two rooms above Czernowski's Bakery, a hot plate and a cot, the radio which he took from home. Every day he felt his step get lighter, he felt admiring eyes on him when he walked to the fire station for his shift. Cocky, he heard the older men say, but he didn't care. He breathed onto the visor of his cap, pulled his jacket sleeve over his palm, and buffed the visor with it until it glowed. They'll see, he said to himself about the older men. They'll see.

They slept upstairs, above the garage where the trucks waited. Bunk beds, not too comfortable, but comfort was for other men, not them, they slept only in fits and starts. They were vigilance made flesh. Their rubber coveralls laid out across the bottoms of the beds, hats and jackets on wall hooks just above their heads. Edmund became so tuned, so sensitized, he could feel the first vibrations of the air before the fire bell rang. He'd be sitting up and pulling on his rubber pants before it sounded. Down the pole, just like you see in movies. Calluses on palms formed early, and made the sliding easier. Once on the truck, he could feel the engines throbbing, hear the screech of the doors as they ground open on their tracks. He saw Eugene, the fire dog, straining at the rope where he was tied so he wouldn't rush into the night to follow them. The priming of the siren, the sudden jerk as the truck lurched forward, out the door, lights flashing, their yellow slickers catching air and billowing like flags. Stopping traffic, stopping time. The intersections they barreled through were still as photographs. The night stopped. In deference to them.

He learned to smell the smoke from blocks away, he watched for the sky to begin to lighten, as if from the tip of a rising sun. Each time, he felt his heart pound, his own heart filled his chest, it echoed in his ears until they made the final turn into the red-hot stunning light.

He was on the job five years when they were called to a three-alarm on Penn Avenue at an old-folks home called Little Sisters of the Poor. Before they were even off the trucks, they heard screaming, saw old men and women crowded into two narrow open windows on the fourth floor. Flames were already shooting through the roof above them and the floors below, fingering toward them up the wall. The nuns who cared for them had tried to save them, two were burned on arms and hands, the others huddled around them, praying, crying, tending. They were like ghosts in their white nightgowns. Their shorn hair made jagged shadows on the sloping lawn.

How many times did they run up the charred, collapsing stairs to carry someone out that night? How many times did they climb those ladders as they trembled in the whipping February winds? Did he go in a dozen times that night? Three hundred rescues in his long career? You don't remember later, you just remember breathing deep and running. He was on the ground easing a half-dead woman from his shoulder when he heard the building moan and crack and splinter as the last of it gave way. And as he looked up, the front wall fell and the top floor folded in and brought the whole roof with it. The earth shook as the blaze mushroomed high into the air and threw a brilliant rain of sparks across the lawn and the bodies lying there. The sky filled with a violent light.

Forty-two old people died. They found them in the early morning, when the fire was out and the heat subsiding. They pulled them from under beds and smoldering mattresses, wrapped them in blankets, lined them up on the trampled muddy grass. It was almost an hour before they realized one of theirs was missing too, their tillerman, Gus Marusic. Edmund's first death. He felt it for a long time. He feels it still.

He volunteered for Gus's job. He wanted to be skillful, steady, fearless like he thought Gus was. And so he became the tillerman, the driver of the rear end of a hook-and-ladder truck. One driver in the front, a fool of a driver in the back, adding to the danger of the flames the danger of the too-quick turns in alleys meant for horses and buggies.

"Don't be stupid, kid," the older men said. "It's a hell of a thing, trying to get around the corners, trying to second guess the guy in the front, while you're going like a bat out of hell." But he knew he could do it, he knew he'd be good. And from the beginning he was a natural, with razor-edge reflexes, a steady hand, a certain spatial sense, a kind of daring that astounded, and then astounded even more as he got better, better, at the tiller, on the ladder, dragging fifty pounds of hose up dark, steep, smoke-filled stairs. He was more careful for a little while, right after he found Fanny, but when he began to lose her, he became a wild man and a fool. Taking corners on two wheels, rushing into burning buildings when there were no lives to save. For the hell of it, for the feel of his heart pounding again, as it did in the beginning when he first fought fire, when he first let Fanny do the tango's backward dip into his arms.

She was nineteen when he met her, with an angel's face, a turned-up Irish nose, curly white-blond hair. Eyes like violet pools. Little, light-boned, made for dancing, and dance she did; fox-trot, samba, tango, waltz. Her hips swung like nothing he had ever seen, when she walked, to the rhythm of the music at the Two Step Dance World, Tuesday nights and Thursdays, too, if she'd worked a double shift and had the cash to pay. He was walking in the snow down Jacksonia Street on his way home from the station when he passed the bright lights of the Two Step. It was new to the neighborhood, a converted grocery, with red and orange lights blinking out its name. There was a plate-glass window facing the street, so passersby could stop and watch, and when he slowed down there was Fanny, thrown back in her instructor's arms: stiletto heels, long leg extended, a flash of thigh as her full skirt flew up around her. Her long hair touched the floor when her back was arched that way. He caught her eye and grinned. She looked away.

He signed up. Feigned interest in the dance, as Fanny would say later.

"You don't know me, but may I walk you home?" he asked after his first class, deciding that he'd take a chance on boldness.

She looked at him and popped her gum. "I don't ordinarily talk to strangers," she said primly. "I've got a reputation to uphold." She used every inch of her small body when she talked, her shoulders shifted, her small hands fluffed at her hair. Proud and sassy, she was something else indeed, in a ruffled blouse and full gored skirt, purple as a plum, or, as she called it, "lavender," a color very big that year. Red lipstick, rouge. No shyness, no pretense, not one shred of Germanic distance, cool reserve. When she walked, she wobbled on her too-high heels. But when she danced, she was transformed.

"You are elegance and grace," he said, a poet in her presence.

She grinned again and took his arm. "Well, I suppose, this once, I could make an exception to my rule."

They stopped for coffee at an all-night diner, another exception to her rule, a good sign. She slid into the booth beside him, ordered coffee and a BLT. She put three packs of sugar in her six-ounce coffee cup.

"I never have to worry about weight," she said when she noticed him watching. "I can eat and eat and eat and never gain an ounce. I'm small-boned. Also, dancing burns up a lot of energy." She touched the sleeve of his uniform. "So, what are you?" she asked. "A cop? A sheriff?"

"A fireman." He placed his blue hat on the table.

"No kidding?" She took her gum out of her mouth and stuck it to her coffee saucer, saving it for later. "An honest-to-God fireman? Full-fledged? Out there on the truck and everything?"

"On the truck and everything," he said. The way she smiled made every risk he took on the job seem worth it.

She bit into her sandwich, chewed but kept on talking.

"So, tell me," she said. "Are you scared? I mean, when you're out there, with your hose and hatchet and all that stuff, do you ever think, 'Oh *god*, what am I doing here?'"

"No," he lied, "it's second nature to me now. I never feel afraid." With another girl he might have said, "Hell yes, I'm scared sometimes." But he guessed right away that that was something Fanny wouldn't want to hear.

"My hero," she said, teasing. She licked the mayonnaise from her upper lip, and let her tongue linger there.

"So, do you really think I am elegance and grace, or is that just a line you firemen use with girls?" Blushing a little, fishing for a compliment. "Now be honest, tell the truth. Am I Ginger Rogers?"

She pushed the sleeve of her blouse up as far as it would go, and held her arm out like a ballerina. He wanted to run his fingers up her arm, into her dress. He looked down at his coffee, sure that if she looked into his eyes she'd know.

"Ginger Rogers, absolutely."

She liked the flattery and liked him well enough to let him walk her home. He took the long way, through the park, and she talked non-stop, fine with him. Her voice was gravelly and gruffly sweet, and since he didn't have to make conversation, it gave him a chance to look at her as they passed under the streetlights. At the corner of Erie and Arch Streets she stopped and pointed.

"There it is," she said. "That's where I live."

He saw the awning stretch from building front to sidewalk. Saw the mortuary sign.

"There?"

"Yeah," she said. "Upstairs. My daddy owns the business."

"An undertaker?"

"A *mortician*," she insisted, and pulled herself up to her full height. "There's a perfectly fine apartment upstairs, big enough for all of us, my folks, my brother and me. Jimmy, that's my brother, will get to join the business when he's older. My dad's training him already."

He tried to imagine it. The sounds of loss and mourning just beneath her feet, seeping through the floorboards. The murmur of the rosaries said, the strangled sobs. He asked her what it was like, and she said it was nothing, that she'd grown used to people wailing, the way they cried and threw themselves on the caskets.

"Which only goes to show you, a person can get used to anything," she said, chewing her gum, swinging her purse at her side, keeping time to the music in her head. He almost kissed her then, he wanted to move her behind the bushes to the summer grass and take her. But he was almost thirty, he'd been chasing girls and women long enough to read them, and he knew that such a move would be too much too soon. But that night he made a vow that before the summer ended, she would love him.

From the start he could tell that Fanny's parents were a little strange. Her mother wore a black high-necked dress all the time, whispered even when she was upstairs, off duty. Her father had the red-faced look Irish drunks get, but his liquor never made him noisy. He got quiet, got a slit-eyed lusting look about him that he often turned on Fanny. Her brother, Jimmy, had greased-back hair, and a swagger when he walked which he no doubt hoped (mistakenly) made him look ominous and tough. Edmund always tried to picture him downstairs, offering condolences to strangers, in a black suit and dark tie, with dirt under his fingernails and acne on his oily skin. But Fanny's dad was optimistic. "He's going to be great," he said, slinging down a shot and gesturing toward Jimmy. "A fine technician."

What living the O'Learys did was done in the kitchen, a whiskey bottle on the table, the smell of sausage and fried bread. Fanny had read somewhere that a man should be kept waiting, so Edmund spent more time in the kitchen than he wanted to. Sometimes Mr. O'Leary tried to make small talk, asked questions about his work. "How's business? Firebugs keeping you busy?" Then he'd laugh at himself and look back and forth from Edmund to Jimmy, waiting for them to laugh with him.

Fanny's dad took Edmund to the basement once, handed him the scalpel that he used to make the small cut in one artery, one vein, and he explained how you inject preserving fluid into the artery, and watch the blood drain from the vein into a bucket. The smell of formaldehyde made Edmund sick, and he hated the way O'Leary nudged him and winked when he talked about Fanny.

"Quite a gal, now, isn't she," he said, as if they were two guys in a locker room, talking about some loose girl. His breath smelled of whiskey. "I've brought her down here, too." He pointed to the table where he laid the corpses for embalming. "Showed her how it's done."

Edmund never knew how Fanny stood it, living there. She played her music even when her mother frowned and shushed her, walked downstairs past mourners, with her head high, in her makeup and dazzling clothes. "We've spoiled her," her dad told him. "Let her have her way." Her parents and Jimmy did their share, her mother kept the books, the record of the Mass cards sent, the flowers. Everyone had work to do. Only Fanny got off free. "She is our little ray of sunshine," her dad said. "Our baby girl. Our star."

Did he come to hate her? Easy enough to say no, no, of course not. How could he hate Fanny when he was crazy in love with her?

"Or just plain crazy." This from his father. Sometimes on his days off, Edmund would go over to work awhile with him. Once he had his own place, he didn't mind going home or to the shop so much. He liked the almost soothing sound of saw and chisel after three months of tango music, six years of fighting fires. His mother cooked for him or mended socks, even when he said, "I'm a grown man, Ma. I'm almost thirty years old, I can mend my socks myself."

"So, why doesn't this fine girlfriend mend your socks?" His father, in a gloating voice, glad to discover that Fanny couldn't cook or sew, glad to have a reason to dislike her. Edmund had brought her by to meet them early on.

"She's cheap and brassy, and you're a fool," his father told him. He was sitting at the kitchen table, carving a cross into the crown of St. Henry, Emperor. "There will be trouble with her later, wait and see." Edmund kept his mouth shut, he'd made up his mind not to fight with him, but the more fault Sir found with Fanny, the more he wanted her. Damned perverse, but there it was. He'd leave his parents' place on Sundays after supper, leave his father in the parlor muttering, and go to Fanny. Wait in a receiving room among the mourners for her flash of color to appear.

Fanny was a telephone operator in the days of switchboards: "Number please?" Making connections by day, dancing by night. Between fires, he'd use the phone; obsessed, eager, hoping that of all the operators working every shift, he'd get her.

He saw her almost every day; she never wore the same dress twice. The way she looked was everything to her. He knew he should regard this as a flaw, but couldn't, it hypnotized him. He volunteered for extra shifts, stepped up his betting in fire-hall pool and poker, trying to save money to get married. He used his father's tools and workshop and started making furniture: a carved frame for a full-length mirror, a bookcase, a dining table with two leaves, twelve truss-legged chairs, a bureau and an armoire for the trousseau he knew Fanny would have. He felt set apart when he was with her. As if she was his reward, his prize, some rare pearl he'd found. She washed her light hair twice a day to keep it shining. He waited for her to get discouraged, about Pittsburgh, about the grimness and the darkness and the dirt, like everybody else, but she never once faltered. She bought a red dress, red shoes, a lemon-yellow chiffon picture hat, one in crème de menthe. Patterned skirts and striped blouses, flowers in her hair.

"I am blinded by your beauty," he told her on Tuesday nights as she spun away from him into the waiting arms of her dance instructor. Mourners in her father's mortuary found the rhythm of bereavement broken by the one-two of the samba as it sounded through the ceiling and quivered in the walls.

She bought him Hawaiian shirts and silk scarves. She didn't like the way the brown stain from the furniture he was making marked his hands. She told him it was unbecoming for her partner, so he scrubbed them till they chafed and bled.

"Give it up," his father said.

He took more chances than he should have on the job so that he could tell her tales of courage. He offered burns and bruises as evidence of daring. In August, he kissed her underneath the mortuary canopy, him in blue serge, her in pink chiffon, the two of them a blur of life and color in the midst of all those dark, veiled figures waiting at the curbside for the hearse.

His fire life, of course, continued. In February 1934, an Akron–Pittsburgh passenger train, speeding into the North Side station, careened off a bridge at Merchant Street and onto the busy avenue below. The whole block burned. Bodies lay in mangled pieces in the crushed and burning wreckage of the train. Nine dead. Scores injured. Then the *Homer Smith*, the boat on which he'd toured his city's rivers as a youth, burned at its moorings. St. Patrick's Church, a public school, homes, saloons, brothels. He was cited twice for bravery, then twice more for rescues made during the St. Patrick's day flood of 1936. He and his comrades saw more death than young men should have. Sometimes he feared that he was becoming hardened to it.

Then, right after Christmas, his father had a stroke that

left him paralyzed completely on one side. Sir hated the hospital, so Edmund's mother took him home too soon. He couldn't speak, and his helplessness and muteness brought forth a meanness in him Edmund had never seen before. Once he swung out at his wife with his good arm when she was trying to feed him. Another time he sent a bowl of hot soup flying at the wall.

Neighbors brought stews, cabbage soup, and dense dark steamy bread. Fanny wouldn't fool with the stuff of daily life; instead, she brought flowers, rescued wreaths and bouquets from caskets, rearranged them, covered coffee cans with colored paper to use as vases, and set them everywhere. "A shame to waste them," she said, pursing her lips, surveying all she'd done. She put eight coffee tins of flowers in the sick room alone, as if wild color and sweet smell was medicine, so good you couldn't get enough. Carnations on his bedside table, next to the jar that held his false teeth, out of reach of his good hand. Sir grimaced, drooled, tried to scream at her but couldn't. Edmund's mother whispered to him. "No more," she begged, gesturing to the flowers. Edmund told Fanny how he loved her.

His father died in May, and as if they'd made a pact, his mother's heart stopped two weeks later while she slept. Leaving him alone in life. An orphan. The only things of theirs he kept were the woodworking tools, and the statues of the saints.

"Saints?" said Fanny, an unenthusiastic Catholic.

"Saints," he said. "My dowry. Companions of my youth."

It took three months to sell the furniture, collect insurance, and when he did there was a little cash. Added to what he'd already saved, it was enough to put down toward a house he'd seen on Jeffers Street.

They married in the fall of 1937, had a fire-hall reception with a Puerto Rican band Fanny's dance instructor found in Cleveland. To please her parents, she wore a long white dress and veil, wishing all the while for shocking pink. She hid her rouged cheeks, kohl-lined eyes, and cerise lips behind a thin white veil. When he carried her across the threshold of the house on Jeffers Street, she giggled like the girl she still was. The mailman stopped them on the front stoop to introduce himself, and Edmund shifted Fanny's weight so he could shake Alphonse's hand. But all the while his eyes were on his Fanny, dressed in a striped orange ensemble, grains of rice still clinging to her hair, a peony big as a grapefruit tucked behind her ear.

After all the months of waiting, they made love like two lost souls who'd found each other. Their best time, the time when they were happy.

Fanny changed almost everything in the house. She painted over paper in the parlor, shamrock green walls with burnt orange woodwork. A saffron ceiling for the eggplant dining room. *"Aubergine,"* she corrected him. "O-bear-jean. I looked it up," she said from the top of a ladder, a paintbrush in her hand, a spot of purple dotting her cheek. They saw every dance movie ever made, went out dancing three times a week or more, and he got better at it, glided with her smoothly, cheek to cheek. Exhausted from those late nights, he got careless at the tiller and almost hit a milk truck once. At dinner (canned beans, burnt chops, Fanny didn't like to cook), he told her what had happened, that he'd lose his job if he didn't get more sleep. She smiled understandingly and nodded, but when he finished talking, she pushed her chair back, took his hand, and kissed it.

"Dance with me," she said.

The days were boring for her once she got the house the way she wanted it. She'd already mastered every dance step that was current. Sirens sounded, he rose to the occasion, became known and much admired for his skill at the tiller, for his bravery and nerve, the first one to rush in to save a toddler or a dog. Addicted suddenly to danger.

He thought a baby was the answer, that Fanny would keep busy with the things a baby needs, but Fanny pregnant was no different than Fanny thin and small. She wore multicolored ruffled smocks, hummed rumba music, stomped out the rhythm in her same stiletto heels. Even in her ninth month, her feet edematous and sore, Fanny swayed.

How could he have known? There was nothing to prepare him for her decline after the baby came. She wouldn't even choose a name, he had to do it. Paul Douglas. What did he know about babies? Nothing. He thought he'd be scrawny, red, and ugly, but he wasn't. A head of fair curls and light eyes like his mama's. A dream baby, Edmund thought, the kind of baby any mother would love. Not Fanny. Her milk dried up in her breasts at the sight of him.

"What the hell?" he asked the doctor the day he was supposed to take her home. "What's going on here? She won't touch the baby, she won't do a thing for him. What am I supposed to do? I've got a job to go to, we've got to eat, I can't stay home. Is she going to snap out of this or what?"

The doctor called it postpartum depression. "Give her time," he said.

"What does he want from me?" Fanny asked, sullen, angry, lipstickless, her hair tied back in a plain dark bow. Driving home in their old Buick, Edmund gripped the steering wheel until his knuckles were white knots. The baby lay between them in a cardboard box he'd rigged to be a carrier when she informed him that she wouldn't hold the baby going home. "Hypodermic syringes, 10cc, #50," the box said on the lid and each side.

"Look at those eyes," Fanny said. "He's accusing me. He expects me to do something, to give up my whole life for him."

"Just pick him up," Edmund said. "He'll be great. *You'll* be great."

Fanny glared at him.

"What do you know about it? I can't take care of him, Edmund. Don't you get it? I've never taken care of anything in my life. How do you expect me to start now?"

Her voice was rising to hysteria's high pitch; the baby jerked awake and started wailing.

"C'mon, Fan. Now you've got the baby going."

"You see?" she screamed. "Now it's my fault that he's crying. My fault! So, Mr. So-Smart-About-Babies, you know so much, you shut him up, you do it!" And he wanted to kill them all then, him, the expert behind the wheel. He wanted to run into a tree, anything to shut her up, to make Paul stop screaming. The truck behind him honked, and Edmund pulled over to the side of the road so abruptly that the box almost dumped Paul on the floor.

Edmund put his head down on the wheel to calm himself, and before he could reach for her, Fanny was out the car door, walking off. Leaving him with the screaming Paul.

"Shh. Shh," he said, and jiggled the box, as if jiggling him would shush Paul, but it only made him scream more, until his little face was red and he looked as if he could hardly get his breath. Edmund didn't know quite what to do, so he offered him a knuckle, the big one on his second finger, and Paul's lips and gums clamped onto it so hard and fast it hurt. Paul sucked and sucked, and seemed to get enough flavor from Edmund's sweaty rawhide hands to satisfy him for a minute. They were only blocks from home, but he was so grateful for the quiet that he sat there for a good long time, changing knuckles when Paul became restless or started whining. Finally, it was almost dark and a light breeze came in through the window he'd wound down, and Paul, who had worked his way on down his hand and was gnawing on his little finger, finally closed his eyes and fell asleep. Edmund closed his eyes, too.

"You're a good kid," he said. "A good strong kid."

He was strong, and it was a good thing, too. Fanny meant what she said. Nothing changed. She took to her bed. Edmund got the wife of a friend from work, Tess Jankovich, to come and take the baby when he couldn't be at home. She had two kids of her own, it was a lot to ask, but she and Mike were friends, they'd gone out dancing together, and she'd always liked to flirt with him. Then after four months Fanny rallied, he came home and found her dancing with the baby in the orange-and-green parlor. Since Paul was born, he'd gotten used to coming home to a dark house, turning on the lights and starting supper before he walked the two blocks to the Jankoviches' to pick up Paul. So he'd stopped expecting lights and sound, and the smell of dinner cooking.

"Edmund, is that you?"

And there was Fanny, dressed and waiting—her hair brushed, a dash of color in her cheeks. Fine, she was just fine, she said. She could not for the life of her imagine what had happened. She had fetched Paul and was just about to feed him. Tess had shown her what to do. She talked too much too fast, but her voice was bright, red lipstick shaped the mouth he'd always loved. He took her in his arms and kissed her hair, her neck, her ear.

"I told you," the doctor said, when he called him later. His voice was smug, self-satisfied. "Sometimes they just snap out of it."

"Yes," he said, "I guess so. But I'll tell you, she seems wound up tighter than a spring."

"Now, I hope you're not complaining. You should be glad she's out of bed."

And he was, he was. Glad enough to think that everything

would be all right now, fool enough to think that they could keep things going. She wasn't great with Paul, God knows, but good enough, he told himself. Sometimes she let him cry too long, or slapped him when he flailed around and knocked a spoon of strained pears from her hand. Another man, a better man, might have noticed, worried more. But he just wanted to be glad and grateful, drive his tiller, come home to a house where things were, if not great, at least O.K.

Paul was kind of fussy, not the easy kid his early good looks seemed to promise. He was tense and edgy, as if he wanted something that he couldn't get. An early walker, he wasn't even a year old when Edmund would go to pick him up and Paul would toddle fast and grab him, as if he was afraid he never would be held again. Edmund asked Fanny what she thought.

"I think you worry too much," she said, crunching a piece of celery between her teeth, doing a little two-step from the table to the stove. "He's just a kid, for God's sake, kids are always scared or fussing or complaining." Then she'd bend to kiss Paul on his forehead before she sashayed to the sink, and Edmund would think, There, you see, she loves him. You're a damn fool, the way you worry. Then he'd put him down and kiss him too, and say, Lucky lucky boy, the way your mama loves you.

Fanny's good times didn't last. Six months of Fanny in her bed, four months of Fanny dancing and O.K. A peak-and-valley life. Why did he stay? Because he couldn't give it up. He'd been raised to be a miracle, a savior. How could he not believe in himself, in the power of his love? Fanny was everything to him. He thought if he stayed steadily beside her long enough, the force of his enormous love would make her whole and his again. So each time she came around he convinced himself she'd come around for good, and nobody would tell him differently. There are names now for what was wrong with Fanny, there are drugs to treat it. But then there was only a general practitioner, the falsely hopeful reassurances of friends. Hormones, nerves, "she's just high-strung." Sometimes she'd be fine so long (thirteen months when Paul was two) he'd think, Jesus, this is it. But when she took to bed that time, he saw the writing on the wall. He hired an Irish girl, Kathleen, to come to tend to Paul, worked double shifts and did without to pay her.

He thought the war would save him. He went to the recruiter the day after Pearl Harbor, thinking he'd just leave, take up a gun and go. But rheumatic fever had left his heart with a murmur that the Fire Department physical had somehow missed, and the army wouldn't take him. He went out and drank himself blind that night, then woke up at the station house, in his bunk, with John Schlusser holding his head while he threw up on the floor.

The last year of the war was Fanny's best year ever. She listened to the radio, made a rough map of the world which she tacked up on the kitchen wall. She used bright-colored pins to keep up with the battles waged on every front, rolled bandages at the Red Cross or poured coffee for servicemen at the USO downtown. She made what she called "connections" there and auditioned twice for dancing parts in traveling shows, as if she'd just pick up and go if she got called. "This is not just fun and games." She lectured anybody who would listen. "There's a war going on, and I'm trying to do my part." Both times, they chose another dancer over her. She pouted, took more dancing lessons, got her hair cut in a short blond bob. VE-Day was crazy on the North Side, car horns honking, strangers hugging strangers in the streets. But Edmund worried, knowing as he did that the war's close would leave Fanny at loose ends. In the middle of that night he woke to see her standing at the window, her arms crossed, her right foot tap-ping, so much restless energy balled up inside her she seemed like someone about to run.

Six months later she was pregnant. The baby was a girl. They called her Anne.

When Anne was ten months old, Fanny's dad died and left her everything he had, having long before decided that Jimmy didn't really have the calling to a life as a mortician. In a surprising show of energy and business acumen, she sold the mortuary.

"A nest egg," Fanny said. "The very thing I need."

And as suddenly as they'd descended, Fanny's dark days lifted. In the wash of light that followed, she saw a new life for herself, unburdened by responsibility. Two weeks after the mortuary closing, she packed a bag and left a note and took off on a trip she said she'd always dreamed of. She'd come to realize that what she'd had with Edmund had been a false and temporary thing, a youthful error, and she had awakened, fi-nally, to her true vocation, she said in a long letter after she was gone. A career in dance, show business, theater, life on the road. She took up travel with a missionary's zeal. Leaving Edmund to manage in that house alone, without even the short reprieves of life and music that they'd had since Paul was born. Reprieves he'd come to count on. Over the next few years she returned from time to time, but only for a day or two. A quick stop, a two-day stint as doting mother. A stranger, really. To him and to love's requirements. And when he thought of how he'd loved her, what he'd hoped for and what he'd lost, his heart grew cold. Alone in bed at night, as weeks, then months, then years went by, he'd lie awake and listen to the city sounds outside his window, and feel what had once been his fierce, firefighting heart grow dull and heavy in his chest.

Just as well, he finally decided. He turned the basement

into a woodworking shop, and when he wasn't fighting fire, he retreated to it. He carved saints and birds and intricately shaped whistles, made furniture to sell for extra cash. He learned to cook, took Kathleen as a lover—easy, convenient, she'd grown thin and kind of pretty in the course of her employment. She'd come early in the morning, and they'd make love in his room in the first light, then be up and dressed and cooking breakfast by the time the kids came downstairs.

And somehow, after Fanny the Heiress took off on her first long trip, he more or less handed the children over to each other—Anne to Paul, especially. Kathleen took care of dressing her or bathing her, but she only worked until four each day, and after that, Paul had to be in charge. He was only seven years older, too young, Edmund realized later, but he was tired, and didn't know what else to do.

Did he love them? Yes, he did. But he thinks now that he was also rather frightened of them. He'd bet on love, and then love failed him. He didn't want to take that chance again. So he kept himself apart from them—fought fire, or spent time lost in reverie down in his basement shop. Imagining the lives of the saints he carved. Admiring their miraculous achievements. Sometimes Anne would come to fetch him in the middle of the night, stand in her flannel nightgown at his elbow chewing on a tendril of her hair, and he'd look up to find her there as if he'd been awakened from a deep protracted sleep.

He tried. The children begged him for a pet, so right after Fanny started traveling, he went out and bought a canary, a pretty little yellow thing to take Fan's place. They called him Schumann. He whistled bars from "Scenes from Childhood" to him, hoping that the bird would fill the house with music. He taught Paul and Anne to dance, and they caught on fast, moved with their mother's natural grace. Sometimes he'd watch them, his dark, German children, remembering how he'd hoped for light-eyed blonds.

He took them with him lots of places that kids shouldn't

go—to Rosie's Pool Palace, to Brennan's place for Friday-night stud poker. But he was gone so much that he thought it was better for them to be with him. When they stayed home he sometimes kept them up too late for company. He showed Anne dance routines that Fanny showed him when they courted. Anne was hesitant at first, but finally, in this one thing, she came to trust him so completely that she'd fling herself into his arms with a wild abandon. She'd arch her back, extend her skinny leg, and let her brown hair touch the floor in the tango's final backward dip. Paul would watch, and change the records, call words of encouragement to her, and keep time to the music with his toe. Or turn away as if it was hard to look. Always glancing instead at the parlor door, as if he was expecting someone, waiting for his partner.

Anne

I WAS NAMED for the saint who was the mother of the Virgin Mary, an old childless woman who, after years of praying, finally and miraculously became pregnant. Edmund carved a wooden statue of her shortly after I was born, put it on a bookshelf in my room beside a stuffed giraffe, a plastic model of a B-52 that Paul had glued together, and a china Blessed Mother night-light. My dad's carving of St. Anne was an old bent woman, one hand on her aching back, the other on her watermelon belly. The plan in choosing saints' names for kids was to offer them a model, give them someone to emulate. Old and cross and pregnant was not anything I ever planned to be.

"Why Anne?" I asked my dad shortly after I began first grade. Those Catholics know the value of early and complete indoctrination. By mid-November, first grade, we'd worked our way through *Miniature Stories of the Saints*, the first three illustrated volumes, and I could see a lot of other names would have better suited me. "What about Agatha, or Joan, or Genevieve?" I pressed. I wanted to be brave and tender-hearted, beautiful and wise.

My dad shrugged. "We wanted something short and sweet," he said.

I was hoping for some more complicated answer. I wanted to hear that he and Fanny had kicked names around for months, done research, consulted seers, made endless lists of possibilities. All for me. It was during the time when I was still trying to believe that I had been at the center of their lives once, the answer to a prayer.

Fanny stayed home for almost a year after I was born. We have photographs to prove it. In most of these pictures, I look like a baby clown, in neon orange pantaloons or a fuchsia polka-dotted sunsuit. My mother used grosgrain ribbon bows to gather my dark hair into little tufts, and they stood out like the bristles of a paintbrush.

"You look like a pickaninny," Paul would tease me every time we saw those pictures. It was my hair, thin and smooth and plain, and I was sensitive about it. Paul kept after me at such times, teasing, goading, showing what would become in him, who could also be so sweet and good, a surprising capacity for hurting me.

The photographs of those early months all look the same. Me and my mother or me and Paul, or me alone with those stupid bows in my straight hair. When I'm ten months old, there is a sudden change. At Thanksgiving, my head is a wooly mass of curls. At Christmastime, my hair is gone. I'm in Santa's lap at Gimbels, crying and struggling to get free, one foot in Santa's crotch, one hand pulling at his beard. Bald and a baby again.

"I told her not to give you that permanent," my dad said every time he saw that picture. "I told her you were too damned young, that baby hair can only take so much." Paul said that it was shortly after that that she left. A straight-haired baby was one thing, bald was something else. She propped a note against the sugar bowl on the kitchen table. "Gone to California which I've always hoped to see." She wrote it on the envelope of my dad's payroll check, which she had cashed and used for her bus ticket. Edmund kept the envelope and taped it in the photo album just beneath the last shameful picture of my mother and bald me.

The house where I grew up on Jeffers Street was a row house. Red brick, one of a group of houses on two blocks on the

North Side of Pittsburgh which became known as the Spanish War Houses because they were built around the time the Spanish-American War began. The neighborhood has become very fashionable now, I hear from Kathleen, who sends a card at Christmas every year. But when I was growing up there, it was a slightly run-down ethnic neighborhood. German and Irish, a few Italians and Croatians. The city streets were cobblestone; streetcar tracks slashed through them. The trolleys made a sound like thunder. Paul woke me up once late at night and took me outside barefoot, in my nightgown. We walked the length of our block to West Montgomery Avenue, a busy thoroughfare by day, not a car or truck or trolley anywhere in sight at 4 a.m., in moonlight. I was five years old, it was a street I had been told not to approach or cross. Paul walked me to the center of it, had me kneel on the cobblestone, press my ear against the track, listen for the vibration of some distant trolley. It's how the Iroquois knew if the cavalry was approaching, he explained. They listened to the earth. "Pretend it's a hundred years ago." He dipped his finger into a small red paint jar he'd brought with him. He made a blood-red mark across my cheek. "Pretend you are a warrior. Pretend you're brave," he said.

Lou Lazarra's grocery store was just around the corner, Rosie's Pool Palace three blocks down Jacksonia Street, Nick Brennan's Beer Distributing was next door on our corner. The Brennans lived above their place, and their son Frankie played accordion—he practiced long and loud. In the summertime, with windows open, I could hear the "Beer Barrel Polka," the theme from *Laura*, "Oh Promise Me." He had plans to get a group together, play for wedding parties held at fire halls or in church basements. "He'll make his fortune," Nick would tell me when I stopped in after school. I liked to watch the conveyor belt move beer cases from the truck, liked to hear the bottles tinkle as the cases rode and quivered. I'd eat the pretzel Nick always gave me, salt first, vow that I'd have

Frankie play if I should ever marry. "I dance good," I would say to Nick, and he'd stop stacking beer to look at me, wipe his sweaty forehead on his T-shirt sleeve, shift the toothpick that he kept between his teeth. "I'll bet you do," he'd say.

Our house had two cement steps that rose from the sidewalk to a small front porch called a stoop. Right inside, there was a little squared-off vestibule with black-and-white linoleum, then a long hall, with the kitchen at the far end, and the stairs rising to the second floor, casting a shadow at the center. Wooden doors from the hallway opened on the left; one set led into the parlor, the other to the dining room. They slid on tracks to close when privacy was needed—on those rare occasions when Edmund wanted to have a talk with Paul or me, or if a fellow fireman died and he wished to be alone. The rooms, like the house, were narrow, but the ceilings tall. Just before the kitchen, a doorway to the right led steeply down into the basement; double doors from that space opened up and out into the tiny bricked-in backyard. Nothing grew there but a single buckeye tree.

There were three bedrooms on the second floor; the front room was Edmund and Fanny's. In the middle was my little box-shaped sunshine-yellow nursery. The back bedroom, Paul's, was a large rectangle cut in two by an open doorway and a wall with a window—an odd design made even more peculiar by the fact that there seemed to be no reason for it. It had never been an outside wall, had never needed windows. The whole divided space had been Paul's for seven years before I was born; he'd used one half of it for sleeping, the other half as a place for play, and there he built block bunkers and block castles, forts from which he fended off imaginary enemies. When I was a year old and Fanny took off for California, Edmund moved out of the room they'd shared and into my yellow nursery, and moved me in with Paul, as if he couldn't stand the thought of sleeping in their room without her. He

locked their bedroom door and kept the key, painted the nursery white, put a cup hook into the wall, hung his fire helmet
on it. My crib was moved to the front part of Paul's room,
requiring Paul to cram himself and all his belongings into
half the space he'd had. There was no exit from his part of
the room into the hall, so access to the hall and bathroom
could only be had by tiptoeing past my crib. Only years later
would I understand how much Paul lost during those months
after I was born: a mother, the space where he could be a
prince and conqueror, the simple ease of walking out the door
and down the hall to pee.

We went to Mass three times a week, Stations of the Cross
each Friday during Lent, confession every Saturday at four.
My dad didn't press too hard about it, but he was clearly a
believer. You could see it in his eyes at Mass, he got an almost
holy look when he received Communion. We had Butler's
Lives of the Saints, all four volumes, on the only bookshelf in
our house, and one hundred thirteen statuettes of saints arranged artfully in every room. Saints on the TV, atop the
icebox, lined up like salt and pepper shakers on the back of
the gas stove. Saints with names like Waudru, Eusebius,
names you never heard of, rescued from obscurity by Edmund
Mueller's skilled woodworking hands.

I took the Catholic stuff to heart. I could say the responses
to the Latin Mass when I was seven. I kept silence for a week
one Lent when I was eight, ransomed forty-seven pagan babies
in twelve years in Catholic school. I used to try to imagine
their lives in Ethiopia, Paraguay, the mountains of Brazil.
Willful pagan children living by their wits. We got to name
them when we ransomed them. At home I used the wooden
saints as stand-ins, gave them the pagan baby names, made
native costumes for them out of dust rags, dish towels, clothes
that I'd outgrown. Bridgette. Estelle. I told them secrets. We

had tea together, I made tea party conversation. "My mother's on a trip," I'd lie. "Her career in dance requires it."

Our elementary school was St. Bartholomew's, the nuns who taught us were Benedictines, a semi-cloistered order; pale, thin-lipped, ethereal. We were six in first grade when they got us; most of us had never been to school before. By the spring of second grade the nuns were supposed to have turned us into reasoning Catholics, capable of knowing right from wrong, worthy of receiving First Communion. First Communion was a big deal, and, given all the fuss and preparation, I began to think that it was going to cause some great change in me, that it would turn me into something special. Edmund even broke with his routine to take me shopping for my white dress and fingertip-length veil. One night when I ought to have been sleeping, I heard him phone his firemen friends, Jack Matranga, Pete Escudera, George Neuse. I knew he was planning a small party with a cake.

I studied hard, rehearsed with all my classmates, held a Necco Wafer carefully and stiffly in my mouth until it melted. (It was a sin to chew the body and blood of Christ.) I excelled at all the ceremonial details.

As the day of First Communion came closer, the nuns became more serious and vigilant about our spiritual lives. They posed questions of philosophy, of morals, devised tests of faith and conscience. Trying to determine, were we ready, were we pure. Sister Leonard had a special skill for weeding out the flawed.

"A little girl has led a perfect, exemplary life," she began one day. "A daily communicant, she honored her father and mother, studied the catechism, performed corporal works of mercy. But one Friday she was tempted by a vender selling hot dogs at a Pirates game. She succumbed to that temptation, bought a hot dog, took one bite, stepped into the path of a streetcar, was struck and killed."

Question: "What is the fate of this child's soul?"

Correct answer: "Her soul went straight to hell."

I knew what the right answer was, but in a choking rush of sympathy it was as if I was there beside that child. I heard the rumble of the streetcar, the thud of impact. I waited for someone in the class to speak in her behalf. When no one did, I raised my hand.

"What if the little girl saw the streetcar bearing down on her and truly repented?"

Sister Leonard frowned.

"Or . . ." In a flash, I thought of fifteen ways to save the soul of that poor girl. "Suppose a priest was on the trolley and gave Extreme Unction to the girl before her soul left her body? Or what if God was feeling merciful that day and gave every good child one free mortal sin, no remorse or punishment required?" I knew from the look on Sister Leonard's face that I had veered onto a rocky path, but I couldn't stop myself. Now, looking back, I wonder if, even at seven, I was anticipating the way my life was headed, and was trying to make a case for a willful girl, stopped in her tracks on the downward path to sin.

The nuns consulted with the parish priests. My First Communion was postponed until the exact state of my mind and soul could be determined. My class went on without me, and I was required to spend my lunchtimes with the pastor, Father Rogers, at the parish house. I brought peanut butter and baloney sandwiches to these lunches; Father Rogers ate tuna salad and drank a dry martini served to him by the overweight, adoring housekeeper. Together we reviewed my catechism.

"Why did God make you?"

"To know Him, love Him and serve Him on earth and be happy with him in heaven."

He lectured me on faith and morals, he cautioned me

against presuming I could ever know what might be in the mind of God. "Sin is sin," he said. "Best not to ask too many questions. Keeping it simple helps God's children keep it straight."

Finally, after eight weeks, he became convinced that I was ready. On a Thursday afternoon he heard my first confession, face to face, without the benefit of screens or secrecy, then invited me to the almost empty 6 a.m. Mass the next day, where I knelt in my glen-plaid uniform to receive my Saviour's body and blood for the first time, without pomp or celebration. No white dress or veil, no ceremony with my class, no sheet cake with a flowered icing cross.

Paul and I had been treated with suspicion from the first day we entered St. Bartholomew's—Fanny gone most of the time, a dressed-up, made-up tart when she was home. Edmund, mysterious, reserved, and darkly handsome. He never came to plays or PTA. What was going on at our house anyway? they wondered. But the incident of the girl, the streetcar, my feverish plea for mercy instead of punishment for sin hardened the nuns' vague suspicions about me into something stronger, and it sealed my fate in Catholic school. From then on, I was treated with a thinly veiled contempt and the sure conviction that the tilt of my chin and the upward thrust of my small nose spoke of a secret boldness, sinful pride. Sure signs that I would grow up to be flip and careless, Fanny Mueller's daughter.

Edmund, driven by loneliness once Fanny was gone, worked as much as they would let him. That left Kathleen, Paul, and me—Paul and me alone once she left for the day. I was the chain around my brother's neck, his little charge. There were days when he looked at me as if he wished that I were dead. I didn't care. He was tall, and older. I thought he was a king. I convinced myself that his disdain was a kind of manly turn-

ing from overt affectionate displays, that he secretly loved me
as much as I loved him. "Disappear," he'd sneer at me, and
I obeyed, biding my time until he realized my worth and
turned to me. While I waited I took up a kind of street life.
After school I roamed the neighborhood, spent time at Brennans (I learned "Three Blind Mice" on the accordion) or at
Lou Lazarra's store, where I swept the wooden floor for him
in exchange for an ice-cream sandwich. Some evenings Edmund went out, and in a fit of guilt over working so hard
and being gone so much, he took Paul and me along.

Rosie's Pool Palace was the firemen's favorite gathering
place, a low-slung, converted warehouse just a block from St.
Bartholomew's. It smelled of beer and cigarettes and cheap
cigars. Paul, by the time he was thirteen, was tall enough to
play. I was not, so, when we went to Rosie's, I hung out with
Rosie herself, the only other woman in the room. She had
blue-black hair, and her eyebrows were dark penciled arches.
Décolletage was the style of dressing she believed best suited
her; the crack between her breasts looked deep enough to fall
into. Rosie liked to think of herself as a businesswoman; she
had a desk with a blotter and a banker's lamp on it and it sat
importantly at the end of the long pool hall, thirty billiard
tables stretched in a double row. When I came to visit, she
cleared a corner of the desk for me and let me sit there, dangling my legs. Because I was made so welcome in the evenings, I assumed I would also be welcome there by day, and
Rosie's became one of my regular afternoon stopping places.
She kept crayons and a coloring book in the top drawer of her
desk for me, served Canada Dry and Wise potato chips, made
book by phone while I had my snack and colored. She smoked
long, exotic, foreign-looking cigarettes and blew perfect rings
of smoke over my head. She asked a lot of questions about
my dad. I came to think she had a crush on him, but she
seemed somehow beyond his notice. She bought me a silk

kimono, antique lace handkerchiefs; sometimes, after my potato-chip snack, she manicured my nails for me. Each fall she had her seamstress hem my uniform skirts. When I hit puberty, she readied me for breasts and periods. Linette her beautician cut my hair.

But Rosie's special expertise was men. On the evenings when I sat perched on her desk, I watched her look longingly at Edmund.

"Men," she almost whispered, blowing a perfect ring of smoke over my head. "Watch it, kiddo. They'll break your heart."

I became the neighborhood pet, breezy, smart, a kid who knew the score. A freckled face, a knowing smile, my hair pulled into what we called "dog ears," two ponytails, one above each ear. The women thought I was running wild; they rolled their eyes when they saw me coming. The men all loved me. When I got tired of roaming, I sat on our front stoop, counted cars, hummed along to the strains of Frankie Brennan's music. I had plans to join his band as his girl singer when I was older.

When I think now of my dad I think of how tall he was, and of how that tallness made him seem particularly able. He was six feet five. His dark hair whitened early, so that by the time I was nine years old, he was totally gray. He looked particularly distinguished in his dress-blue uniform, frowning, silver-haired and proud. He surprised me once in third grade by getting time off and coming to our Christmas pageant because I had a speaking part as an angel, and even the young chaste nun who was my teacher blushed and stammered when she shook his hand at the end of the performance. Elizabeth Anne Spillar, who played Mary, brought her arm out of the blue folds of her costume to stick her elbow into my ribs. "Your dad's some looker," she whispered to me, grinning. It was the first I'd really thought of him in terms of how he seemed to others, and it made me see him in a new light, as someone to be watched.

Paul became an altar boy in elementary school. He said it was because of Father Tim, who was young and brash, with a crooked nose he'd broken boxing. He cursed, he drank, he flirted with the nuns, who loved it. All the kids adored him. When he took charge of acolyte training, the boys at St. Bart's clamored to sign up. Paul joined the ranks when he was only ten and endured two years of apprenticeship, memorizing Latin rhythms and responses, learning how to swing the incense lamp and hold the paten.

"He lets us taste the wine," Paul said one night, over the wooden screen he'd rigged up in our room for privacy. "And he's going to take us to a camp for altar boys this summer, in the mountains, and we'll sleep outside like pioneers under the stars."

When I was old enough to read—I did that early, I'd do anything to be like my brother—I forced myself into Paul's male world by being the only one who would coach him in his altar-boy responses. Night after night, I played the part of priest, he my young attendant.

"Dominus vobiscum."

"Et cum spiritu tuo."

I spurred him on to learn more complicated prayers so that he could serve at special rituals, like the Mass on Maundy Thursday, the opening prayers of Forty Hours. I loved the quiet in our room at night, the closeness, the sound of my own droning voice as we rehearsed.

"Quare tristis es anima mea, et quare conturbas me?"

"Why art thou sorrowful, O my soul, and why do you trouble me?"

For three years, beginning just after my fourth birthday, we heard not a single word from Fanny. Usually she sent post-

cards chronicling her travels—Belvidere, Wisconsin; May-
field, Missouri; Normal (no doubt a bitter irony for Edmund),
Illinois. They were sent erratically, arrived with postage due
or with nothing more than "Greetings" dashed boldly, in
some brightly colored ink, across the message section. But
they let us know that she was alive and out there, and when
none arrived in three years, I began to think she'd never come
home again. Still, her mark on the house on Jeffers Street
seemed permanent. We kept everything exactly as she'd left
it. The Little Miss Toni permanent-waving rods she used on
my baby head were in a junk drawer in the kitchen. The colors
she chose for the walls and ceilings were nicked in spots and
faded, but were never changed. The ruffled curtains she'd ordered from Sears were taken down twice a year and washed,
then hung again. She had used the wooden saints my grand-
father and Edmund had carved for decoration. Saints as kitsch,
paper flowers in St. Jerome's folded hands, a pink chiffon scarf
around St. Cecilia's martyred neck, blinking Christmas lights
adorned the suffering Jesus' crown of thorns. In a moment of
religious fervor right after he started serving on the altar, Paul
declared this to be sacrilegious. Edmund conceded that it
might be, but he did nothing to change it. He always claimed
he didn't have the time, which was true enough, he worked
so many double shifts it seemed like we hardly ever saw him.
Then he worked in his basement woodshop almost constantly
when he wasn't fighting fire. Still, keeping the house so much
like she left it created for Paul and me the sense that he was
waiting for her. It was as if at any moment she might come
waltzing through the door. I'd made myself ready for it. I'd
memorized her face from photographs, found the key to her
room in Edmund's sock drawer where he'd hidden it, and
went through her things whenever I was alone. Paul always
laughed bitterly when he spoke about that room, he called it
"The Shrine." And so it was, and I a pilgrim to it. I tried her
dresses on, I lay down on her side of the bed, let my head

rest on her pillow. I pressed my face into her underclothes, wanting to know her smell, to be sure I'd recognize her when she came back to me.

And I did. When I was seven, shortly after my First Communion, Fanny came home and surprised me. I was playing hopscotch by myself on the sidewalk in front of the house. She stepped out of a long black car and opened her arms wide to me, as if she'd been gone twenty minutes, not three years. She kissed me hard and cooed my name. "Oh, how I've missed you, little bird, sweet Anne, oh, look at you, you are the sweetest thing." Amazing words, words that no one ever said to me. She took my hand. "Come on, now, Mama has a great surprise for you." And, mesmerized, I went right with her. Kathleen was gone for the day, Paul was at the park shooting baskets, Edmund would be coming home soon, I should have left a note but didn't. "Come on," she said, and without a second thought I was in the seat beside her. Karl was the name of the man who was driving—strands of black hair were combed from a low side part to cover his bald head; he smoked a fat, chewed-up cigar, flashed a thin and unenthusiastic smile at me. The car was his. My mother ran her hand across the dark upholstery.

We went around West Park, across the Duquesne Bridge, downtown.

"So you're *not* dead?" I said. On Paul's last birthday, after we'd had cake, he said he was sure she was, or else she would have called or come. She laughed out loud and Karl laughed with her.

"No, I'm not dead, am I, lover?" she said, leaning across me for a wet and greedy kiss from Karl. Then she placed her thin hand on my shoulder. "Do I look dead to you?"

I smiled uneasily. "No, ma'am," I said. I almost asked where we were going, but it didn't really matter. All I knew was that I'd waited and she'd come for me.

Fanny smoothed my hair. A light snow had begun to fall,

patches of fog were gathering along the river. We were down-town, driving past lit shops, barred windows, an old man sleeping in a doorway. Fanny pointed to the blazing lights of a movie marquee. "Lovely to Look At" was the film, Ann Miller the star.

"I named you for her," Fanny said proudly. "Just wait till you see her."

She was beautiful, all right. Dark hair upswept, the smallest waist. Her shoulders were white, bare, and shimmering. Red Skelton and Howard Keel couldn't take their eyes off her. Fanny swooned over the dancing and the songs. "Smoke Gets in Your Eyes," "The Touch of Your Hand."

"Isn't she something?" Fanny whispered. She rested one hand on Karl's knee, used the other to take popcorn from the box she'd gotten me. Along with Tootsie Rolls, and Good & Plenty, and black cherry soda, food I loved and rarely got. The man behind us shushed my mother when she whispered, but she went right on. "Except for her coloring, I think she looks a lot like me."

I looked up at my mother. Her fingernails and cuticles were bitten, her hair was white-blond, wildly curly, a wisp of a woman, pale compared to Ann Miller's dark charm. She looked a good bit older than the mother in my photographs. I feared she might be sick, then I convinced myself she was just tired and that's why she'd come home. I thought of ways I could take care of her, make her life easier, be so good a daughter she'd never dream of leaving home again.

"Oh yes," I said, the picture of cooperation. "You look exactly like Ann Miller." Then I sucked hard on a pink Good & Plenty, until the coating melted and licorice taste came through.

It was almost five when we got home. I got out of the car, expecting her to follow. I thought how surprised Edmund and Paul would be. But she said she and Karl had to be in

Wheeling, West Virginia, later that night, they'd better hit the road. I almost said "Why Wheeling?" but never got the chance, her getaway was well rehearsed and fast. Lies and promises—how soon she'd come back, how splendid it would be. She rolled her window down to wave goodbye, and blew light kisses through the air.

I don't know how long I stood at that curb before I went into the empty house. But it was dark when I stepped inside, and I had to fumble for the light switch. I heard the fire-whistle sound at Edmund's station, No 12, and knew from long experience that he'd be late. So I found an apron and started peeling carrots for the stew Kathleen had started. Thinking all the while that I was tired of stew, tired of cooking. Thinking of Fanny on the road. Wondering if she and Karl would stop, what sort of place a traveling mother goes for dinner. Wondering what Ann Miller eats when she's tired and by herself, after she's spent a long day dancing.

Kathleen came to care for the house and Paul and me before I was even born. When I was eight she left to marry Sean O'Hare, the butcher.

"I have got my future to consider," she said to my father, and I heard his voice go icy, as it does when he is proud.

"If that's what you want, I'd never dream of standing in your way."

I've often wondered why Kathleen never meant more to me. She was constant and reliable, she did what was required. But she was brusque and edgy with me, as if she was always in a hurry to get to Paul. Whom she loved. No, whom she frankly and irrationally adored. The first winter that I was in school, I was bundled up, in leggings, boots, overcoat, and hat, two pairs of mittens, hot as hell and champing at the bit to go. Waiting in the vestibule for Paul, so we could walk together.

"Do you have your lunch, now?" Kathleen said to him. "And your thermos? God knows you'll be needing soup by noontime, don't be forgetting your soup."

"Thank you, Kathleen, I won't." Paul was thirteen, polite, unsmiling, and, in his own small wounded way, intensely loyal to our mother. He'd had her longer, missed her more. So much so that he refused the little loving gestures coming from Kathleen—hot soup, ironed handkerchiefs folded in his pants pocket, mittens placed on the floor registers and warmed by the heat from the basement furnace. He slipped quickly out of reach each time she moved to touch him. On that morning when Kathleen gave him soup, and he turned coldly from her, I could still feel her hurt eyes on our backs when we were halfway down Jeffers Street.

"Don't you think that you should be nicer to Kathleen?" I asked. The wind was blowing hard and swirling snow into our eyes. I had to shout to be heard above it.

"I'm as nice as I can be," he said curtly.

"Oh, come on, you could smile at her at least. Or thank her for the soup. She doesn't make *me* soup. If you're not nicer to her, maybe she'll quit or something. We'd be in a real fix if that happened. We'd have to cook, and do laundry, and mop the floors. You want that?"

"Who cares?" he said defiantly. His favorite retort. "Who cares? Who gives a damn?" With anybody else I would have nagged and argued, it was part of the tough-kid way I saw myself, but I knew Paul wanted me to be quiet, and with him I always acquiesced. For him I'd bite my tongue or cut it off.

It was a long walk to school, made longer by Paul's sullen silence. Young as I was, bundled up for winter weather, sometimes on these morning hikes I tired out, slowed down as we got closer to school. And every single time I did, Paul took my strapped-together books and carried them for me, or took my hand and pulled me along a little faster. Small gestures, nothing really. Evidence, not of fondness perhaps, but of impatience. But they felt like love to me; he must have known that. And the memory of those things, my hand in his or the sudden lightness I would feel when the books were taken from my shoulder—those memories kept me going, far into the time when I was grown.

After Kathleen left, my father took up cooking with the fierceness that he brought to fighting fires.

"I'll need your help," he told me. "You're the girl."

He bought two new aprons and three cookbooks. Tess Jankovich came by. She kept tabs on us, especially after Kathleen left. Brought casseroles from time to time, even fresh flowers once, the only time they ever graced our house.

"Good idea," she said about the cooking. "But keep it simple. No need to make it harder than it has to be." She helped us decipher instructions that seemed beyond us.

"These books aren't for beginners," Edmund complained. "They act like you know a lot already. Dice, julienne, shred. What the hell is julienne?"

"You can count on me." Tess offered to come as often as we needed her. "I'll teach you everything I know." She stroked my hair and smiled up at my father.

She came almost every day at the beginning. She showed me how to scoop and whisk and measure, on the days when Edmund had to work and couldn't be there. She smelled good, and I liked her, but after we got the cooking basics down, I wished she'd leave us alone in the only thing Edmund and I had ever had between us.

I thought we'd stop at stews and soups, but he got interested and decided there was no end to our talent. Macaroni and cheese. Salmon patties with canned mushroom soup for sauce.

"Not so vigorous!" Tess cautioned him about the egg whites he was beating for a cake. "They need a gentle touch," she said sweetly, and she came up close and held his hand to show him. Her voice was velvety and low as she pressed closer. The two-cup measure slipped from my fingers and shattered on the floor.

We went from cakes to canning. Putting by, stocking up. We made more food than we could ever eat. We bought tomatoes by the bushel, stewed them, made spaghetti sauce, with meat and plain, tomato soup and juice, our own tomato ketchup. Canned bread-and-butter pickles. Also dill. Rhubarb and jams and jellies. My dad built shelves in the corner of the basement and filled them with the bounty. Glass jars, sterilized and labeled. Things we'd never eat. Food we didn't even like.

Paul came in late one night, after basketball, after a big loss for his team. He was in eighth grade, on his way to high school. Winning was everything to him. He looked mad and tired that night, and it was nine o'clock; I guessed that he was hungry. He threw his books down on a kitchen chair, and jars that we had sterilized rattled as the chair leg bumped the table. Edmund and I had two big vats of applesauce going on the burners of the old gas stove, and we'd been so busy that I'd forgotten to make dinner—something that seemed to happen more and more.

"What is this?" Paul shouted. "What are you getting ready for here, the end of the world?"

A raised voice. Unheard of in our house. We'd all been made subdued and cautious. Loss can shut you down that way.

I looked up at Edmund and wondered what he'd say. He was putting cooked apples through a food mill. I was sitting on the white enameled sink beside him, stirring as the apple goo fell into the vat. Steam flushed our faces, made strands of my straight hair curl lightly at my face. I could see the muscles in his tanned neck tighten.

"Leave it alone, Paul," he said without turning toward him. "I'm just trying to see that we have enough, that's all. I want to be sure there's enough."

"Enough for what?" Paul shouted. "Are we expecting someone? Do we have some kind of plan that I don't know about?"

Paul stepped closer to Edmund and screamed at his broad back. "Look at me. What do you think you're doing, anyway?" Paul's leg brushed my knee as he tried to push past me. He was reaching out, about to yank the slotted spoon from Edmund's tightening grip.

"No!" I cried out in a voice that didn't even sound like mine. It filled the little kitchen. Then I reached out from my sink perch, put my hand on Paul's far cheek, and turned his face toward me. "Here," I said. With my other hand I reached a wooden spoon into the vat I'd been stirring, and brought it up full of applesauce, thick and steaming. "It's good." I kept my hand and eyes on Paul, and blew on the spoonful of applesauce, cooling it so it would not burn. I felt a little rough patch, the first signs of a growth of beard on his soft cheek. "It's good," I said it again, and I held the spoon up to his lips. "It's applesauce, made just the way you like it. With cinnamon and cloves, especially for you."

He looked hard at me. There was so much anger in his eyes, I braced myself. I feared he'd push the spoon away, I even thought he might hit me. Then I said, "Please, Paul. Trust me," in a pleading, quavering voice, and, like a child, he opened wide. He let me feed him.

Paul rose steadily in the acolyte ranks, excelled in basketball with Father Tim as coach. He was a forward, he took the ball downcourt, dribbling while he gestured his teammates into position with his free hand. The one in charge, the spirit of the team. A whole new life for quiet Paul, the life of someone tall, important, with a fire-breathing mentor on the sidelines,

Father Tim in a sweat-soaked sports shirt, cursing at the other coaches, gesturing with his fist. Paul at the foul line, Paul's shot sweeping through and making the hoop rattle in its hinges; Paul in mid-air, his hand hooking the ball into the basket like a giant swooping crane. St. Bart's cheerleaders, pre-nubile babies from the eighth grade, in St. Bart's blue and gray, shaking their small backsides to the rhymes they chanted.

"Paul, Paul, he's our man. If he can't do it, nobody can."

A different brother from the one I knew, fifteen, then sixteen. His voice deepened, dark hair sprouted on his legs. He started to smoke cigarettes, spent all his free time at the park without me, playing basketball, practicing for his new life as a star. I followed him, he sent me away, he fell in love, I would have killed her if I could have found a way; instead, I bribed an upperclassman, a small-scale Catholic hood, to dump ketchup and applesauce in her locker. At home, Paul kept to himself and brooded. I lay awake most nights, afraid that if I fell asleep, he'd leave me.

My mother spent four days with us when I was eight, two nights when I was nine, a long weekend the year I turned thirteen. The doors of "The Shrine" swung open, and briefly she resumed her role as reigning princess. Edmund moved in at the station at those times. Unable to turn her out into the street, unwilling to spend one minute in that house with her. Perhaps he was afraid he'd fall in love with her again. From the fire station, he checked on Paul and me each day by phone. Sometimes, when Fanny was at home, she did the things that any other mother might. She permed my hair again, made oatmeal cookies. She smocked a dress for me one spring. The house hummed with her presence, and then, just like that, she was gone. I'd come home and find an empty place, a note. "There is a tango club in San Juan that is looking for a talent

such as mine," or "I hear Miami is as pretty as a picture in
the spring." Sometimes my dad searched for her, sometimes
he just let it go, knowing she'd turn up at some point in a
shelter or be picked up by police as years went by and she
got worse. He used most of his savings for some psychiatric
treatment when I was ten, and for a while we organized our
lives around twice-weekly visits to her in a hospital near La-
trobe. It was the closest thing to a family time I ever remembered. Not quite *Leave It to Beaver*, but for those few months,
during our visits to her she was present, she was ours. The
medication stilled her. The strain in her face eased, and I got
a glimpse of who she'd been, and why Edmund had loved her.
She asked questions about school, watched me closely as I
answered. She seemed interested in me. In the patient lounge
we made a life together, we played Chinese checkers and Mo-
nopoly. We took fudge to her and peanut brittle, and even
Paul, who had become so skilled at feigning cold indifference,
let her smooth the collar of his shirt, and stroke his hand
when he sat on the couch beside her.

But she wasn't even home a week when she stopped taking
her medicine and disappeared in the middle of the night.
Leaving us to try to take up our lives again, to try to remember our old routines and go back to them. In truth, in time,
we had no energy for old routines. Because every time Fanny
came and left, we were diminished by her; the air in the house
seemed stifled in her presence, was thin and would not support
life when she was gone. Sometimes I think that's why Paul
left. Because he couldn't breathe.

Paul left home to join the seminary when he was eighteen.
He did it suddenly, secretly, by night. Taking only the things
he thought he'd need for a life of prayer and contemplation
—his First Communion prayer book, a rosary with onyx beads
that Fanny's dad had stolen from a casket, and a basketball

for the hours when he wasn't on his knees. Paul packed them in an orange canvas duffel bag he'd used on the rare occasions when he spent the night with friends. He left the way my mother did, propping a farewell note against the sugar bowl. He must have tiptoed past my bed, moved slowly down the stairs. He closed the front door so carefully behind him that although its hinges often creaked it didn't give him away. Even I, who slept fitfully at best, woke just once that night, and only because I had been frightened by a dream of falling.

I was first downstairs the next morning. Eleven years old, the breakfast maker. I was the one to find the note.

I've gone to join the good Dominicans. Don't try to come for me or change my mind. You can get rid of everything I've left in my room. Anne should spread out and use the space. We've both been cramped and crowded for too long.

I turned the paper over, thinking I'd find more. Paul had never said a word about being a priest. Of course, I'd been in Catholic school a long time, I'd heard the stories of a sudden unexpected call from God. St. Paul knocked from his horse, the Virgin Mary surprised at prayer by news of her divine insemination. I knew how capricious God could be. However, I wasn't interested in God's will in this matter. All I knew was that Paul was gone. When he left, it marked the end of faith for me.

My dad read the note again and again. "I can't believe this," he kept saying to me or in the parlor to himself. I had half believed he would think it a privilege to have a son become a priest, the way Catholics are supposed to, but all he felt was loss. He called Father Tim, and asked him where to go to find Dominicans, as if he'd get in our old Buick and bring Paul home. Father Tim came to the house to reassure him. "God's will," he said, and took the glass of whiskey Edmund

offered him. He stayed late, and the two of them got drunk
and sentimental and reminisced about Paul and St. Bart's winning team.

At midnight, I helped Father Tim in his stagger toward
the door. I had my arm around his waist, he had one arm
slung around my shoulder as we weaved toward the vestibule.
But once we got to the door, he stood straight, blinked his
eyes purposefully as if to get them into focus, and seemed
suddenly sober. He bent toward me, I thought he meant to
whisper some small consoling blessing into my ear, when he
tilted my chin up and kissed me. Hard and on the mouth.
My first kiss, not what I'd imagined it would be (a drunk
priest, my dad sprawled out on the sofa in the next room just
a dozen steps away). I ducked and managed to avoid his second pass, then in a complicated shuffling two-step I moved
behind him and pushed his weaving frame through the front
door.

I thought one drunk was all I had the strength for in one
night. So I brought a pillow and a blanket, arranged Edmund's sprawled limbs on the couch. It had been a long day,
and I was about to go up to my room when he reached out
in the dark to take my hand. I sat on the edge of the couch
beside him.

"I can't believe it," he said for the hundredth time that
night.

"Don't worry," I said with a certainty I didn't feel. "He'll
be back. He's not the type to be a priest. Not our Paul."

He held onto my hand for a long time. Finally his grip
loosened a little. I thought he was asleep, but when I moved
to go upstairs he called to me.

"Promise that you'll never leave me."

A maudlin, silly thing, the kind of thing he would never
say if he was sober. It was too much to ask, too much to
promise, but it had been a hard day for both of us. I would

have given him anything he asked that night. I didn't even hesitate.

"Cross my heart," I said, and I made a giant X across my chest.

Paul finally sent his address on a postcard, nothing more. I kept thinking he'd write a letter, that he'd have some long and satisfying explanation. Mad as I was, I swore he'd have to make the first move, but after three months passed, my resolve weakened and I began to write to him. Long, exhaustive recapitulations of the happenings at home; short, cheerful notes; stupid greeting cards; self-addressed stamped envelopes with letters to myself I'd composed for him, so that he would only have to sign them and drop them in the mail. "I'm happy here," they said, or, "I think of you a lot and miss you." Alone so much, I began imagining that he'd come back one day, and bring a power that he'd found in God and share it with me. I spent my first two Christmases and birthdays after he had gone expecting him, stubborn as only I could be, refusing gifts and celebration as I watched from the window for him —a thin black priestly streak against white snow.

At fourteen, I began to babysit. I didn't like the kids much, the way they whined and wanted. But I had a plan. I spread the word through Nick, through Lou, through Rosie; they spread it to their customers. In one year I made more than a hundred dollars, saved every dime. Then, on my fifteenth birthday, I broke my heart-shaped bank, took the cash, and bought a ticket on a Greyhound bus to Cincinnati to the Dominican monastery where Paul was. I packed my toothbrush, hairbrush, and a change of clothes into my school book bag. (Standard issue, a dark blue fake suede shopping bag, "St. Bartholomew's" in gold flocked lettering across its side.) Not the stylish luggage I would have preferred for my first great adventure, but I wanted to look inconspicuous. I left for school that morning as if it was any other day.

It took five hours on the bus, and I was too excited to read *Rebecca* as I'd planned. So I sat back in my seat, bit my nails, and watched the landscape change, from the western Pennsylvania hills on through the flat Ohio wheat fields. The monastery was just beyond the city, and wasn't a place that the bus routinely stopped, so I had to watch the signs as we came closer and remind the driver. He let me off at an Esso gas and bus station. The man who owned the gas station and garage was about Edmund's age, balding, red-faced, pleasant. He was getting into his truck to go pick up a part he needed, and when I told him where I was going, he was kind enough to offer me a ride.

The drive was short. The monastery sat on a small rise in plain view of the interstate. A dirt road cut a path through what must have been a farm. There were cows, a herd of grazing sheep, a rusted wheelbarrow left next to a sycamore tree. I guess in Catholic school I'd seen too many pictures— I expected hand-built stone walls, spires, fretted windows, the Sankt Gallen plan—with a cloister common room, and a chapel with a window facing east. This looked more like a factory, or an asylum, blood-red brick, bars on the upper windows. Only when I heard a chiming bell, a call to prayer, was I sure I'd come to the right place.

"You sure you're expected here?" My driver turned in his seat and looked over his glasses at me.

"Absolutely," I said with a fixed, determined smile. I put my book bag on my arm. "I'm sure I'll be staying for a while."

There was a giant knocker on the door. I slammed it hard against the wood. I heard a dog bark inside, but no voices or footsteps. I knocked again, then heard a shuffling sound, a muffled call—"Coming, coming." Then the door swung open and an old monk squinted through the sunlight at me. In a rush of words I told him who I was and why I'd come.

"Sister?" he said. "Sister?" As if I was speaking in a foreign language, as if he had forgotten that women or blood relatives existed.

He motioned me in. "He never said a word about a sister."

The habit he wore was brown and hooded. He smelled like herbs and dirt and just-cut grass. I guessed when he wasn't minding the door he tended the garden. He kept a careful distance from me, as if I was the carrier of some rare disease. Fine with me. I'd kept my own safe distance from priests since my midnight kiss from Father Tim. I tagged along behind him, glad I'd worn my school uniform. I thought I looked more like a seminarian's sister in my plaid skirt and blue wool blazer.

We walked down three long halls; the old monk's cane clicked on the dark linoleum. We passed no one. "Vespers," he rasped at me, as if he knew that I was wondering where everybody was. As we made our last turn, I heard, just barely, a chant, an almost ghostly sound. Monks in some far corner of the grounds at prayer in a vaulted chapel. My monk guide paused, opened a door, and told me to wait there, in the library.

"Sit down," he said. "I'll see what I can do."

The library had two straight-backed wooden chairs, one on each side of a giant yawning fireplace; a long table with low benches on each side stretched down the center of the room. To the left of the door through which I'd entered there was one slipcovered sofa, the only spot that looked the least bit welcoming. The books were in glass-fronted cases; French doors at the room's end let in the only light. I chose a wooden chair to sit in, afraid that God would frown on my mission if I opted for the comfort of the couch. After about ten minutes, the door creaked and another younger monk came in with a tray of tea and tiny almond cookies. He didn't speak or introduce himself. When he left, he closed the door behind him.

The room got darker while I waited there alone. I ate my cookies hungrily, having had a turkey sandwich early in the day and nothing since. The almond-cookie crumbs made a fine beige dust on my skirt. A bell tolled loudly, marked the hour, then the half, then the hour again. My tea got cold. I stood at the French doors and watched the pink and orange and purple sunset as the sun slipped low in the western sky. I began to panic, imagined a scene in which he'd stubbornly refuse to see me. I felt stupid, like a baby, began to wonder why I'd come, where I'd spend the night, fifteen years old in a strange town alone. As I was reaching for my book bag, about to run, the door opened.

"Hello." The first thing I thought was that his voice would be good for giving sermons. Deep, commanding, clear. I turned to see him. He looked taller to me, and so thin, I thought, so slight in that floor-skimming habit. When I'd imagined this moment I'd always imagined myself playing it cool, holding back, insisting that he make the first move. But once I laid my eyes on him, I wanted hugs and kisses, a crazy, jubilant reunion. I took a step toward him, but he held his breviary to his chest as if it was a life vest. It seemed to fill his arms and I could see there wasn't room for me.

"You've really gotten big," he said.

I felt tears cloud my eyes, and looked down at the floor, so he wouldn't see. Then for several seconds we just stood there, across the room from each other, neither of us having the first clue what to do. Finally he made a move toward the French doors.

"Come on," he said. "Let's take a walk."

We spent about an hour roaming through a funny little garden that Paul said the older monks tended. Old and blind,

I thought—it was thick with weeds and wildflowers. Mums they'd planted didn't stand a chance. I saw a wild straw-colored orchid, the top of its hooded blossom trying to rise above the weedy tangle. Hooded ladies' tresses. A flower, a name that I'd picked up in a romance novel I'd read.

And what to say? What was there to say? He talked about his studies and his plans, the gift for languages he'd discovered in himself.

"I think they're going to send me first to Africa. Then maybe to the jungles of Peru. The dark interior."

I nodded approvingly. "My brother the linguist. That's great."

"Do you know the nickname for Dominicans? Domini canes. Hounds of God."

I laughed. "Why's that?"

He smiled. "I guess because we're like bloodhounds sniffing out the faithless. One of the first orders to unleash missionaries on the world."

"Saviors," I said.

"Or so we hope." He nodded.

"So, Mr. Linguist. Say something for me."

"What?"

"Say something for me. In . . . oh I don't know. How about in four different languages."

He blushed, reluctant to perform. "What should I say?"

"Oh, anything. It doesn't matter."

"No. Really." He stopped suddenly and for the first time that day looked directly at me. "I'm serious. What do you want me to say?"

I brought the end of my ponytail around and began to chew it. He pulled it gently from my mouth.

I thought for a few seconds. "How about, 'I am very happy here.' "

He said the words in Greek. "What else should I say?"

I clasped my hands behind my back, and rocked back on my heels, as if this was a game we were playing. "How about, 'The sky is very blue here in the spring.' "

This time he spoke in Latin. "And what else, Anne? What else should I say?"

It broke my heart to look at him. I dropped down to one knee to tie my shoe.

"How about, 'My sister is very beautiful and I've thought about her every single day since I've been gone.' "

He bent toward me, took my elbow. "Let's go in," he said. "It's getting cold."

The October night was crisp and clear. A single star had risen in the sky to be a partner to a slice of moon. Lights had flicked on in the monastery's upper windows.

"How's Dad?" he asked finally.

"He misses you."

He nodded. I'd come to question him, to fight; once I was with him, it seemed impossible and pointless.

"And what are you doing?" he wondered.

"Nothing. You know, school. Junk like that."

"So you're O.K.?"

"Yeah." I'd been suspended from school twice in a month, once for smoking, once for cursing the principal. "Everything's just great with me."

"And Fanny?"

I shrugged. "We haven't heard from her at all these last two years. She came home for Christmas right after you left, and wondered where you'd gone."

"Should I be touched?"

I stopped and looked at him. "I don't know Paul. How should I know what you should or shouldn't be? Be touched, be mad, don't give a damn. You asked, I answered. What do I know about you, anyway? How should I know how you feel?"

"You don't have to get so pissed, Annie." Annie. He sounded like my old Paul. It made me risk all and touch his arm. I feared he'd bolt, but it was a chance I had to take.

"You could have written," I said when he didn't pull away. The reason that I'd come, the confrontation.

"I thought a clean break would be better. I was afraid if I wrote you'd want me back, and I couldn't stand it. I just didn't have it in me anymore. Not for you, not for Dad. We should have painted the house, given up on Fanny. As long as I lived there, I felt I was waiting for her, and I finally just got sick of it. I had to get away."

I reached up and pulled a leaf out of his hair. "You never even said goodbye."

"You were eleven years old, for Christ's sake. What was I supposed to say. 'Goodbye, good luck'? I had to do it like I did. For me, there was no other way. And you know what's strange? It wasn't any great religious passion that inspired me to come here. Really. I just wasn't sure where else to go. After all that time in Catholic school, with Father Tim, it was the only thing I could think of. And in spite of that, by some great stroke of luck, I've been pretty happy here. There's a routine I can count on, people I can trust. I can't tell you how much I love that part of it. The regularity and order. Prime, the Angelus, matins, vespers. Every day's the same. Sweet sweet predictability. That house, our crazy mother, our life on Jeffers Street seems like something I just dreamed. And that's the way I want it."

Paul stopped to open the door for me. My tea and cookie plate had disappeared. Small lamps with yellowed shades made little aureoles of light around the room. Paul listened as the tower bell chimed ten times.

"It's late," he said.

"Yeah." I could see I wasn't going to be asked to stay. I put on my red pea jacket, buttoned it, pulled the collar up around my cheeks and neck. It would be a long walk.

"So you're happy now. Great. What about me?" I asked him. "What am I supposed to do?"

"You should get away from home. You're almost old enough. You'll go to school or something. Make another life."

"I see." My head ached.

"Do you have a place to stay?"

I lied and said I did.

"Can I come back for your first Mass?"

"Sure. Why not?" He smiled.

"And will you baptize my first baby?"

He pulled my ponytail. "That's pretty long-term planning, don't you think? Let's just wait and see, O.K.?" He stood at the door when I left, waved as I walked down the road, as if he was unaware—that I was just a kid, that he ought to be frightened for a baby sister walking in the dark.

The owner of the gas and bus station had left a light on, left the door of the little waiting area unlocked for me. I guess he'd seen through my false confidence. I slept in one of two vinyl-covered chairs. Stuffing poked out of a large hole in one of its arms. I woke up with a crick in my neck, and the first signs of a head cold. I took some change out of my pocket and bought my breakfast from a vending machine. A stale sweet roll, some pretzels, and a can of Welch's grape juice. A scrawny gray dog wedged through the half-opened door and sat at my feet, begging with his eyes, so I used the last of my change, bought him a sweet roll, too. He ate his in two bites, and fell asleep at my feet, using my saddle shoe as a place to rest his head. My feet were cold, and he felt warm and good, while I waited for the bus to take me back to Pittsburgh.

Edmund

WELL SPOKEN? Why, thank you," Edmund says. "I like to think I am. It's a result of years of reading. And also a concerted effort on my part to change, to shape myself, to become an adept." He stops abruptly, not wanting to get ahead of himself.

From his desk he takes a sheet of paper. "For you," he says. A spell. From *Egyptian Secrets or White and Black Art for Man and Beast*, St. Albert the Great, Albertus Magnus, author. A loan from Lucy.

Edmund knew early on that alchemy would be his focus; the spells were always just a hobby. But years ago, as soon as he began to read them, he could see that, besides being intriguing, they might also be useful. And so, when he was stricken by a toothache just after he'd acquired the book, he searched the pages for a spell that might address his problem. He'd been warned by his dentist that root canal was the only treatment that would solve the problem, and in the face of such a diagnosis, what had he to lose? The spell entitled "For the Toothache" was straightforward and simple; he followed the instructions given. He wrote, "Quosum sinioba zenni tantus lect veri" on a little scrap of paper, hung it on a string over his back, and within hours he was pain-free, the swelling had subsided.

Success inspired him, led him to wonder. If this works for a toothache, how about for other pain? Backache? Heartache? The dull pain of regret? He could take the piece of paper on which the spell was written and wear it like a scapular, much like the one he'd worn as a child in school. He could have it laminated, find silk cord to use instead of kitchen string. Place it carefully around his neck.

As years passed, and he read more closely, it began to seem to him that, beyond the spells, there was a kind of magic in the book itself. Whenever he turned to it he found something that he hadn't seen before, a spell or a turn of phrase that seemed particularly apt to whatever problem was at hand. It was, he thought, as if the book *knew* him. So it was last night when he flipped through the pages and found a spell that he thought might be useful to a doctor. A gift. For his young doubting Thomas, Dr. Currie.

To See What Others Cannot See
Take a cat's eye, lay it in salt water, let it remain there for three days, and then for six days into the rays of the sun, after this have it set in silver, and hang it around your neck.

Currie reads it, looks up skeptically at Edmund, but Edmund stops him before he has a chance to speak.

Don't feel that you need to comment now. Just keep it. Why pass judgment when there is still so much you don't know? Such as how it was for me after Anne left home. Or how I chanced to meet Lucy.

Duquesne University, Pitt, Mount Mercy. Pittsburgh was a fine city, full of colleges, stay here, commute, he told Anne. During her junior year in high school, he got brochures from all the local places, left them in her room or on the hall table.

"She's got it in her head to go away," he told John Schlusser. They'd been playing poker on the night shift, waiting for the sound of the alarm. Those Pittsburgh winters were the damnedest things. The wind and water tore right through their rubber suits and froze them. Every minute that was quiet seemed like a sweet reprieve, a blessing. A kind of other-worldly silence settled on the firehouse on a fireless winter night.

John shook his head. "It's kids, Ed. They all do it. Not like when we were young, when you got a job, stayed home until you found a girl to marry. Kids today are not like us, Ed."

"Yeah. I guess." He took a big gulp of his coffee, thought about how eager he was to get out of his parents' place when he was young.

"Also, this is a lot of money we're talking about here. My kids are young yet, but . . . college? We're talking big bucks. You got that kind of money?"

"I've got some put by. You know you can always get some money if you want it enough. Work double shifts, do without."

A small shaded lamp hung from the ceiling over their pocked wooden table and their game. The worn cards, buffed from so much handling, seemed to gleam. Most of the guys were trying to sleep, dozing on their bunks. "Pipe down," somebody groaned.

John leaned closer. Whispered.

"The telephone company. Tell her to get a job there. Good benefits, good pension. They stand by their people, Ed. With the phone company, a person can't go wrong."

He thanked John for his advice, then doused the light. In the dark he spread his rubber coveralls across the foot of his bunk, lined his boots up on the floor beside them. He pulled his blanket up, folded his arms behind his head, wanting sleep to come. But for the longest time he lay awake and thought of Fanny at the switchboard, *Number please*, the calls he made when they were dating. All night long he dreamed of tangled wires, and Fanny's voice echoed in his ears.

He met Lucy during Fire Prevention Week of 1964. Early summer. Warm and dry. Firemen from all over the city went in groups of three to neighborhoods, in polished trucks, in fire-fighting gear. They let kids try on their helmets and climb around on the trucks. Then they rang doorbells, introduced themselves, asked fire-awareness questions. "Have you memorized our number? Do you have an escape route planned?" Hard for someone shy like him, but people are friendly to a public servant, glad to shake his hand. He thought that's what Lucy meant to do when she reached out for his. Instead, she turned it palm up and traced the lines she found there. "Amazing" was the word she used for what she saw. She lived on the second floor of a duplex just beyond the park, behind the Aviary. When he told her who he was and what he wanted, she asked him to come in. She said there could be fire hazards anywhere.

She was forty-six then, with straight black hair pulled back in one wide barrette, the bare scrubbed face of someone young. Her ponytail hung to her waist, she wore a ring on every finger. Long, dangling earrings shaped like stars grazed each cheek when she moved. Thin and olive-skinned, she had pale lips, a graceful neck. She was the only woman he'd ever met almost as tall as he. The first thing he thought was how good it was to look a woman in the eye.

She took him from one room to another, each jungle-thick with potted plants. She stroked the leaves; she told him how much she liked living things. Dried herbs hung from the ceiling; sixteen candles, all lit and placed about the living room, made it look like a shrine. He had to step across an astral chart spread on the floor, wedge past a trestle table strewn with books and tarot cards. He bent close to admire a globe-shaped object, which she called an armillary sphere.

He checked her space heaters for gas leaks, inspected the fire escape. On a bookshelf in the corner there was a porcelain skull divided by black lines into labeled sections. He had to squint to read them. Hope. Ideality. Philoprogenitiveness.

"Some place," he said. A fire trap if ever he'd seen one. He looked up at a star map tacked to the wall, then looked at her. "What is all this?" he asked.

"My work." She handed him the morning paper, pointing to an ad she'd underlined in red.

Know thyself. Fortunes Told. Charts Read. Phrenological Measurements Taken. Interpretations Made.

"You tell fortunes?" he asked.

She nodded. "Fortunes and much more. You should come for a consultation. You might find out surprising things about yourself."

He fingered the hard edge of his helmet. "Thanks, but I'm not interested. I just don't think it's for me."

The truck horn honked outside. He knew Matt and Jim were ready to move on. Her hair swished against the back of her white shirt as she walked him to the door. He left her with a list of what she needed. Two extinguishers, a new gas jet for the space heater in the bedroom, a light fixture to replace the bare bulb in the hall. Attention, caution, care.

Six weeks after Anne left home, the district chief had called Edmund into his office. Edmund was fifty-nine years old. He knew what was coming. He started talking before the chief had a chance.

"I'm strong as I ever was," he said. "My eyes are good. I'm quick. There's no one better on the tiller. I sure as hell am not ready to give it up."

"Well, ready or not, in this business, you're getting old, time to slow down, ease up." Edmund had known him for thirty-seven years, they'd been rookies together. His belly made a fold over his belt, his eyes were bloodshot, his fingers were stained from nicotine. Time spent behind a desk had aged him.

"Jesus Christ, Ed, I thought you'd be glad. No more shift work, no more wrestling with that damned hose. Straight days. Warm and dry. You've got close to forty years in. We need someone like you to interview these kids we've got applying. That preliminary screening is the real key. We can give them tests and train them till hell freezes over, but it takes a pro to tell if a guy has really got what it takes. Take the job, Ed. Give yourself a break."

"I don't want a break." Edmund knew they'd let him stay out, drive tiller longer than anybody else because he loved it, it was everything to him. Early on, he thought he might make captain, but then in '54 he got involved in that union business when he should have kept his mouth shut, put in his time, gotten his promotion and a car with "District Chief" on it.

"Look." The chief leaned back in his chair, put his feet up on his desk. "I'm not trying to be a bad guy. I'm just telling you the way it is. This is a promotion, for God's sake. Take it."

So he did. He did. Eight to four-thirty, Monday through Friday, raise in pay to help with Anne's tuition, extra time for woodwork in his basement shop. What the hell, he said. But he thought of fire, dreamed of fire, woke up screaming . . . *The wall, the wall! Move, get out, the wall is coming down!* Panting, sweating, sick with the smell of singed hair, burning flesh. Staying awake all night to keep from dreaming.

"No crystal ball?" he said, looking around.

Six months after he started his new job, he went back to see Lucy. Since he didn't know her number, he couldn't call. He just showed up one day.

She didn't seem the least surprised to see him; she stepped aside and showed him in.

"No crystal ball." She clasped her hands behind her back. White shirt, black pants, a kind of uniform. Except for her gold hoop earrings, she might have been a nun.

"What, then?" He traced the sections of the porcelain skull with his finger, feeling foolish for being there at all.

She cocked her head. "Well, that depends. What do you want?"

He pointed to himself. "Who, me? I don't know. I just came back because I'm curious, that's all."

"I see." She smiled, then closed three open books and cleared away some papers so they could sit down on the couch. He had never been looked at so directly; no matter how she moved or what she said, she never took her eyes off him. The afternoon sun brought a red sheen to her hair.

"If you don't know what you want, why did you come?"

"I guess I thought it was better than doing nothing."

She frowned and eyed his wedding band. "Are you married?"

"Sort of."

"Children?"

"Two. One's grown up and gone, and the other's on her way."

She took his hat from him and hung it on a clothes tree in the corner; then told him to wait while she disappeared into the kitchen.

He called after her. "That ad you showed me said that you tell fortunes, that you can help me know myself. I guess that's what I want. I want to know if my future is going to be any better than my past."

When she came out of the kitchen, she was carrying a pot of tea. "Darjeeling," she said. From a glass-fronted cabinet she took a cup. "In my long experience, I've found it works best. The leaves are fuller, settle into patterns that are more distinct. Drink it," she insisted. "The leaves will know you better once the tea has touched your lips. I'll take some measurements while you're drinking."

The tea was warm. She brought a wooden chair in from the

kitchen and placed it in the center of the room so she could walk around him. The afternoon sun sent shafts of light through the half-closed venetian blinds, and gave the room a hazy look. She used what she called a craniometer to measure his head, stopped to jot down figures on a lined pad. With her fingertips, she felt her way, behind his ear, across his forehead, pausing when a hollow or protrusion was of interest to her. She smelled like some exotic flower. Her small breasts rose and fell at the level of his eyes. When she was finished, she took his teacup and held it to the light, studied it, then put it down and studied him.

"I see you coming back to me tomorrow," she said, and she shook her head no when he reached for his wallet. "We'll run a tab," she told him. She reached over and with a light touch brushed a tea leaf from his cheek. "We'll work on this together. We'll settle your account when your future is complete."

So they started. Tea leaves and tarot cards. His stars observed and followed, his profile drawn on parchment, matted, framed; the place above his eye that the phrenological map says houses harmony was located by measuring and mapping, then massaged in the hope of making it expand. At first he saw her once a week, more often if she had an unexpected cancellation. He brought lunch sometimes, knowing when he did he'd be asked to stay.

She sold hosiery at Gimbels, told fortunes and guided futures on her days off and in the evenings.

"I like my job," she told him over hot pastrami and iced ginseng tea. She served the simple meals he brought on flowered china, folded linen napkins in the shape of tulips, lit candles as if he was a special guest, as if he'd brought a feast. "Gimbels has the best hosiery department in the city. I know my customers and I know my merchandise. Seamed, plain, mesh or ultrasheer, neutral and in the colors of the season. Fishnet is very big right now, but it's a passing fad." Anxious to know everything about her, he paid close attention.

"Never married?"

"No. I could have. I've had great loves, I've had offers, but they never seemed quite right. I got so close once that I had my white organza gown and veil and invitations ready to be mailed, but then I changed my mind."

"How come?" He watched her, checking for some sign of longing or regret.

She raised her shoulders in a "Who knows?" shrug, but when she looked at him her eyes were clear.

"The stars were wrong," she said. "I looked at the charts and looked at them, I even thought of pretending that what I saw was wrong. But in the end I knew it would have been a bad match if I'd made it. I liked him, he was good to me." She took one last sip of her tea. "But in the end, Edmund Mueller, I had to face the truth. A person has to trust in something and I trusted in the stars."

And so she opened up some other world, a world of thought for him, he said to Currie. He felt as if he was moving with her into something larger than himself, some truth that had up until that time eluded him. She displayed the heavens on a chart, she called stars by their names—Sirius, Aldebaran, Alpha Centauri—then said they moved across the sky for him. *For him.* And he was hungry for it. He had long since given up the Catholic Church and God; he'd become a faithless, bitter cynic. Until he met Lucy, and the more he saw her, the more she eased the dull regret of his old life. He waited for her the way he had, as a kid, looked forward to his first breath after swimming underwater. He dreamed about her, long and lustfully, and woke up to find his penis standing rigid underneath his sweat-soaked sheets. He was impatient as a schoolboy, waiting for Lucy to give some hint that she might care for him, but there was always another client waiting when his hour with her ended. On his walks home, he tried to imagine Lucy reading tarot cards for someone else, her fingers tracing sections on another person's skull. He took to stopping at the Aviary on his way home, to sit, to remember all the things she'd said to him. The walls and ceilings of the Aviary rooms were made of glass so the birds could get some glimpse of sky. There was a man-made waterfall and an array of broad-leafed jungle plants, and wooden benches for visitors where he could be alone and think of Lucy. Her black hair stretching like an arrow down her back, her slender neck, the softness of her voice. Her simple sure insistence that he was meant for greatness, that the stars and sun had shifted at the moment of his birth.

Anne

BOWLBY AND A GROUP of his British colleagues de- voted whole lifetimes to the study of young children— the nature of their fierce attachments. He wrote three long volumes entitled *Attachment*, *Separation*, and *Loss* in which he gives case histories, talks about childhood depression, fear, the ways early loss shapes lives forever. I've studied Bowlby closely, almost memorized his books. *Loss* has a photograph of a small boy on the hardcover edition. A child no more than four years old, standing at a door, hand on the knob, nose pressed against the glass pane, eyes fixed on a point somewhere outside. All of him poised in an attitude of waiting. His is a serious and solemn face, and he looks so much like Paul when he was young—the curve of his ear, the light thin bangs, that look of worried waiting—that every time I see that photo- graph I have to look away.

I never felt afraid when I was young. I kept a slightly wise- ass attitude I'd developed in high school. I taunted my dad by staying out all night, was suspended from school six times for my bad attitude. I learned to be provocative and smart about the ways I chose to hurt him. If asked, I would have shrugged and said I didn't miss having a mother, that it didn't matter when my brother went so far away. I felt re- lieved when it was time to go to college, free of the burden of trying to be a daughter. I would have said I never felt afraid. I would have been lying.

———

Penn State seemed the perfect choice for me. Far enough away, good tuition rates for residents, scholarships and loans so plentiful in those days that they even offered one to me. I was a good but not great student; the scholarship surprised me, and for the first time in my life I became deadly serious about my work.

Because my life began on the Penn State campus. It was the farthest I'd ever been from home, anonymous among strangers. Reading the college catalogue that last summer on my bed, I thought, This is my new life. I can do anything now. Study fields I'd never heard of, learn ancient languages considered obsolete. I flipped on my back, looked out my window, and said to myself, *Anything can happen now.*

My dad drove me to State College, Pennsylvania, for Freshman Week in our old Buick, an act of great love, I realize now. He rarely left the North Side (except, of course, when called to a fire); he found his greatest pleasure in the small routines he had there. He must have hated crossing the river, leaving town, the strangeness of the autumn countryside, the almost overpowering sweetness of clean air. But he did it, with a tight-jawed stiff-upper-lipped good humor.

"Right or left or what?" he asked me when we got to Blairsville, or Wheatfield, or any of the tiny towns that marked our way. Me, the navigator, with the Pennsylvania map spread across my lap. He, the expert when he drove through the narrow streets he knew, reduced to novice status when the last of the Pittsburgh boroughs disappeared behind us. I tucked my hair behind my ears to aid my concentration, and spoke as if I knew the way.

"Left," I said, and he ground the gearshift into third to round the corner.

He'd made a big to-do about my going, pored over lists the college sent of what I'd need.

"A typewriter? Snow boots, rain boots, slacks and skirts and jumpers? Do they think I'm made of money? I thought you went to a place like this to learn, not dress up and run around." So I went without the things the college recommended and it made the packing of the car a simple operation. My hot curlers, a sack of favorite books, and a valise, as Edmund called it, the only one we had, since Fanny had the other.

"You'll be without a suitcase," I said when we were planning. "Suppose you want to go somewhere."

"No problem." He watched me fold my two skirts and only sweater. (What need had I of more in uniforms in Catholic school?) He was sitting on the edge of my bed, at my elbow, as he'd been for days.

"Maybe when I get there I could unpack fast and send the suitcase home with you."

"Forget the valise," he said. He had walked over to my bedroom window and was standing, looking out, his hands clasped behind his back. "Put the suitcase underneath your bed and keep it. I'm planning to stay put."

My first roommate was Val, from East Orange, New Jersey, a smoker, drinker, party girl, with long blond hair that she ironed every morning to make it perfectly, stylishly straight. She had a lot of girlfriends who gathered in our room, girls who'd been to public schools, who'd dated boys and worn their rings on chains around their necks, and wondered about going "all the way." They talked about their lives at home, family vacations, mothers who cooked roasts and played piano, fathers who held court at family dinners. Knee socks and pleated skirts and sweet, round-collar blouses. It was a world that differed totally from mine, and I felt like a spy sitting on the edge of my bed, listening, knowing that I'd never quite belong. I didn't have the clothes for it, and I didn't have the heart.

From school, I wrote weekly letters home. I tried to keep them short and snappy, I thought an upbeat motif was expected of me. After we lost Fanny, Paul somehow won the right to be the pensive one; it fell to me to be overly knowing, witty, flip, a style that served me well. But when I first got to Penn State, I suddenly felt cut off from everything I knew, as alone as I had ever felt in my whole life. There were too many buildings, people, classes, sounds. Too much activity. Life on Jeffers Street had been subdued and slow. I knew, of course, that when Edmund went to work, danger was his heart's companion, that in his fire life he thrived on mayhem, chaos, and terrifying unpredictability. But on Jeffers Street he kept all that at bay. There peace and order took the place of passion, quiet was his one necessity. Now I often think that if anyone had seen us then, the muted way we lived in those silent rooms, we would have looked as if we were moving in slow motion, two divers weighed down with equipment, weaving through their cloudy underwater world.

Because of that, right after I left home, I had no filter in place for processing experience. All the light and color at Penn State hurt my eyes after the dreariness of Pittsburgh. I didn't want to, and I never would admit it, but I missed my father, and that missing took me by surprise. I, who had so longed to go away, began to wish that he would come and get me, and as the days passed, my need to speak to him developed into a physical sensation—a dryness in my mouth, a thirst. But he told me not to, so I did not call. Nor did I sleep. Or eat. In the first month I lost twenty pounds.

Somehow, I got through those weeks. Every morning I gathered the pieces of my self together, got out of my thin-mattressed bed. Walked as if in some drugged stupor from class to class, took notes as was required. Then one day a girl in my English class asked me to go for a Coke with her, and a few days later the boy who sat beside me in chemistry asked me to a party. The layout of the campus began to be familiar, so that getting from class to class became easier, more automatic. Ordinary, small things, but they combined to make life seem livable, and by mid-November I was myself again, the kid who knew the neighborhood, who knew the score.

Edmund never knew, of course, how much trouble I had had. Because, throughout those early weeks, and in the midst of all the existential terror that went with them, I played what I thought was my role, kept my part of our unspoken family bargain. I might have been hungry, sleepless, frightened, and alone, but Sunday after Sunday I kept writing snappy, witty, clever letters home.

I took my first lover in the winter of the snow. I was nineteen years old, a sophomore. He was someone that I'd known my freshman year, my German I instructor. Martin Becker. A long-haired, noisy radical who taught us German verbs and sentence structures, and took time out of every class to give short impassioned speeches against the war in Vietnam. That whole long semester, he barked at me for my stupidity in German, a language that ought to have come naturally to me with a name like Mueller. But the more he pressed, the more my mind closed against the sounds of German. I switched to French after I barely got a C, knowing as I did from long experience when it was time to give up and cut my losses. At the end of the last class that first semester, Herr Becker asked me to have coffee with him. I said no thanks. His bold eyes and sharp tongue were unsettling to me. He shrugged and said, "Your loss," before he gathered up his books and walked away.

But by the time I saw him again, that second snow-bound winter, I'd changed a lot. I went one evening at the end of my freshman year to a teach-in at the student union, held by faculty opposed to the war. I sat on the floor surrounded by blue-jeaned students with disappointed eyes and worried frowns, people who'd found a way to use their anger in the service of a cause. Only curious when I first went, I was surprised at how easily I fit among them.

A new life, and I took it up eagerly. Because I didn't get much money from my home, I'd had a part-time job since I started college, shelving books after the library closed at midnight. That first spring I took what little money I'd saved, gave half to the peace movement, and with the rest bought new clothes for the new me. Jeans and sweaters, dangling earrings, my hair cut to chin length, shining. I demonstrated at an army base, went to Loch Haven State and Slippery Rock and other college campuses to pass out anti-war material. I studied when I could—in the library when I ought to have been shelving books, by flashlight in the buses we rode home from demonstrations.

I had seen Martin Becker a few times since class ended, at the far end of a courtyard, across the room at a lecture on the history of Vietnam. It surprised me when I heard his voice behind me that cold January night. It was a little after midnight on the second day of snow. The library had just closed and I was on the steps.

"A real mess," he said. His cheeks were chapped, snow clung to his short beard. He had the same bold eyes.

"Hello," I said. Then, thinking he might not remember me. "I'm Anne Mueller. I was in your class last year."

"I remember. You've changed, Miss Mueller, but not so much you need to introduce yourself." His voice half serious, half teasing.

"In what way have I changed?"

"It's hard to say, you just seem different. Are you still so serious?"

"Was I serious?"

"Very. Also very careful. When you said no to coffee after class that night, I thought you were a little afraid of me."

I bent my head. The hair I'd tucked behind my ear fell

forward on my face. "Afraid? No. You're wrong." I looked up at him. "I'm not afraid."

There were few people in the library on so bad a night. The janitor had locked the door behind us.

"Do you have far to go?" Martin Becker asked.

"Not so far." I pulled my gloves out of my pocket.

"So tell me, have you changed so much that you drink coffee now?" He was watching me.

I smiled. "Yes, I drink coffee. But I never did learn German."

His turn to smile. "No problem. I speak English very well. And I live nearby. We could walk there. It wouldn't be so good for you to go out into this alone. I think you ought to come with me. Just until the snow stops."

We both knew the snow was only getting started. I thought of setting out alone across the lawn, of finding my way as I knew I could, even though the paths were covered. But I'd felt fumbling and foolish for too long when it came to sex, knowing just the things that boys my age and I could show each other. Recently I'd wanted more. Looking at my naked body in the mirror, I'd been wishing to be admired by some different eyes, eyes and hands that had known other girls and women, that had explored, compared, and even after so much sampling wanted me.

It only took me moments to decide. I took the arm he offered me.

He had a big bed, a bed for explorers, a bed to be lived in, and so we did, for days. Hardly in the door, he slipped his hand beneath my coat to touch me, to unfasten and unhook me. I made it easy for him. Kissing his fingers when they fumbled, guiding his hands. I wanted him to say my name —to hear his voice caress it, love it. Anne. In bed in moments, unashamed in bright light, wanting to be pleased and pleasing. On top of him, beneath him, surprising him with so much willingness. How had I become so willing? So eager for so much from a stranger? He asked me, he whispered to me, loved my ear and abdomen, what he called my long and lovely thigh. I said yes to everything. Is this good? Do you like it? Liking everything, his voice and touch, his surprising tenderness. Does it hurt? he wondered when I, a virgin, bled onto the sheet. But nothing hurt. I was hungry for him, glad to have him. Amazed at having someone so desperately want me.

We ate in bed, we talked in bed, I watched him sleep, so pleased to be so near. I called my roommate on the second day, told her I'd gone home unexpectedly. Don't worry, I said. Tell the counselor, I said. I'll be back as soon as the weather breaks, I said. Then I hurried to Martin Becker's bed, afraid I'd lose him if I left his side too long. He served sweet German wine to me, then we made love again with a slightly drunken freedom. So much yearning in his eyes, as if he couldn't get enough of me.

It was hard to think of ending when the sun came up the fourth day. He watched me dress. "You'll come again," he said. I pushed his long hair back and kissed his forehead.

"Of course," I promised.

And I did. But it was different later. We had dinner twice, made love by candlelight one evening, then later in a thicket in the park at noon. But nothing seemed the same without the darkness and the snow, and I soon figured out that a long affair wouldn't suit me. The I-want-you's that had pleased me so much early on began to sound like the claims of someone who wanted much too much from me. So I was relieved when he got his Ph.D. that spring and took a job in Kansas. We celebrated with champagne and kisses and promises to write that I never planned to keep.

———

Paul was ordained a priest in the summer of 1965, and my dad, persuaded to give up, briefly, the grudge against him for ever having left, came with me to Washington, D.C., to the Dominican House of Studies for the ordination. We took the train, something we couldn't afford, but we were sure the Buick wouldn't make it. (Our second Buick, the first one wore out finally and he got another, second-hand, twelve years old.) I wore a new dress for the trip—a pale blue linen sheath with matching jacket. I felt worldly and sophisticated, fresh from my affair, long-haired, long-limbed, pretty.

We had dinner on the train. Pork chops and baked potatoes, radish roses and celery curls on the relish tray. Silver-plated forks and fine cloth napkins. My father unfolded his with an uncharacteristic flair.

"Very nice," he whispered to me. He pushed his wire-rimmed glasses, which had been slipping, back up onto the bridge of his nose. The glasses were new to him, and he said they made him feel like someone growing old. He didn't like them, and was always doing battle with them, taking them off or cleaning them, or rubbing the sore place they made behind his ear.

"Get contact lenses," I said after dinner, when he was fussing with them. The worldly college girl, full of high-cost smart advice. "Or go around half-blind. How much do you need them, anyway?"

"I need them for reading," he said, as if that settled the question.

I'd never in my whole life seen him read. Now I know I should have asked: What are you reading, anyway? I should have cared more. But I was caught up in the pleasure of traveling, of eating on a train.

"Pie?" I asked him, sure we'd splurged too much already. But he surprised me and said, "Sure. Why not? A la mode, with ice cream." He laughed when I did, as if it was a pleasure to be so generous with me.

The ordination was on Saturday. Then, on Sunday, Paul said his first Mass robed in white chasuble with gold embroidery, the priestly garb of celebration. It was a High Mass, and when Paul sang, his voice was a pitch above his speaking voice, mid-range and melodic, nothing like the voice I remembered. It made me wonder if Paul had changed that much, or if I'd never really listened to him during the time we were growing up.

After Mass, the lawn outside was filled with a crush of happy milling relatives. We waited there for Paul to come, to give his blessing. I hadn't seen him since my trip to Cincinnati; my dad hadn't seen him at all since the night he left us. Edmund looked unhappy in his coat and tie, unused to crowds, craning his neck, wanting nothing but to see his son. There wouldn't be much time to tarry, Paul had explained in the letter of instruction. The meeting on the lawn, a photograph of my dad, Paul, and me that we could look at later and remember. He was off to his first mission that very day. A short ride to the airport, a plane to New York, another to Nairobi, and then a bus, a jeep, a mule? "Who knows?" he smiled as he stood beside us.

When the time came for his blessing, I knelt down in the grass in front of him. His hand was heavy on my head. He smelled like Ivory soap and incense. He leaned close and almost whispered when he blessed me. His warm breath blew against my hair. Then I turned my head to watch him move the few steps toward my father. Expecting I don't know what. A flash of light, some sign of forgiveness between them. But Edmund was too proud, he simply dropped down to his knees and closed his eyes when Paul's hand touched him. But as he was getting to his feet, he stumbled, and instinctively Paul reached a hand to help him. It was only then that my father pulled Paul toward him in an awkward, fumbling wish to hold him.

"Well." Paul blushed and took a step back. "I guess it's time to go."

"Yes. You wouldn't want to miss that bus." Edmund cleared his throat.

Two more young priests appeared as if to save us. Introductions, awkward jokes, the last-minute search for bags and passports, the pointless pretense of farewell instructions. Take care, send photos, be sure to write, goodbye.

Easier this time for me than when I went to him by bus before. Perhaps because I hadn't expected much. So I could be there in some small way for Edmund. I told him college stories on the train ride home. Of football games and student-government debates about the war, science labs and late-night practices for chorus. Things he'd never thought about, things that made him smile.

"Tell me about the laboratories," he said. And I described the old science building with fairy-tale embellishments. With flasks and vials and steaming potions foaming at the rims, and a Bunsen burner that you didn't have to share (as we always did in impoverished Catholic schools). Your own Bunsen burner, I said, with a good high flame. I let my voice drop to a murmur, but kept on talking until the sun set and the train lights dimmed, and my dad's head fell to his chest as he drifted off to sleep.

Martin Becker was my first but not my only lover. Each quite different from the last, part of my new life plan to find out what was out there, what I'd missed and what might be in store. Promiscuous? Perhaps. But I liked those brief affairs; it was love that suited me, intense, consuming, brief. There was a sweet shy boy who flew small planes on weekends, who slid his hands between my legs and kissed me in the cockpit. A football player, who almost crushed me with his bulk and passion, not my type I knew, but I was eager to experiment. Which is what I did with men and jobs and majors. I considered being a marine biologist, imagined myself a forest ranger with a forest-ranger husband, searching with binoculars for signs of fire. I changed jobs often. A campus tour guide, a cocktail waitress when I came of age, a dog trainer (no experience but how hard could it be, I said when questioned). An assistant to the dance instructor in P.E. "Where did you learn to tango, Anne?" she asked me. I held my hair up from my sweaty neck.

"Who knows?" I said. "I guess I've just got rhythm in my soul."

At the end of my sophomore year, I took a job in the local hospital, drawing blood at 4 a.m. for fasting blood work, last-minute pre-op checks. I was a quick study, learned how to use the tourniquet and find the vein in one afternoon, and was on my own the second night at a job nobody wanted, the graveyard shift. I stalked the dark halls with my flashlight and equipment tray. Consulted my patient list, woke the sick from sleeping.

"Your doctor's ordered some blood work." I was sorry to bring bright light and pain and then just leave the patient wide awake when I was finished. I knew how long sleepless nights could be. I looked for ways of being less intrusive. I learned to hold the flashlight under my chin and aim at the arm, so that I wouldn't have to turn on the overhead light. It was an odd time, the whispering, the waking, the intrusion into moments of half sleep, where one foot is awake and moving, one foot straining still in that hopeless non-productive running we all do in dreams.

Some people woke up frightened.

"I didn't do it," said one old black man, pulling back his hand as if to fend off blows. "I wasn't even there." A begging, desperate voice.

"Take it all," said a woman, offering her arm. "I've got no need of it, I'm dying." She was young, with a sallow, wasted face. There was a picture of two little children on her bedside table. Somebody's wife, somebody's mother. "They won't tell me, but I know. What does everyone think, that I'm some kind of moron? Tell me the truth. You. You." She reached out and pulled the flashlight from underneath my chin, aimed it at my face. "Don't I deserve the truth?"

I drew blood for almost two years, the longest I'd stuck with anything, and because of that, I began to think I'd like to be a doctor. Did I have a calling? Such a question never crossed my mind. It just happened that when it was time to think about my future, medicine presented itself to me.

"Nurse," said Edmund in answer to my letter. "A girl should be a nurse. Something to fall back on. Forget this doctor business. It takes too long and costs too damned much money."

His disapproval strengthened my resolve. I tried other jobs around the hospital, a nurse's aide, a tray deliverer, a ward clerk in acute care when the one they had left to get married. I'd heard from pre-med students in my dorm that to get through medical school I'd need compassion less than I'd need tenacity and will, two traits I was long on. I began to wonder where I'd get the money, if I could pass the exam for getting in.

"Doctor? Jesus, Anne. Sounds hard to me."

This from my football-player lover, after sweet sex, his big head resting on my breast, his giant wearied penis lying softly on my thigh.

"Sure it would be hard. But I've got the brains for it, I've got the grades. And as often as I've changed my major, I've got all the courses that I need."

"I know." He rolled away, pushed himself up on his elbow to look at me. "It would just take so long, four years. I don't want to wait."

"Wait for what?"

"To get married."

"Who said anything about getting married?"

"Well, we've been going together for a while now, we've been screwing, we're both seniors. I figured we'd get married after graduation. Besides, I'm crazy about you. You know that." Just speaking about his passion for me made his penis stiffen.

I sat up in bed. "I know you're crazy about me. Marriage is just something I've never considered."

"Well, start considering." He reached to pull me back down to him. I should have gotten up and dressed. I should have said, I've lived my whole life in close quarters and it's not what I ever plan to do again. But he was on me suddenly, hard and eager, his lips against my neck, the hand he used for passing spreading my legs, making way. So that it was too late for stopping, too late that day for anything but bringing him inside again, and coming.

I knew I'd have to work awhile and save my money if medical school was what I wanted, so after graduation I kept my night job drawing blood and waited tables during the day and in the early evenings. My dad said, Come home, rent paid is money wasted, but I knew I'd come too far for that. I found a room on the third floor of the home of a philosophy professor's widow, worked at my two jobs, slept in the first few hours of morning, or when I could. I introduced my football player to my old friend Val, and they fell in love at once and deeply and were married right after graduation, with me as maid of honor. I was happy for them and a little jealous too, as they held hands and kissed, certain that only happiness could come from so much love.

I had no friends and wasn't eager for a lover. I lived quietly and simply, like an athlete in training or a novice on the eve of taking vows.

Once Paul went to Africa he began to write to me as if closeness seemed possible because he was so far away. I thought I had resigned myself to the loss of him, and only became aware of how much I'd missed him when I saw his name, the return address. I felt a kind of lightness in my chest, I didn't care what caused his sudden change of heart, I just felt lucky, and didn't want to wonder at its source or worry that luckiness would leave me. Careless about my mail before, I met the postman at the sidewalk, the way Paul and I had as kids when we'd sent away for a prize that was offered on the back of a Wheaties box.

Ethiopia is fine, he wrote. *Not at all what I expected. The capital is Addis Ababa, fairly modern, pretty in its way. Or it was when I first came here. I haven't been back since my plane landed. We're too busy. Besides, the roads are poor, and when the rains begin in June, they become impassable. I'm in the town of Goba, one of three priests and two nuns. We manage a church, a very tiny school, and what we call an infirmary, although it's really just a hut with a first-aid kit and two cots.*

All the languages I learned in seminary seem pretty useless to me now, although the language of this country, Amharic, is a bit like Hebrew, and that helps some. The weather where I am is temperate, but I'm told the deserts can be hot as hell.

Your letters take a long time getting here. So you shouldn't be discouraged if I don't answer right away. Write often, watch the mail. Don't give up on me.

Edmund

WHEN HE FIRST CAME HERE, the doctors suggested that exhaustion might have played a part in all that happened. Edmund shrugs; he doubts it, even though for years he had been troubled by insomnia. He all but stopped sleeping right after he became a fireman and never really took it up again. There always seemed to be so much to do, at the station, in his old house, then in the basement, first with wood, then with his laboratory. But it hardly matters now, he's sleeping better every day. The talking, the confiding has been easier than he thought it would be, and he is feeling lighter, as if words had weight and he was emptying himself. Laying down burdens. And he likes young Dr. Currie, ponytail and all. At least he doesn't seem inflexible and thickheaded the way the others did. Of course, Edmund thinks, he and Currie haven't gotten to the hard part yet.

The winter of the second year that Anne was gone was as cold a one as he remembered. It snowed, then froze, then warmed up enough to snow again. Snow drifted, trolleys stopped, plows and salt and cinder trucks barely scratched the surface when it began to snow again. He played his radio, tried to stay tuned in. City workers who had nonessential jobs stayed home. He was, God knows, nonessential.

"I could get there," he said on the phone to the district chief on the third full day of snow. "I walk, it's easy, a little snow never bothered me."

"Come in and interview who? Everybody's home, Ed. Everything's closed down."

"Well, if somebody at the station can't make it, if you need someone on one of the trucks, call me. I can be there in five minutes. Any shift. Call me."

"Yeah." The chief hesitated. "Thanks, Ed. I'll put your name down here. In case we get into a bind."

"Great," said Edmund, but he knew the phone would never ring.

He worked in the basement on a linenfold panel for a large chest he'd been making, but he felt sick of it that day. The saw's buzzing filled his head. So he went upstairs at seven to reheat potato soup he'd made the night before. He ate it slowly, took a long time washing his few dishes. Trying to make his dinner hour last, so that he could go to sleep and pray for sun and a thaw tomorrow.

It had been five years since he'd heard anything from Fanny, and he'd come to believe that she was gone for good. He'd had no word from Paul in the two years since his ordination, and he pined for him; he'd cursed God a hundred times for taking Paul away. Now, with Anne gone too, he was more lonely than he could ever have imagined. She wrote from school, but almost never called. "Money doesn't grow on trees," he'd told her sternly, in a churlish wish to punish her for leaving him, for going so far away. Long-distance was a tool for the rich, not for the working man. "Write to me," he'd said in her dormitory room that first day, helping her plump the thin, dank pillow on her thin and creaky dormitory bed. It had been a long ride and a long day of unpacking and helping her arrange her few things in her room. He felt as if he was in a foreign country trying to speak an unknown language. He smiled politely when introduced to her resident advisor, struggled past the banners and balloons that enthusiastic upperclassman had strung in welcoming array across the dormitory entrance. He tried to take his cues from other parents when it came to chitchat and cordiality, but what did he know about college, really? Posters for the walls, lap desks, bolsters shaped like easy chairs propped on the bed for studying—he brought none of these for her and he felt angry with himself, inadequate and stupid. He had to fight the urge to whisk her up in a fireman's carry and take her home with him where she belonged. Then, as it was time to leave, he wanted to take back what he'd said earlier, to press her hand and plead with her, "Call every day, call twice, a hundred times a day, I'll miss you too much if you don't." But instead he said O.K. when Anne asked if it would be all right if she didn't walk him to the car.

Once home, he tried to be satisfied with letters. She wrote to him as if it was her job to entertain him.

Dear Pop, (Do you like that salutation? It's what Joyce, the dim-witted girl in the room next door, calls her father.) Penn State is really something—big and noisy, and crammed with so many people that half my time is spent waiting in line, for food, for gym locker keys, even for the answer to a simple question. It's also brighter, more wildly colorful than anything I'm used to. I guess my eyes are out of practice when it comes to color's intensity and variation. Twelve years in Catholic school looking every day at dark plaid skirts, gray blazers, and two-tone saddle shoes will do that, I suppose. The grass is an altogether different shade of green than it is in the city, and the tree branches full of fall leaves make dense brilliant arches over all the footpaths. It's the custom here, if you have a date for a football game (I haven't yet), for the boy to give the girl a mum and pin it to the lapel of her coat, and in the stadium the sight of all those flowers is really something, like a million burning suns of color. It may sound silly, but even the clothing the other kids here wear seems dazzling. My roommate has different colored shoes to match each of her sweaters—red and pink and oxblood and, are you sitting down? three different shades of blue.

She wrote on Sunday, as if by requirement, as she did when she was at Camp Fatima. During her twelfth summer, he had splurged and sent her there for two weeks, but the Christian counselors wouldn't give dinner to anyone who hadn't written a letter home.

In English the professor recites Keats for us from memory. In my History of Science course we're reading Darwin's Origin of Species. *More and more I realize how much I didn't learn in Catholic school. All I seem to know about is sin and theology. Until yesterday I'd never heard of Percy Shelley or Linus Pauling. I'm going to have to work like crazy, that's for sure. I've got a lot of catching up to do.*

Anne's letters were delivered to Jeffers Street on Wednesdays, answered by Edmund at the rolltop desk he'd made. He tried to be interesting for her, shared news of Lou Lazarra and the goings on at Rosie's. But when he lost the tiller, excitement of any sort had left his life, and he quickly realized that he didn't have much to say. So he wrote less frequently, and over time he found that his letters, which had always been short, had also become stiff and awkward, empty of the love he felt but couldn't seem to put on paper.

On the cloud-filled Wednesday of the snowstorm he took up his pen and tried to write—about the weather, the paralysis it brought with it to the city. But in the quiet house on snow-clogged Jeffers Street he drifted into sleep instead of writing. His head bent to his chest, he leaned forward in his chair. And an hour later, when he awakened, he saw dimly, through the haze of half sleep, that snow crystals had frozen into opaque sheets on his windowpanes, so that now the blizzard had blocked not only his passage out into the world but his view of it as well. His isolation made complete, he thought, and that thought sent a shiver through him.

To dispel the gloom, he turned on lights, retrieved the newspaper. He'd counted on it to bring news of the world to him since his young manhood, but on this day, instead of easing the cold monotony, the newspaper only added to it. All the news was news of snow. The Northeast quarter of the continent was shrouded in it. Roofs collapsed, pipes burst, cars skidded into bridge abutments. And fires, of course. Twelve major fires in three days. Extreme cold required extreme measures to counteract it, and Edmund knew from long experience that the wish to keep warm bred a carelessness about the overuse of furnaces and heaters. He remembered how hard it was to fight those fires, how hydrants froze sometimes, how hoses grew stiff and unyielding as ice clotted in them. The way icy water blown by icy wind rained over the trucks, then coalesced into a lace-like frozen web over the hulking forms—the ladder truck, the fire chief's car, the pumper. Edmund opened the paper, winced at the sight on page 2 of a dead baby in a fireman's arms, and was about to turn the page again when a story in the bottom right-hand corner stopped him. A fire had destroyed a dancing school near Albany. A woman instructor was burned beyond all recognition, found on her knees, with her head tucked down against them, her arms and hands stretched out on the ground before her, like a Muslim turned toward Mecca. He closed his eyes and formed a picture of her, prostrate, in his mind—a supplicant to the fire gods, pleading for her life. He remembered how it is with fire, how the smoke stings at your eyes and keeps sweet oxygen from entering your lungs; the way every surface, every wall and floor, the door-knobs, the very air sears at your skin; the solid world seems about to melt into you. Edmund imagined the sound of her screams as she cried out for help, for mercy. He pressed his hands against his ears. He would have saved her had he been there, he said to himself. He was always good, the very best at saving.

His house felt colder every day. The oil furnace couldn't fight the cold. It just drank oil, used it up and gave him nothing back but creaks and groans and long metallic sighs. He woke up shivering, wore two sweaters, three pairs of wool socks, lit the oven in the kitchen to make biscuits, then kept it on all day for the warmth of it. The third night he lay down on the kitchen floor and fell asleep in front of the open oven door, not willing to go upstairs, imagining he'd freeze in his own house and bed.

In the *Post Gazette* he saw an ad for firewood. There were fireplaces in the parlor and in the bedroom just above it, but in the time he had lived on Jeffers Street they never had been used, soot and ashes being things that went out of fashion when Pittsburgh cleaned up right after the war. He just kept artificial logs in them, and forgot that they were even there. But as it got colder, the fireplaces began to seem like dark caves of possibility. He called the number in the ad, long distance, a number in Altoona. "I saw your ad," he said to the man who answered. "For wood. And I want a cord."

He was a country man, he kept the conversation short. "Where're you calling from?"

"Pittsburgh."

"Most city folks want half," he said. "Half's enough."

"Whole," Edmund answered. "I need a lot. And I'll pay cash. Just bring it."

He said he'd load it up and come down the next morning, so Edmund set to work making a place for it in the back yard. He pushed the snow aside and made a shelter, working that whole evening well past dark, in moonlight. He shoveled snow until the bricks were clear, brought old wood up from the basement, and built a raised platform so his logs wouldn't have to sit and rot in slush. Three wooden sides, a slanted roof of lumber scraps and shingles. A place where wood could dry and age, get more and more combustible. The work felt good, the labor warmed him. Even when the temperature dropped further and a single thick cloud rolled through the sky and hid the moon, he worked on, past midnight, in the dim reflected light of stars on snow.

As soon as the snow stopped, he resumed his visits to Lucy.

"I need to find some project," he told her after the eighth day of snow. "I'm spending too much time in that old house alone." The sound of his own voice was reassuring to him, after so many days without human contact.

She cocked her head quizzically. "What about your woodworking?"

"It's not enough," he said emphatically.

She nodded, not needing to probe or question, then led him into her spare bedroom to a bookcase made of cinder block and boards where she kept her texts and tracts and manuals. "Help yourself," she said. "Choose some things, become a student. There's great wisdom in these books. But you've got to find the kind that suits you, Edmund." She smiled encouragement. "I can do a lot of things for you but I can't do that."

He'd never been much of a reader. He ran his fingers down the row of spines, and chose three books, knowing nothing about them but their titles. *Transcendental Magic*, *Paracelsus: Selected Writings*, and *Egyptian Secrets or White and Black Art for Man and Beast*, Albertus Magnus, author. And then, as he was about to go, he chose one more, arrested by its title. *The Book of Mercy*. Indeed, he thought, as he ran his hand across the rust-red waterstained cover.

Lucy offered him tea, but for the first time in many months he felt an eagerness, a sense of urgency about returning home. He said no thank you to the tea, shook her hand warmly, booked a return visit for himself for two days hence, then pulled his muffler tight around his neck and headed home to Jeffers Street.

He'd thought to have the chimney cleaned two days before.

He'd laid the wood out in the fireplace before he left, opened the flue, listened to the sound of wind whine across the roof and chimney. So when he returned from Lucy's, opened his front door, and stepped inside, the house was cold, but everything was ready. He left his wet boots in the vestibule, threw his coat on the couch, blew warm breath into his hands. He took the matches from the mantel, struck a long match, threw it in, and watched maple shavings flare, then the kindling catch and spit and spread the flames along the length of logs. Until it caught, and with a sudden whoosh of sound and light, the fireplace was alive with fire, so hot so fast that he was forced to take a step back from it. He sat on the floor for a long time, watching, prodding the logs with his poker when the flames seemed to flag or hesitate. Then he took up one of Lucy's books and began.

Philippus Aureolus Theophrastus Bombastus von Hohenheim, known as Paracelsus, was born at Maria-Einsiedeln in Switzerland in 1493 in a house near what was called the Devil's Bridge. The cottage stood next to a path which led to a holy place for Christian pilgrims—a shrine to the Mother of God —and as a boy he watched from his gate as the pilgrims returned from their devotions, flushed and bright-eyed, suffused with a belief in miracles, transported by their brush with the divine. His mother was a peasant woman who died just after he was born, his father was a licentiate of medicine and town physician, as well as a dabbler in alchemy. Paracelsus was slightly built, with a large head, unruly hair, deep-set pale eyes. Strange in appearance, a little wild in temperament, he was much loved by his father, who had great ambitions for him. So much so that he named him Theophrastus after Tyrtamus Theophrastus of Eresus on Lesbos, a highly regarded follower of Aristotle.

When Paracelsus was nine, he moved with his father to

Villach in southern Austria. Like other boys, he attended the Bergschule there, and was trained in metallurgy, it being assumed that the students would become overseers and analysts for mining operations—gold, tin, mercury, and alum—which flourished at that time and in that place. After school, when he returned home, he watched his physician father minister to miners—men who talked of metals "growing" in the earth. In the classroom, he learned the language and science of metals; then, when visiting the mines, he saw the hot transforming wonder of the smelting vats.

He was seized early by a wanderlust. At the age of fourteen, he was exploring the universities of Europe, seeking famous teachers. His curiosity led him to Wittenberg and Leipzig, Vienna and Cologne. He shared his father's passion for medicine, but his search for knowledge left him frustrated and disappointed. He always wanted more. "Universities do not teach all things," he wrote. He believed there was knowledge to be gotten from simple men, "old wives, gypsies, sorcerers, wandering tribes." He wanted to develop in himself the haptic sense, to learn by touch, experience, and observation. His was a search for a higher, more profound wisdom, one not gotten in schools or from scholars.

He studied intensely, though erratically, in Rhodes and Crete, Padua and Paris. He was bold and overconfident and, despite his youth and inexperience, rash and bombastic in his self-promotion. When he chose to go by the name Paracelsus, he smugly placed himself above the learned Celsus, renowned first-century Roman physician.

In Italy he took up natural science, read Greek philosophy, immersed himself in the writings of the great physicians Hippocrates, Aretaeus, and Galen. Finally, in Ferrara, he settled long enough to win his doctoral degree, and then, as a licensed and practicing physician, he felt even freer to question every orthodoxy. He tried to raise the level of discourse among physicians. He wanted them to *love* their patients, to think of man as a wonder of the universe, a heavenly creature. "Man is a star," he wrote, and "the mysteries of the firmament are revealed by the physician."

Paracelsus went to Ireland, then Scotland, served as an army surgeon in the "Netherlandish wars." He was held captive in Russia, then escaped to Lithuania. While in prison, a Russian gypsy read his palm, discovered that his Head and Heart and Life Lines joined and predicted that he'd die violently if he didn't settle down. Intrigued by her and her predictions, he took up the study of occult philosophy, including alchemy, and other mysticisms of the day. He, too, began predicting futures by astrology and chiromancy. He studied the patterns of the veins of leaves, drew diagrams of hands—the Mount of Mars, the Line of Saturn—mapped what he believed to be the landscape of the soul. He spent time in Egypt, and went with the son of the Khan of the Tartars to Constantinople, in search of alchemic wisdom, the secret of the tincture of Trismegistus.

He ought to have established a medical practice, but, as was his wont, he moved against the current of the time, believing that a physician should be a traveler, embarked on a constant search for wisdom. "Learn and learn, ask and ask, do not be ashamed" became his motto, and so he did. He studied with pious abbots, herbalists, unholy fools. He knew no prejudice, discarded nothing. Everything in the world was created by God to be known and used; therefore, everything was worthy of his interest.

Still, he settled long enough in Strasbourg to prosper briefly as a practicing physician, and while there he developed an expanding reputation. So much so that in 1525 he was called to Basel to treat the renowned printer Johannes Froben, who had had an apoplectic stroke. The famous humanist, Erasmus, who was living with Froben at the time, fell ill shortly thereafter and sought the young physician's advice as well.

The details of the treatment administered by Paracelsus are not known, but both men recovered, and as his reward, Paracelsus was appointed city physician and lecturer at the University of Basel.

Students flocked to him, and from the outset he invited those who attended his lectures to join him in his rejection of the order of the day. The herbal remedies so highly regarded and so widely used were worthless, he exhorted, insulting both the apothecaries who made them and the physicians who prescribed them. He insisted that his medicines, ones made from minerals, were superior. He lectured in German rather than in Latin, an offense against the custom of the day. With boundless energy he theorized and wrote—about diseases and their remedies, "worms, consumption, gout," and the treatment of external injuries. He stressed the healing power of nature; prevent infection, he suggested, and nature will do the rest. To that end, he thought wounds should be allowed to drain, not packed with moss or dung. Illness, he wrote, is caused by some specific outside agent rather than by an imbalance of "humors"—the unsubstantiated theory of the time. The more he lectured, the more rowdy and enthusiastic his students became in their response to him. He declared all universities, all teachers, to be less gifted than the hairs of his beard. If another physician disagreed with him, he was dismissed as a "wormy, lousy Sophist." He wished to cast aside the Hippocratic oath; he had one of his own design in mind and rashly pinned it to the university's notice board, much as Luther, ten years earlier, had tacked his Ninety-five Theses to the cathedral door. The comparison between the two was quickly made by growing ranks of enemies. It was said that he was drunk when he lectured. Or perhaps simply made wild by his own passion, driven to a mad recklessness.

As was I, thinks Edmund, looking at Currie. As was I.

Currie puts his pencil down, furls then unfurls his fist to

work the writer's cramp out of his hand. Edmund fears that
he is bored by this, the necessary history, that he'll bring the
session to an end now, get up and go. Instead, he takes his
pencil up again and nods. And then? he asks.

Interest, thinks Edmund. Encouragement. The very things
I need. He licks his lips and clears his throat, preparing to go
on.

"By nature I am not subtly spun," wrote Paracelsus, but
subtlety, by then, was hardly the issue. On St. John's Day in
1527, surrounded by a crowd of cheering students, he threw
copies of Galen's works and Avicenna's classic text on medicine into a student bonfire, screaming that the ratchets of his
shoes were better instructed than those two admired men. Just
two years after he'd arrived in Basel, he was driven out, de-
prived of income, work, and all respectability. Unemployable.
His reputation ruined.

His life became that of a recluse and wanderer. Comar,
Nuremberg, St. Gallen. He had no friends, seems never to
have had a lover. After leaving Basel, he never again stayed
long in any place. But wherever he went and however long
he stayed, he never stopped his reading or his ceaseless writing. There were periods of brilliant synthesis and great dis-
covery. In 1530, he wrote a treatise on and described a cure
for syphilis (carefully measured doses of mercury compounds,
taken internally), foreshadowing the treatment established in
1909 and used for decades. He returned to his work with
miners, and theorized that "miner's disease" was caused by
the inhalation of metal vapors, rather than by a curse delivered
by the mountain spirits. While working again with miners,
he renewed his interest in minerals and metals. He prepared
new remedies containing mercury, copper sulfate, iron. Alone
so much, he grew estranged from the daily intercourse of men;
he moved deeply into himself, remembering from his youthful
travels the tales he'd heard of other learned men's experiments

with metals. He imagined he could know the "truth" of matter, metal's essence. More and more, he turned to alchemy.

Aristotle was his alchemic inspiration, and like Aristotle, Paracelsus was compelled by the logical possibility of transmutation. By Aristotle's reckoning, the basis of the physical world was a primitive matter which could take many forms. Aristotle described four elements—fire, air, water, and earth—then ascribed qualities to them. Hot, cold, moist, dry. Each substance in the world is comprised of all four elements. The only difference between one physical substance and another is the proportions in which the elements are present. Thus, by altering the proportions, one could transform any given substance into another. Lead, for example, could be changed to gold.

Alchemy's goal is the preparation of the agent of that change—the Philosopher's Stone, the Elixir of Life, the Tincture. The smallest portion of this can transmute base metals (lead, tin, copper, iron, and mercury) into gold. It can also cure disease, or make an old man young again.

Paracelsus was well suited to this thinking. He knew about ores and alloys from his days at the Bergschule; he'd seen firsthand that metals can be altered, their forms and colors changed. The study of the possibilities of physical transformation made perfect sense to Paracelsus, and meshed, on a higher plane, with his belief in God and magic and man's perfectibility. The wish to find the golden core in all earth's metals paralleled man's desire to find the god-in-himself, his shining core. "Alchemy," wrote Paracelsus, "is the art which makes the impure into the pure through fire." If that seems a bit like magic, Paracelsus said, why not? "Magic has a power to fathom things which are inaccessible to human reason, for magic is a great secret wisdom . . ." Without the magic of alchemy, all is meaningless, he said. Believe in it and become like the blind man who has been given the gift of sight.

Edmund paused in his reading to stoke his fire. The embers glowed as he turned them with his poker. Beautiful, he thought, about their colors: the reds and oranges and ambers, the dove-gray of the accumulating ashes. The flutter of the lambent flame along the parched, disintegrating length of log. He leaned closer, blew softly, and watched the fire rise up on the gust of air his breath made, and it occurred to him that there might be real pleasure in this, in slow and careful fire-tending. He'd known fire all his life, but he'd known it as an adversary and he'd loved it for the rush it brought, the frenzy. Now, as the firebricks glowed white and hot, an arc of warmth spread from the fireplace to wash over and surround him. He took his sweater off. The chill that had seeped into his very bones was disappearing.

Would that he'd been able to create this soothing warmth in his house before, he said to himself, thinking of Fanny. Would that he'd known better how to calibrate the passions that had burned in his young heart. He thought of how ob-sessed he'd been with fire—the desperate race to every blaze, the heated stumble into the hot light of Fanny's arms. He'd known the dangers of fire; he ought to have been more careful of her. He ought to have seen from the beginning that she was making too much friction in her mad career through life. He should have saved her from her own blistering brightness. Instead, he'd been a Daedalus, a failure, unable to keep his wild child from the sun.

Outside, the day was fading. A pink and golden light suf-fused the room. "Like a blind man given the gift of sight," he read again. With a pencil he placed that phrase in brackets. Then he folded back the corner of the page for future ref-erence.

Palingenesis was one of Paracelsus' special interests, a cousin to his alchemical musings. By reconstructing plants from their own ashes, alchemists hoped to prove that the soul, the consciousness of a thing, could survive, even when the physical structure has been destroyed. In hermetic language, the tree of the soul is burned by human weakness; palingenesis proves that, no matter how low man may descend into vice or folly, the essence of him is never lost, and can be reassembled by the art of alchemy.

Base metals transformed into gold, new life born from a fistful of ashes. Amazing things, thought Edmund.

You smile, young Dr. Currie. You ask, did I *believe* this? Greater men than you or I believed it. It was the obsession of fine minds for centuries. Men who lived alone, thought deeply, made furnaces, built complicated laboratories. Who spent lifetimes in small quarters, tending vials and flasks and smoldering embers, hoping to find the Philosopher's Stone, the instrument of transformation. Hermes Trismegistus, Zosimus of Panopolis, Geber, Thomas Aquinas, Raymond Lully. Even Goethe. Saints and scholars. Men known for their diligence and patience and for a certain skill with fire. Attributes of mine, Edmund thought; small things compared to all his failings. But there it was, a magic for which he seemed eminently suited. He read until his eyes ached, still he only scratched the surface. He vowed he'd learn all there was to know.

And so reading became his great preoccupation. Just alchemy at the beginning, then philosophy, religion, history, Robert Browning's poem on Paracelsus, anything that seemed even remotely pertinent to his course of study. The Chinese *Book of Furnaces* and *The Investigation of Perfection*; the Arabic *Emerald Tablet* of Hermes Trismegistus. The works of Roger Bacon. He filled his house, his time, himself with all he read. Remaking himself in some other image, someone fit to be a father to smart children, an able, knowing wise man.

Throughout the next few months he spent his free time reading in the book of spells, *Egyptian Secrets or White and Black*

Art for Man and Beast. He was in the midst of trying to decide how far to go with his interest in alchemy, wondering if he had the spirit required by the Magnum Opus. It seemed wise to try a few spells first and use them as a kind of test of whether or not he had a special power in him. Some were simple, so he thought he'd start there, hope for some small success. Consider such success to be a sign.

One night, while baking, he was in a hurry and grew careless, burnt the soft flesh of his forearm on the oven door, raised a blister bigger than a dollar bill that stung and pained him even after he spread butter on it. So he found the burn instructions in the book and intoned the spell three times according to the text. He looked over his shoulder as he spoke, knowing he was alone, but checking anyway, feeling foolish talking to himself in his own kitchen.

For Burns
Away burns, undo the band; if cold or warm, cease the hand.
God save thee, Edmund: thy flesh, thy blood, thy marrow, thy
bone, and all thy veins. They all shall be saved, for war and cold
brands reign.

The blister was gone before he finished. The pain was gone. He felt encouraged, inspired to go on.

"To See What Others Cannot See," "To Understand the Song of Birds," "To Restore Manhood" . . . so many spells to try, so many things to ponder. A remedy for back pain, a magic for one infatuated by illicit love.

That night, on his way to bed, as he walked toward the little room that had been Anne's nursery, where he still slept, his eyes fell on the locked door of the master bedroom. For years, he'd lived in this house as if it wasn't his; perhaps, he thought, he should reclaim it. Reenter what his children called "The Shrine," face the memories he'd left there. But when he went to his sock drawer, searching for the key, he couldn't find it. He had always believed that no one else knew where it was; surely, he said to himself, it had to be there. Only after he'd dumped the contents of the drawer across his bed, squeezed every toe in every sock, was he convinced that it was gone.

He could have called a locksmith, but his growing faith in the book of spells made him turn to it instead. He paged quickly through it, his index finger skimmed the pages, but he found nothing specific to lost keys. So Edmund settled finally on "If Something Is Stolen from Your House." A stretch perhaps, but he was game. Lost, stolen . . . what did it matter? He told himself that it could do no harm to try it.

> *If Something Is Stolen from Your House*
> *Inscribe over the door of the house these names, and it will be found*
> *again.* ✝ *Chamacha,* ✝ *Amacha,* ✝ *Amschala,* ✝ *Waystou,*
> ✝ *Alam,* ✝ *Elast Lamach.*

That was what the spell required of him. And he did it, laboring over each letter to be sure to make it big enough, lovely to the eye. He used a tiny chisel and a hammer, leaned a ladder on the stoop, carved it into the wooden arch above his door. He supposed he could have painted it, but he wanted something permanent, protection for a lifetime from thievery and loss. It took him days. Neighbors stopped by, asked what he was doing. He said "Spiffing up the place. It's been too plain too long around this door." He worried that they'd be more curious, look more closely at his work and wonder, so he used his woodworking skills to make each letter curlicued and quite ornate, unreadable to passersby. Unreadable, he hoped, to anyone except to whatever Force or Spirit roams the world tending to spells.

He felt peaceful in the house the night he finished, and walked through it in a way he hadn't done in years, touching the arms of chairs he'd built. He straightened antimacassars, blew dust off photo albums. It felt to him as if the house was his again, and just as that thought came to him, in the corner of the vestibule, on the floor, he saw the key, a bright brass glint against the dark linoleum.

All right, he said, bending to retrieve it. How the key got to the vestibule, he did not know, he only knew to take it as a sign. He'd found it, now surely he was meant to use it. Time to dismantle "The Shrine," move himself back into the front bedroom, into the four-poster bed he'd made the year he married; to give Paul back his room, move Anne across the hall into the "nursery." His mind raced as he planned it.

All week, the second floor was strewn with boxes as he moved and packed and put away. Fanny's clothes, and Fanny's quilt, and Fanny's perfume bottles—folded, wrapped in paper, carried carefully up to the attic, in case she ever returned. Except for work and seeing Lucy, rearranging was the only thing he did.

He bought rye whiskey the day he finished, he felt inclined to celebrate. He toasted his room first, his fireman's hat on a hook beside the door, his certificates of merit in the line of duty framed and filling one whole wall. A dark quilt on the bed in place of Fanny's ruffled bedspread. Anne's few things fit fine into the room where she'd slept as a new baby. As he toasted her room, he could see himself standing at her crib, his rough hand on her little newborn head. He went to Paul's room last. He'd put Paul's desk and chair and model shelves back where they were before Anne was born, then took his building blocks out of the attic and set them about as if a young boy lived there still and was simply at the park, shooting baskets, due home any time. "To Paul," he said, and raised his glass, a little drunk by then from all his toasting. Instead of going to the front room to the big bed, he decided that he'd just stay in Paul's room for the night. He lay back and watched the moonlight fall across Paul's models, making giant airplane shadows on the wall.

He woke up early, headachy and raw, went downstairs to make coffee before the sun was up. Hungover or not, to Edmund the world seemed new. The house was his again. He'd found the spell, and found the key.

He was pouring his third cup of coffee, strong and black, when the doorbell rang. It was Alphonse, the mailman, his friend ever since he introduced himself on Edmund's wedding day.

"Look here," Alphonse said, grinning, handing him an onionskin letter. "Very important, from far away. I thought I'd better ring the bell and put it in your hand."

A return address in Ethiopia. Edmund's name written in the small cramped lettering he knew.

Dear Dad, he read.

Dear son? he whispered softly. He couldn't breathe, his heart burned in his chest; Alphonse, the vestibule, the world around him blurred, then spun away.

Edmund reached for Alphonse's arm, and with his help eased down slowly toward the stoop, reading all the while, Paul's letter trembling in his trembling hand.

Anne

TOO HOT, too flat, the sky too big, the air too thick and humid. But they took me. Make me a doctor, I said in my applications, and just one place said, Fair enough, we'll do it. A school in Houston, Texas.

"Texas?" My dad looked at me as if I'd said I was going to another galaxy. I thought it best to tell him in person, so I'd gotten a ride to Pittsburgh from the cook in the restaurant where I waited tables, who was heading to McKeesport for a family wedding. Edmund and I were sitting on the front stoop on Jeffers Street, wrapped in warm sweaters, wanting to be outside because a winter's worth of snow had melted, the sun was out—just the slightest hint of spring in the second week of March. I told myself that the chill in the air, not my news, had drained the color from his face.

"I guess I'll never see you now," he said, and the flatness of his tone, his passionless expression, was not what I expected.

"It's not so far," I said briskly in response to Edmund, turning my eyes from him, amazed at what an able, facile liar I'd become.

"Not far? It's half a continent," he said, but without the warmth of feeling that I had come to expect when the subject turned to how far away I lived. "What is this wanderlust?" he pressed. "Where does it come from? There is nothing wrong with Pittsburgh, Anne."

"I know that," I said defensively, sliding a little farther from him on the wide cement step. I liked it better when he was feisty, when he banged pots and pans around like he did when I first mentioned college. I'd created an image of him for myself and I didn't like him veering from it. In my mind he was independent, self-sufficient, not given much to need or longing. Years earlier, when I was nine or ten, Rosie had suggested to me that Edmund was complicated and unreadable. A man of mystery.

"Very deep," she'd whispered, with a wise slow nodding of her head.

I'd tossed my hair, put my hand on my little bony hip, and hotly denied it. "He is exactly like he seems. He doesn't need anyone or anything. He's so strong even fire is afraid of him." I can still remember how the words rushed out, how determined I was, even then, to ignore any signs he showed of needing something from me.

"I had no choice. I didn't get into Pitt," I said, continuing to justify myself. In fact, I hadn't applied. I wanted to go as far away as I could get. "Besides," I offered lamely, "it'll be a chance for you to travel. You'll come see me. There'll be cows and oil wells and cactus, a different climate, a new world view."

"Indeed," he said. An Iron City beer truck turned the corner onto Jeffers Street and lumbered loudly past us; its brakes let out a tortured high-pitched screech as it pulled up to the curb in front of Brennan's. When Nick came out to greet the driver, and saw us sitting, he took his toothpick from his mouth and blew a kiss to me.

Through college I'd dutifully gone home for school breaks and holidays and in the summers, but in the year and a half I'd been working and saving, I used my two-job schedule and the inconvenience of the long bus trip as excuses for staying away. So I hadn't been home since Christmas, and although Edmund didn't know it, I wasn't planning to come back again before I headed for the Lone Star State. I think now that I should have been ashamed for keeping myself from him, but the new life I'd cobbled together still felt pretty tenuous and fragile, not yet fully mine, and I imagined that any close attachment to the past would spoil it.

"And how do you plan to get to Texas?" asked Edmund in that same calm voice.

"Fly."

"And where will all this money come from?"

"I've been saving like a crazed fiend," I said impatiently. "All I do is work and sleep and count my money in my room at midnight like some old hunchbacked miser."

"You know I'll help you," he said simply. "As much as I can. I always have."

I could tell that he was hurt by my complaining. "I know. I know," I said, guilt rising like bile into my throat. "I didn't mean that like it sounded. I'm not worried about money. I've arranged for loans and I've got savings. I'll be fine."

"Of course you will," he answered.

I looked carefully at him. I'd noticed something different about him since I'd been home, a deliberateness that had been missing since he took his desk job shortly after I started college. He'd been so peevish then, so cross and restless. Even the basement, where he'd always, in the worst of times, found solace with his rasps and saws and chisels, offered him no comfort, could not soothe him. I returned to school as fast as I could after that first Christmas, eager to be out of the house, too callow, too insubstantial myself to try to be of any use to him. But by the next Thanksgiving things were different. Paul was writing regularly to Edmund, a fact which pleased him greatly, and without warning or explanation, three years ago he'd rearranged the house, moved himself back into the front bedroom he'd so despairingly abandoned all those years before. Twice since I'd arrived for my spring visit he'd made vague references to reading he was doing, "compelling new interests" he'd acquired. Interests that kept him up late into the night, I found, when a slit of light from beneath his bedroom door cracked the darkness of the hallway as I came out of my room at 2 a.m. to use the bathroom.

"Are you mad at me for going?" I asked him on the stoop, a child again, all of a sudden, wanting him to reassure me. Are you there, Daddy? Is it O.K., Daddy? Tell me, Daddy, I used to say to him, standing at his elbow in the basement. Tell me that everything is going to be all right.

He cleared his throat. "Mad? No. Never," he said distract-edly, pulling the collar of his sweater up, looking off into the middle distance.

He rose then, took my hand, and pulled me to my feet. So easily—it was as if I weighed nothing. He was as strong as he had ever been, his arms and big hands still powerful from gripping, in his dreams, the tiller's wheel.

I let him go inside before me, and stood a minute by my-self, looking down the length of Jeffers Street. No telling if or when I'd be coming back. Goodbye cobblestones, goodbye stoop. Goodbye, house, I said as I was crossing the threshold into it. And when I paused there, briefly, to run my hand down what had once been the smooth wood of the doorframe, I felt, for the first time, the densely chiseled pattern. The raised arched A, the humpbacked M. The beautiful, the lab-yrinthine carving.

When I arrived in Houston to start school, July heat rose and quivered from the pavement, yards and fields were jungle-wet and green, anything could grow in all that heat and sun. Live oaks and palm trees side by side, plants called elephant ears, and they weren't kidding when they named them. It was cool when I had gone there for my interview in late November, no one said a word about July. Or August, or all the weeks from April through September. At the airport, my luggage stacked around me, waiting for the bus to take me into town, I lifted my hair from my neck, stuck my lower lip out, blew damp bangs from my forehead. Heard the Stetson-hatted man beside me try to give directions to a woman from L.A. in a slow, deliberate, Texas kind of drawl. "Just take the freeway right on in, follow the signs, before you know it, downtown will be there, right in front of you. Nothing to it. Easy as pie." Life in the Sunbelt, the great Southwest.

I looked for an apartment close to school, in a neighborhood near Rice University, where the streets were all named for English writers. Dryden, Shakespeare, Swift. Charming, I thought when I started. After two days of looking, I found a place at the not-so-charming end of Dryden, where the street backed up against a run-down garish peach-and-blue motel. The top half of a duplex, one room with a bath and tiny kitchen, yellow cracked venetian blinds that wouldn't raise or lower, a white-tiled shower laced with so much mildew it made Rorschach patterns, potted plants in plastic baskets hanging from hooks stuck in the ceiling, roaches bigger than my thumb, ten of them at least, belly-up inside the greasy oven.

The landlord, who'd been giving me the tour, hooked his thumbs through the belt loops of his jeans.

I let the oven door slam shut, smiled with what I hoped seemed like enthusiasm. I needed a place right then, the price was right, it was close enough to school to bike or walk.

"I'll take it," I said and Mr. Landry flashed a toothy prideful grin, wiped his hand on his shirt, and stuck it out for me to shake.

He pumped my arm. "You're going to love it here."

I cleaned the stove, got a coat of off-white paint up fast before classes started. Posters on the wall: Chillida, black on white, a Magritte window, a photo of a Joseph Cornell box with glasses, marbles, celestial charts, and a picture of the sun. In my first week in Houston, I found an old daybed that could double as a couch, got a table and two wicker-seated chairs third-hand from Blue Bird Circle. The night before I had to be at school for orientation, there was a summer storm, rain heavier than any I'd seen in Pennsylvania, with a wind that made it lash and heave against the windows. I realized that the hanging plastic baskets were there to serve a purpose, catching rain that dripped down through the ceiling. I'd made fried rice, my first real meal in my new home, and I used my only place mat and cloth napkin and lit a tapered candle that I planted in the center of a saucer, as if I expected company. Then I ate the rice alone and listened to the rain, and watched two brazen roaches march across the ceiling toward the dark moist safety of a plant.

Anatomy, physiology, cell biology, and histology. All mysteries to me. To all one hundred fifty of us first-year students. The days of equality hadn't yet arrived. Only twenty-seven of us were women.

Orientation was on Monday, and on Tuesday we got right to it, eight hours of lecture with a thirty minute break for lunch, three hundred textbook pages covered, all about the cell. Cell structure and division, cell injury and death, hypertrophy, hyperplasia, agenesis, necrosis. Cilial propulsion, mitochondrial formation of adenosine triphosphate, better known as ATP. The ways cell nutrients pass through the membrane. (Diffusion, active transport, pinocytosis.) Start with the cell, all four professors said. Dr. Davies in cell biology paced back and forth, his hands clasped behind him, pausing now and then to write with great exaggerated flourish on the board. Red bow tie tied perfectly, overhead lights reflecting from his smooth bald head. A condescending smile for anyone who asked him to slow down.

The cell. The cytoplasm and its organelles, lysosomes, perxisomes, microtubules, 0.005μ across. Consider the Golgi apparatus, the flattened cisternae, membrane bound, their parallel array, the many fenestrations on the outer surfaces, the vesicles at the periphery, some bristled, others smooth. Dynamic equilibrium its business, the balance kept by Golgi's complex between the cell's rate of accretion of new membrane and the rate of membrane loss.

"Balance," said Dr. Davies, about the pathological basis of disease. He held out both hands, palms up, scale-fashion. "The business of the cells, the organs, the body as a whole. When the scale is tipped too far in one direction"—Dr. Davies lowered one flat palm—"the body struggles in every way it can to get things evened out again. Remember," he said. Then he clasped his hands behind his back, resumed his pacing. "Balance."

Two nights before school began there was a party, planned and executed by Administration. Beer and tamales, timid introductions, tentative approaches, the careful looking one another over, checking with a few well-chosen questions who was a smart-ass, who was a gunner, who could be counted on for a hand, good notes, a ride on rainy days. A careful formal stiff affair that ended early, with mutterings and sighs and palpable relief. Then the Friday after we'd been there a week, someone named Mike had a real party at his place, three blocks from mine, and everybody went.

Mike's apartment was the first floor of an old house with a porch that wrapped it, and a big front yard, where people sat or sprawled on blankets, talking, drinking beer. I was heading for the keg when someone took my arm.

Her name was Jill Cooper. "From Dallas," she said. She asked about me and, after I told her I'd come from Pittsburgh, introduced me to everyone around her as "this Yankee." All the faces looked familiar after just one week and I was glad to have a chance to put some names with them. Leo, the little guy with horn-rimmed glasses, who took notes faster than anyone I'd ever seen. Lynn, with straight Joan Baez hair, a practiced plainness I'd seen a lot in peace marches. Larry Kline, sharp-tongued, serious, his lean body taut as a coiled spring. A gunner, I suspected. No nonsense, no smile, the slightest nod as greeting when Jill introduced me to him. Kate Corcoran, red-haired, fair-skinned, with an absolutely stunning smile, the beauty among us, fairly dragged away from our short talk by two dumbstruck admirers.

"Let's have dinner," she called back to me as she moved with them across the lawn, and I said "Sure." Surprised at the shyness I felt, aware of how few friends I'd ever had.

I stayed late; we all had too much beer. Joe Tucker did a Dr. Davies imitation, singing out "The cell, the cell, the cell" as he staggered back and forth across the lawn. Mike put on music; after all the jokes, there was dancing. Tall Sam Atkins, blue-eyed, cowboy-booted, with the sweetest drawl, said I was pretty as a Picasso, kissed me, held me close and hummed while we were dancing. I closed my eyes and let him lead me. Pretty. Yes, indeed. There'd be a lot of pairing off that year. Alone and stupid-feeling, many of us would find somebody, hold on tight, have sex and romance taken care of, time for work and concentration guaranteed. Sam kissed my ear. I opened my eyes long enough to see Mike and Jill, entwined and groping, moving toward the bedroom. I pressed myself to Sam. It had been a while since I'd had a lover, and I felt ready to have someone wrapped around me. I would have gone to bed with Sam that night if he had asked me. But he walked me home instead, those few blocks, his arm around my waist, his shy voice singing Willie Nelson tunes into the night.

"Watch the stairs," I said when we got to my place, warning him against the second-from-the-top step, missing. "A trap for burglars," I joked, as he stretched his long leg across the space and pulled me up beside him.

"And suitors?" he said. We were just inside the door, the

lights out still. He pressed against me, placed his hands against the wall behind my head. "Stay awhile?" I said.

"Too tired, too drunk, too late." He grinned. "But I take rainchecks."

Histology lecture right after lunch. A mistake. Boring at best, it was excruciating with our stomachs full. Dr. Levinson, fat and red-faced, boomed at us; his enthusiasm for his subject knew no bounds.

"Cells form tissues. The basic tissues are . . ." Dr. Levinson liked to surprise us with questions in class, see who was keeping up with reading, who was slacking off.

"Miss Mueller?"

I woke suddenly to the sound of my name.

"Uh, yes?"

"Would you care to answer the question for us, Miss Mueller?"

I blushed. "I'm sorry. I didn't hear the question."

His face reddened even more than mine.

"Well, I think we could safely say, Miss Mueller, that you are not alone in your inability to hear the question. It seems to me that there is quite a bit of sleeping on the job here.

"WAKE UP!" He slammed the text down on the table next to him. People around me, not forewarned by the sound of their names being called, started, jumped, dropped pencils, knocked binders to the floor. *Do you people think I'm talking in order to hear the sound of my own voice? You people are going to be tested on this! You'll have to take a board exam on this! You'll have to* know *it, for God's sake.*"

His voice dropped. "Now," he said. "Has anyone in this room done the reading assigned for today?" He looked down at his class roster. "Mr. Kline?"

All eyes turned to Larry Kline. He didn't flinch. "Yes, sir?" said Larry.

"Tell me, Mr. Kline. Do you know the answer to my very simple question?"

Larry shifted in his chair. "Yes sir, I do. The basic tissues are epithelium, connective tissue, blood, muscular tissue, and nervous tissue."

Dr. Levinson's face relaxed. He smiled like a happy child. "Thank you, Mr. Kline," he said. "And could you also tell us, by any chance, which of the types of epithelium is shown in this photomicrograph, and where in the body it might be found?"

Dr. Levinson was pointing with a long stick toward an enlargement of an illustration from the book that was hanging on the wall.

Larry frowned, leaned forward. "Yes, I think so. That looks like ciliated pseudostratified columnar epithelium, which can be found in the trachea."

Dr. Levinson's grin broadened. "I thank you, Mr. Kline. Your class thanks you. You have saved them from my further wrath, and for that they should be grateful."

"Gunner." Mike, beside me, glared at Larry.

When class was over, everyone came toward me, rallied round, pissed with Larry for breaking the unspoken rule, for showing up a classmate. But I didn't want their sympathy. I felt exposed and stupid and furious at anyone who offered comfort. "Forget it," I said. "He knew it, I didn't." I was pushing past them, wanting to be left alone. As I headed out the side door of the building, I slammed right into Larry at the bottom of the stairs.

"Careful," he said, grabbing at my arm to keep me from falling. I looked at him. It was the same unsmiling face I'd seen the week before at Mike's party. He was picking up my binder, which I'd dropped, and when he handed it to me, he seemed to realize for the first time who I was. The stupid one. The girl without the answers.

"Sorry," he said, brushing dust off the edge of my binder. About running into me, about class, I didn't know what he regretted, I didn't give him a chance to say. I just took the binder and ran outside, around the corner of the building, where I leaned against a tree and did what my dad told me Muellers never did. I cried.

We became the walking wounded, backs bent by the weight of textbooks, lab manuals, and notes. Hands cramped from taking notes, vision blurred from too much reading, eyes, raccoon-like, ringed in black from too little sleep.

Where are the patients, we all wondered, not a sign of one, more reason for discouragement.

"Forget it," Kate Corcoran said. "Who could manage one more thing, anyway? Who needs people to worry about?"

It was 2 a.m., we were eating Wheaties with bananas and half-and-half. Resting before we took up biochemistry again.

"Well," I said, my mouth full. "That's why we're here, after all. You know. Healing the sick. That stuff."

"Are you sure this is all you've got to eat? No wonder you've lost weight."

Cereal, bologna, some moldy bread were all we'd found in my kitchen, shopping and cooking being things I'd given up for lack of time. Cold cereal, black coffee were my staples.

"Breakfast of Champions." I washed my Wheaties down with coffee. "It could be worse."

Kate smiled her stunning smile.

"You can't fool me, kid." She shook her red hair from side to side. "Wheaties, biochem, a test tomorrow and I don't know a thing, a tire on my bike is flat, it's raining, I haven't had a date in weeks, and I almost broke my leg on that damned step of yours. You can't fool me. This is as bad as it gets."

———————

The anatomy lab was on the sixth floor. No windows, bright lights, bare walls. Our rubber-soled shoes squeaked on dull linoleum. We'd been given our dissecting kits that morning, a lab coat with a name pin on the pocket. Divided into groups of twenty-four, then four, assigned to an instructor. "Dead is not the kind of patient I had in mind," I heard somebody whisper, but still. It was something.

My lab instructor was a woman, a third-year student used to rapid motion, I could see, no time to waste. "Follow me," she said, and took off fast, with us hurrying along behind her. Like kindergartners on a field trip, hanging on her every word, off the elevator, down the hall, through the locked door to which we'd each been given keys.

"We keep the doors locked for protection against abuse of the cadavers. You can come here after hours to work, but *only* you. Don't get any smart ideas about bringing dates or friends up here for cheap thrills."

Someone snickered.

"Don't laugh, it's been done." Ms. Alvarez was unamused. She wore a black turtleneck and slacks underneath her lab coat, her blue-black hair was parted cleanly down the middle, pulled into a bun. She hadn't smiled yet. I'd begun to think that no one found any pleasure in medical school, and when that thought occurred to me, I wondered how I'd stumbled into this—a system meant to break you, wear you down, when worn down was the thing I'd sworn I'd never be.

She paused again at another door, opened it, and flicked the light on as we entered.

"Get used to the smell, you'll be living with it for a while. It's formaldehyde. The preserving fluid. Wear old clothes when you come here, things you don't give a damn about, because you'll want to burn them when you're through."

She gestured toward the tables spaced around the room. "There are six cadavers to a room, four students to a cadaver.

Today is just orientation. On Thursday you'll begin. We'll start on the arm. The lab manual will tell you everything you need to be looking for. Read it before you come. You'll save yourself a lot of time. I'll be here to answer any questions. But you should think of this as independent work." She smiled then, slightly. The smug smile of the initiated faced with the anxious pilgrim.

My cadaver was Amelia. A name tag tied to her toe. Floating in formaldehyde, preserved in a coffin-shaped tank. A tight fit, no room to spare, none needed. She lay on a sieve-like platform with a lever at each end, so that she could be hoisted up out of her tank to work level, drained, dissected, then lowered back into her vat at the end of every lab session. The lifting was hard work, death made her weighty, it took two of us to raise her, cranks squeaking as she surfaced. The smell of formaldehyde burned my eyes, permeated all the clothes I wore, my hair, its very shafts; even when it shone from clean-ness it stank. My fingers had a slimy feel that wouldn't go away. I wore old clothes under my lab coat, as Ms. Alvarez had said to, kept them in a box beneath my kitchen sink. But still, I smelled like Amelia.

I guessed her to be fifty, maybe older. The formaldehyde gave her a yellowish cast, her face was bloated, her features puffed and thickened by death and preservation. Hard to know what she might have looked like, who she'd been. Ame-lia. A pretty Southern name. As weeks passed, sometimes I'd be there working, late at night, and find myself imagining a life to go with such a name. Dances, garden parties, children and a husband. In those late hours, I'd let myself forget what I knew—that the cadavers were most often derelicts, bodies found in the streets, picked up, left in the morgue for days unclaimed.

Larry Kline was my partner on Amelia's left side; Dave

Bizinski and Leo Michelson took the right. Dave and Leo seemed just fine, but I wasn't happy to find Larry right beside me. The day after orientation, we all got there early, scalpels at the ready. We were to start on the forearm, and when I hesitated, Larry jumped right in.

"I'll do it, I've read the manual, let me make the first incision."

A hotshot, I thought.

"Be my guest," I said, mocking him. But it was wasted, I could see. He had made his slit already and was pulling back the skin. The mush of subcutaneous tissue glistened in the light, a pale gray muscle layer stretched out just below it. The mystery unraveling before my eyes.

I bent closer, took my probing instrument. Began.

Larry Kline was a gunner, all right. Dave, a flirt; Leo, a mustached, frowning scholar. If we needed extra lab time, which I often did, we'd try to come in pairs, since cranking up Amelia was a two-man job. At first the pairing off was random, but since I went so often after hours, and Larry, always eager to learn more, went often too, we ended up together quite a lot.

"I don't know why you spend so much time here," I said one night, straining at the crank at Amelia's head. "You know all this stuff, you're ahead of the rest of us."

Larry secured his end of the platform. "The reason I know so much is *because* I spend so much time here," he said. "You think I absorb this, get it by osmosis? I study just like everybody else."

"No, I think you get it by pinocytosis." One of the ways a cell ingests things, by engulfing what it wants and taking it. I imagined Larry engulfing his books, and the thought made me smile.

"Not funny," Larry said curtly.

"Just a joke. It was nothing."

"Forget it," he said. "Let's get going on this, or we'll be here all night."

We were in the upper arm, separating muscle layers, trying to distinguish arteries from veins. We worked a long time silently.

"Damn," I said. "I can't tell one from the other."

"Sure you can." Larry picked up a vessel with a probe, cut through it with his scalpel. "The arteries have that pumping action, so the walls are thicker. Take a look." He moved his head so that I could get down closer. Larry had long, slender hands; the vessels looked like threads next to his fingers.

"It's hard to see," I complained, and Larry used his free hand to move my head.

"It is if you block your own light." He laughed. I'd never heard him laugh before. I looked at him again. He was just about as tall as me, with sand-colored hair, a narrow face. He wore rimless glasses that rested on the bump at the bridge of his long nose. His face relaxed when he laughed, his smile became him.

I turned my attention back to Amelia's artery.

"You're right," I said. "The light helps a lot."

Money was a constant problem. Edmund had always sent me what he could, two hundred dollars a month sometimes. Once in a while he'd send a large check proudly, when he'd made and sold a table or a bed. But I was feeling less and less inclined to accept his money. A nagging worry about him was taking root in me. I'd talked to Edmund only once since I'd left home; mostly I got letters from him, and lately he'd been ending each one with some random quotation, apropos of nothing as far as I could tell, attributed to people whose names were not familiar to me. Paracelsus, John Dee, Henry Cornelius Agrippa. "Until the Astral Fire is kindled . . . there is work for us to do," or "There is nothing that man is unable to discover." They gave his otherwise straightforward letters an odd, disjointed quality, and I worried that hard work was taking some unanticipated toll on him; I wondered if he ought to be slowing down. So in November, when he sent five hundred dollars, which I needed badly, I sent it back. "You should save some for yourself," I wrote to him in my short weekly letter. "You'll be able to retire soon."

So it went. I had loans, and lots of them. But the money I had saved from working the last two years was dwindling, I knew I'd have to find some way to work while I went to school. Rent, tuition, books, and lab coats; I'd need a stethoscope right after Christmas. So, early in November, I decided to give myself the gift of a quiet Christmas, stay in Houston through the break, find work in a shop that needed extra help, catch up with my studying, and start the January quarter with a clean slate. Then be ready when the new year came to face the music. To draw blood again at 4 a.m. By flashlight.

The day Larry sawed through Amelia's ribs, Dave Bizinski asked me out.

"What?" I shouted, to be heard above the noise of sawing. "I can't hear you."

"I said, there's a Latin band in town. I hear they're good. They're playing at this place in the Heights. We could have some beers. There'll be dancing."

Larry had stopped sawing. Leo made a crack about romance. "Hear that, Amelia?" He bent to whisper loudly in her ear. "Love is blooming right here across your knees."

I gave Leo a drop-dead look and pushed my hair back with my forearm. I was glad to know that somebody could see beyond the bone dust in my hair, the tissue fragments under my nails. But I had too much to do to take up the business of flirting with him, tempting him, seeing how long it would take to win him. There was a histology exam at the week's end, biochem lab in the morning. Dancing seemed like something from another lifetime, out of place in the world of cells and organs, foreign to me, me who'd spun to tango music in the womb.

I heard Amelia's last rib crack, give way. Leo made a microphone of his fist, held it to his mouth, and dropped his voice to a serious, news-commentator tone. "Ladies and gentlemen," he said into his fist. "We are pleased to report here from the medical center in Houston, Texas. The operation has been a success." He gave a cheer, and we applauded. Larry put the saw down, took a bow. Then I watched as Larry lifted our half of Amelia's rib cage out of her chest cavity and held it up in front of him. It looked as if it were a barred cell, he a prisoner.

"So, what do you say?" Dave leaned across Amelia's knees toward me.

With our half of the rib cage removed, I could look into Amelia's chest. I saw her heart and thought if I came back that night I could get started on it.

"It's a nice offer, Dave," I said. "Thanks a lot. But I don't like Latin music much, and I don't dance."

Larry was the son of a violist, a New Englander. But his parents were both German-born.

"Survivors," he told me one night in the lab.

"Mine are, too," I said.

"No, I mean concentration-camp survivors. Auschwitz."

I looked up at him. He was squinting at Amelia's abdomen. "What are they like?"

He went on working. "They're very . . . gracious. Very formal, actually. And very introspective. Their Jewishness is everything to them. It kept them alive in the camp, it's become sort of the essence of them. Their faith and their children are their great preoccupations. My younger brother got married while he was still in college, dropped out, never finished; now he's a clerk in a clothing store. His wife is a nice girl, but not Jewish. A very big problem. Disappointment in my brother has practically killed my mother. Now their highest hopes are pinned on me."

I handed him an instrument he needed. "Sounds hard," I said.

He shrugged. "What's 'hard'? Anything they ask of me seems easy, compared to all they've been through. Nothing's hard compared to that."

Larry had a girlfriend. He talked a lot about her during our late nights in the lab. Elana. The girl he'd met at Harvard. The daughter of a rabbi, ambitious for herself and him. She was in law school in Boston. The perfect girl, he said, the girl he loved and slept with any weekend he could get away and go there. Fine with me, I needed help with bones and muscles, someone to lead me through Amelia's heart. Larry relaxed a little the longer I knew him, I even thought we were becoming friends, and I regretted having called him a gunner.

"Well, he *is* a gunner, or was one, or whatever. He knew more the first day than I'll ever know, and he's not afraid to flaunt it. Don't torture yourself about it." This from Kate. We were cooking dinner in my kitchen.

"I'm not torturing myself, I just think I wasn't fair. He's helped me a lot. I'd still be in Amelia's forearm if it weren't for him."

"I wish he'd been my lab partner. God, could I use help."

Kate and I had bought the smallest turkey we could find and were stuffing it. Thanksgiving. Larry was in Boston. We'd flipped a coin for where we'd eat, and even though I'd chosen heads and tails came up, we were at my place, because Kate didn't have a table. I'd thought of trying to figure out a way to go home and be with Edmund, especially since I knew I couldn't go at Christmas, but I'd finally told myself the time was too short. Just as well, I was happy where I was. Kate was chopping sausage. We'd had trouble deciding on the dressing—oyster, corn bread, sausage, sage and thyme.

"Maybe we could put in everything," Kate said finally, and I said, "Good idea. Let's do it."

I was cutting celery. "Do you think this is a bad sign, this not being able to decide about the stuffing? I mean, in another eighteen months we'll be doing our rotations, asked to make decisions that will matter."

"All the more reason to be indecisive now. Rest our brains. Save them."

I laughed. But I guessed that Kate was having a lot of trouble with her grades. She was the first close friend I'd ever had and I didn't want to lose her.

"What are you doing the rest of the weekend?" I asked. "We could go and work in the anatomy lab for a while, or go check out those slides that Levinson wants us to look at for histology. Catch up a little, take advantage of everybody being gone."

Kate shook her head, vehement. "Not me," she said. "I've got to have some time off. I swear, I'll go crazy if I don't. If I see one more slide, I think I'll vomit. Besides, I'm going away. With Dave Bizinski."

I raised my eyebrows. "No kidding. I didn't know you two had something going."

"Neither did I till he asked me to go to Austin. So, tell me, you know him better than I do, you've shared a cadaver with him. What do you think?"

I looked at Kate. She'd had her red hair cut the week before, she was wearing lipstick for the first time in a while. I noticed when she put a fistful of stuffing into the bird that her fingernails were manicured and polished. It made me think that it was time to pay attention again to the way I looked.

"Well, what I think is that you look great. And what I

hear is that our friend Dave is very good in bed. Lots of experience." I nudged my elbow to her ribs and we both laughed.

"It sounds like just the ticket," Kate said. "I believe I'm ready for some exploration of the body that doesn't involve a scalpel."

We spent the evening trying to imagine Dave in bed, picking out what Kate might wear. Laughing, talking. Like two much younger girls, with nothing serious to do. Drinking wine and eating ice cream, up till 3 a.m., cross-legged on the floor in cotton nightgowns.

It's the rainy season here, Paul wrote in early December. *No snow, no shovels, no need for Kathleen clipping mittens to our snowsuits. We'll have a simple Christmas. For dinner we'll have wat, a spicy stew of vegetables and meat, and injera, which is a native bread. Forks and spoons aren't used much here, the bread is good for scooping food. Sometimes I think of sauerkraut and wieners with a certain longing (hard to believe, I'm sure, considering how much I loathed them when you used to cook them).*

Besides this Mass card, I've sent you a necklace under separate cover, made of tiny metal beads, and a shamma, an Ethiopian dress, with instructions for the way to drape it. The beads are made by women in our village and are supposed to bring good luck, fertility, and God only knows what else. The women here look very beautiful in their shamma and beads, and I thought that you might, too. Have someone take a photo of you. A lover or a friend. P.S. I've installed a basketball hoop, and we've started a village team. But the hardest things to find are those pins that you stick into the hole in the basketball to inflate it. If you have time, find some for me, will you? We've got the pump, the ball, the coach. But if we can't get air in, none of the other things matter.

My dad called the night Paul's letter came, and I knew I'd have to tell him about Christmas. There was a lot of static on the line at first, it sounded as if he was calling from the moon.

"I can't hear you," he kept saying, whenever I said I wasn't coming home. "I'm waiting till you get here to pick out the tree. Like you and Paul and I did when you were little."

"I don't have the money, Dad. I can't come." I was shouting.

"I found a recipe for goose. I've never tried goose before."

The line cleared suddenly.

"I can work here through Christmas break. All the stores need extra help. As soon as finals are over, I'll work extra shifts."

I thought about Christmas at home. The long quiet day, me upstairs, Edmund puttering in the basement. The fear that Fanny would pop in, the certainty that Paul would not. I leaned against my kitchen wall and let my back slide down it until I was sitting on the floor.

"I just can't come," I said.

He wasn't listening. "I brought the creche from the attic just today and found Mary's right arm broken. So I glued it and I'm hoping it'll hold."

"Listen to me," I said. *"Listen to me. I'm sorry, Daddy, but I just can't do it. I'm not coming home."*

Silence. Then, "Oh. Well," he said. "Well sure, I mean that's all right." He used his fireman's voice, the voice I'd heard so often when I was small. The ringing of the phone at midnight, his voice on our end. The fire station. "Sure," he'd say. "No problem, Jim, give me two minutes. I'll wake the kids and tell them. I'm on my way." Quick'itches up, suspenders on his shoulders. Big-voiced. Brave. It was my fireman father who spoke into the phone.

"You're not crying now, are you?" he asked.

"No."

" 'Cause you sound like you're crying and I don't want that, no crying now, you know how I hate crying. This is fine. No problem. I have things I need to do here, too. And I'll have a friend to dinner, that's right, I'll have a friend come over, cook that goose anyway, don't you worry about me. No problem here."

"I wish I could do it, but I've got all that I can manage here, Dad."

"Sure," he said. His voice trailed off. "Sure."

The next day, on my way to my exam in anatomy, I walked through the back lobby of the Administration Building. The giant Christmas tree was up. Tables with green cloths, red punch bowls, poinsettia centerpieces. A party. Faculty wives. Their annual event for students.

I tried to hurry through, avoiding the women with Christmas-tree-shaped name tags on their chests. I'd been up all night trying to study, distracted by my conversation with Edmund. I panicked and called Larry twice, and when I called a third time, he came over, 3:15 a.m., and we went through Amelia's upper body one more time.

"Take it easy," he kept saying. "Relax. You know it. It's all right."

The people in the lobby blocked my way. "Excuse me, excuse me," I said, pressing through, shaking my head no to a cup of punch and a Rudolph the Red-Nosed Reindeer cookie. The faculty wives were dressed for Christmas, high heels, angora sweaters, tailored skirts. Well-meaning, I knew, taking up the cause of suffering students, but it reminded me too much that morning of the kindness strangers showed me as a child, poor Anne, her mother gone, her clothes not right, in need of some attention. A woman not much older than me came up—pink-lipped, red-sweatered, smiling, a tray of cookies in her hand.

"No thanks," I said. "I'm in a hurry."

"Surely," she said sweetly, "you have time for just one cookie."

I stopped and turned on her. "Look," I said. The months

of edginess, the money worries, the pain in me found focus. "I've got an exam in five minutes, I don't have time to talk to you, and it's not even eight o'clock yet. It's too damned early for a party and I don't want a cookie."

Stunned silence. Another of her number standing near us overheard, and walked quickly toward me. "There is absolutely no reason to be so rude," she said.

She was older, with white, bouffant hair, pearls that fell into the folds of her silk blouse. She could have been anybody. Old enough to be the wife of Dr. Levinson or Davies, old enough to be my mother.

"Shut up," I said. Then I turned, walked fast away from them, and took the stairs by twos.

I passed the exam, and the first term ended. And while I wasn't looking forward much to the holidays, I forced myself to make some effort, bought a small tree, one string of lights. Sam Atkins's parents lived in Houston, and he invited me for Christmas dinner at his house. I wore a red wool dress I found on sale and the beads my brother sent me, took time with lipstick and mascara. The Atkinses were quite Southern, very charming. His father clearly found it odd that a woman would want to be a doctor, and asked me a lot of questions with a puzzled, vague expression on his face.

"You were a hit," Sam said late Christmas night, driving me home. "They loved you. Your only flaw is your strange preoccupation with medicine."

We were passing houses with lavish Christmas decorations. Thousands of blinking white lights spread across the eaves and over the shrubbery of a large house set back from the road.

"Yeah," he said. "You've passed inspection. Too bad I don't want to get married. You'd be perfect."

"Is this supposed to be a news flash, a warning, what?" I

looked across the gearshift at him, amused. Our romance had never come to much. Shortly after that first party at Mike's house, he'd taken up with a nurse he met, and, when that broke up, another. In between we went out a few times, saw some movies, had a drink one night when the last nurse, Lulu, told him they were through.

Out of the back roads, he swung the car onto the freeway.

"Neither a news flash nor a warning," he drawled. "I just didn't know what you were thinking after all those probing questions my dad asked. The thing is, they'd just love to see me married, find some nice girl who would keep me on track, see to it that I finished school."

"Doesn't sound half bad," I said. "You should think about it. But trust me when I tell you. I know that nice girl isn't me."

Sam relaxed then, took my hand out of my lap and kissed it, off the hook and free with his affection.

It was late when we pulled into my driveway. Sam held my hand as we went up the steps, and helped pull me over the broken one, just as he had the first time he walked me home.

"You should get that damned thing fixed," he said about the step.

"I know, I know. I guess I'm still warding off burglars."

"And suitors?"

I'd opened the door and Sam slipped inside behind me.

"Listen," he said softly. "We're both unattached, alone. It's late, it's cold, it's Christmas. Why don't I stay. No strings, no problems, just a warm bed in the morning." I felt his lips against my neck. I let myself relax against him, lonely suddenly. What he said made sense. I wanted someone with me.

He fumbled with the zipper on my dress. I turned around to him and reached up in the dark to unknot his tie.

"All right," I said. "You can stay." He worked the zipper

down. He slid his cool hand along the full length of my spine. "But just this once," I whispered. "Because it's Christmas."

I woke up halfway through the night, with my back to Sam. I eased away from him, slid out of bed, pulled my robe around me, and tiptoed to the kitchen to make tea. My hands were cold, I cupped them around the mug for warmth. Then I sat in the chair beside the Christmas tree, across the room from Sam. I was glad enough that he had stayed, but I wanted morning to come quickly, so I could be alone again. I watched the tree lights blinking, sipped my tea and planned my day. And I thought about my brother and decided I'd go shopping in the morning, get those pins Paul needed for his team, so that he could get a whole life started and teach the Ethiopians everything he knew.

Second quarter, new year, January, seventy degrees and sunny. Introduction to diseases. Stethoscopes, white jackets. A book called *A Guide to Physical Examination*. Word spread fast among us. By God, they're going to let us see patients.

Just for interviews at first (what would we have known had we wanted to examine them?). Then we did health histories, height, weight, pulse, gross physical exams. It was what we'd all been waiting for, and finally, the thing I'd hoped for all my life. A place where I showed promise.

Was it the time spent as a child trying to guess what Edmund felt or what Paul wanted from me? Or later, the hours I'd spent drawing blood, waking people up, then listening? In the clinics finally, listening paid off. I was prepared to wait it out with people, not push too hard. I'd introduce myself, explain why I was there. Then I'd lean forward, spread my hands, palms up. "What seems to be the problem?" No special brilliance. I simply asked. The patients told me.

My preceptor, Dr. Abrams, sat behind his desk, thumbing through the histories I'd taken. He'd made some notes in the margins. "These are quite good, Miss Mueller. Interviewing is important. What the patient says is what the doctor has to go on. And you're doing a fine job."

"Oh. Thank you." He was the only person since I'd started medical school who told me I was doing well.

I ran into Larry on my way out of the building. "Have dinner with me," I said. "My treat. I don't want to go home and start studying right away."

Larry looked at his watch. "Sure," he said. "I could do that. But tell me, what's the occasion?"

I might have told him, but I thought he'd think me foolish, Larry the genius. I imagined Dr. Abrams's praise would seem a small thing to him.

"Nothing really," I said. "I'm just feeling good. Like things are going to work out. That I'm going to be a good doctor, after all."

Larry smiled. "Well, I could have told you that."

So much praise in one day. So much pleasure.

After that first dinner, Larry and I began eating someplace once a week or so, mostly burgers, the occasional splurge on Italian food at Nino's. Sometimes we'd go early, then go to work on Amelia; sometimes we'd study together (not so much, though; I knew I slowed Larry down) and eat late. So much time away from Elana made Larry lonely, glad to have the chance to talk. Already he was making decisions that I didn't want to face. He said he'd like to be a thoracic surgeon; he knew which residencies were best. He hoped to go back East again, be close to his family and Elana's. They'd marry as soon as they both graduated.

"Was there ever anybody else?" I wondered one night. We were at his place, studying physiology. We'd ordered pizza.

"A couple of girls in high school, quite a few my first two years in college. Why?"

The double cheese was stringy. I had to twirl some that had fallen on my chin around my finger.

"Just wondered," I said. "You just seem so *sure* about everything—Elana, your career, where you'll be and what you'll do. I'll bet you even know how many kids you want. Look, you're blushing. You *do* know how many kids you want!"

Larry rolled up an issue of the *New England Journal of Medicine* and slapped me with it, laughing.

"Knowing what you want is not so hard. I knew I wanted someone Jewish, anything else would be impossible for me. I knew I wanted someone smart. If you'll pardon the expression, 'an intellectual companion.' " He was teasing now, half serious, half smiling. "I knew before I applied to med school that I'd choose either medicine or surgery. It's not that I'm so clever or clear-thinking. Some things just fit, others don't. It's not very complicated."

"Then why do I have such a hard time? I have no idea what I want. I haven't thought one minute beyond medical school."

"You're funny," he said. "Sometimes in the lab, when I glance over at you, you have this burning look, as if every moment of your life requires some fierce concentration. The way you focus makes you seem as if you've always known what would be required of you."

"I guess that's true. I do try to pay attention to what's required of me. But that doesn't necessarily have a thing to do with what I want."

We talked most of the night. He told me about his life, the years after his bar mitzvah, men gathered in the temple for daily prayer. He called it mystical, the way it felt then, as if all Jewish men who had ever gathered that way were alive in him, speaking through him.

I spent a long time listening. And when it was my turn for talking I told him things I'd not told anyone before. About my mother, and brother, fire trucks and sirens, tango dancing in the parlor, my mother's lover, the way she permed my hair. He pushed his chair back on two legs and listened. It rained. No leaks, no hanging plants to catch them, Larry's place was modern, ordered, warm, and dry. He made coffee, real, not instant. I was sitting on the floor and he propped a pillow at my back against the wall when I grew tired. After I went home I worried about all I'd said, and when I saw Larry going into class the next day, a paralyzing shyness gripped me and I hesitated, wondering how he'd be, if I'd talked too much, said things he didn't want to hear. I stood back while everyone went into the classroom. Larry waited for me at the door. My hair fell forward and I let it hide my face when I came up beside him. He pushed the door of the lecture hall open, and touched my back to gesture me to go in before him.

"Thanks for last night," I said.

"Thanks for what?" He pushed my hair behind my ear so he could see me. "Good pizza, good talk . . ."

"Good friend," I said.

"Boston's too damned far away." Larry took a whack at Amelia's portal vein, close to the point where it leaves the liver. It was almost midnight.

"Take it easy." I reached down for his hand. "We all need to take a look at that, you know, find the point of entry. It won't be easy if you've ripped it out of her abdomen."

"I'm sick of telephones and travel, screwing every six weeks, a celibate between. Shit. I wish exams were over, I wish I was in Boston."

I was checking out the veins that form the portal system, the superior mesenteric, the splenic. The cystic was the one I had to find. Everything in the cadaver had the same gray look, and I was leaning in close to get a better view. My hair grazed Amelia's liver.

"Elana should move here," I offered without looking up. "City this size. There must be a law school here. Isn't there a law school? Where is that goddamned vein?"

Larry bent close with me.

"Sure there's a law school. But not one as good as B.U. Move your hand. I think I see it."

"Well, you go there, then. Transfer. Gotcha." I had the cystic vein between my forceps.

"Not so easy and you know it. Are you sure that's it?"

"Of course I'm sure." I pointed with my elbow at the opened page of the lab manual. "From the gallbladder into the vena portae. Take a look."

We bumped heads, my fingers slipped. I lost it. I put my forceps down.

"Look," I said. "You two should be together. Forget school, forget your long-term plans. Get to work on this, figure something out. Passion. Where's your passion?"

"My passion is in passing this exam."

"Okay. Okay," I said. Then I watched Larry's hand disappear into Amelia's belly.

The second year was much like the first, but with more patient contact, and without Amelia. Toward the very end, we cut her into pieces, sawed through her pelvis, took her legs to separate tables for closer examination. I hated that, the final mutilation, the end of her.

Larry and I had dinner once in a while, or a quick lunch on the run, but our schedules were different and we weren't together as much as we had been when we shared a cadaver. So I was glad to have a chance to talk when I ran into him that second spring. We were both going to Ben Taub Hospital to do histories on clinic patients, and we were walking together, catching up, when Larry stopped abruptly and looked at me.

"So, what's this about you and Sam?" he asked, an edge in his voice.

"What about him?"

"Are you two serious, or what?"

I laughed. "No one's serious with Sam. I just see him when he's at loose ends."

"Are you sleeping with him?"

I stiffened.

"What business is that of yours?"

"Never mind the injured sense of propriety. Are you sleeping with him or aren't you?"

I could have made light of it. Instead, I flipped my hair back. Turned my burning focused eyes on him. "Why? Are you jealous?"

"Fuck you," he said. "No. I'm not jealous. I'm in love with someone else, remember? I just think you could do better, that's all."

"And just what's wrong with Sam Atkins?"

"Nothing." He was looking straight ahead and walking fast as if he wanted this conversation to be over. "But if you take up with him you'll be short-changing yourself. Settling. You shouldn't do that."

"Don't worry, I don't plan to."

He was going to surgery. Me to medicine. He got to the door before I did, but he didn't wait.

Clinical rotations started in our third year. Medicine, surgery, O.B., psychiatry, pediatrics. I got medicine first.

Each student was assigned to a team. Each team consisted of a student, an intern, and a resident. For the first few days I mostly watched the others, followed them around, did small jobs they gave me. At rounds the attending asked a lot of questions, what labs were ordered, what were the results, what do you think should be done next for this patient. I'd thought

there might be a period of grace where I'd be spared that kind
of grilling, but in two weeks' time I went from "new kid,
give her time," to doing some part of the history and physical
on new admissions, drawing blood, dictating discharge sum-
maries. More than once I had to say, "I'm sorry, I don't
know," to the attending. "Then look it up," he'd say, "and
know it by tomorrow." The phrase "eating humble pie" took
on new meaning. I gorged on humble pie, overdosed, was
finally numbed to the taste of it. "I'm sorry, I don't know."
I knew the next day. "I'm sorry, that lab result isn't on the
chart yet." I was sent to find it. Twice a week I slept in the
hospital, took call with the intern, learned to wake up quickly
to the sound of the ringing phone, be coherent enough to take
a message from the operator, alert enough to call the nurses'
station, wake the intern, get moving. More than once I
thought of my dad, sleeping at the fire station. As I brushed
my hair, and forced myself awake, I imagined him already
down the pole, on the tiller, eyes narrowed to slits, the better
to see through freezing rain.

On my birthday, Kate and Larry had a party for me. Kate
brought wine, Larry did the cooking with his usual culinary
flair. He made quenelles of fish. I'd never even heard of them
before.

"I'm impressed," I told him in his kitchen.

He bowed. "I bought a book," he said. He was in his surgery rotation, distinguishing himself with all he knew, busy
at Ben Taub or in Boston on a lover's mission. I'd hardly seen
him since the argument we'd had in the spring.

"You look good," I said.

"You think so?"

"Yes. Different. Like your hair is longer, or you've lost some
weight or something."

He shrugged. "I don't think so. Maybe it's just that I
haven't seen you. Maybe you've just missed me."

He was right. But it was not the kind of thing I was inclined to admit.

The steam rose from the saucepan full of cream sauce, fogged his glasses. I handed him a pot holder when he gestured to it with his chin. I watched him while he poured. The sauce washed over the quenelles that he placed at intervals in a buttered Pyrex dish.

"Maybe I *have* missed you a little," I said after a few minutes of silence.

"No need," he said. "I'm here. I've wondered where you've been."

"Busy learning to deliver babies," I said.

"Good," he said. "That's good. I was afraid you might be carrying a grudge."

"A grudge?" I asked.

"Yeah. Against an old friend who had no business meddling in your love life."

I smiled.

"I was stupid," he said. "You ought to find somebody. I'd like you to be happy. Everybody should be as happy as me."

There was a picture of Elana taped to the cabinet above the sink. Her blue eyes smiled out at me. I looked back, unblinking.

Kate had decorated Larry's apartment. Crepe-paper streamers, helium-filled balloons. Jill and Mike came over later, bringing carrot cake and candles.

"I love celebrations," Kate said, while I sliced the cake and served it.

"Well, then, you'll love our news." Mike reached for Jill's hand. "We're getting married."

They were the first in the class. Someone cheered. Kate cried in Jill's arms. "Larry's next," I heard Mike say. Larry grinned.

"To love," I said, and raised my almost empty wineglass.

"To love." The chorus. Larry was beside me. He reached his arm around my shoulder like a brother. Then he turned my head and kissed me.

I didn't sleep that night. Out of my window in a winter sky, I saw Venus, the Big Dipper, the star Antares glowing in a cloudless sky. My pilot lover from college had taught me everything I knew about the stars. At the airport before a night flight. Stars can take you anywhere, he'd say. He gave me navigational charts and showed me which constellation to find where in spring, summer, fall, and winter skies. Or skip the charts, he said one night, just marry me, I'll do the navigating. I said no. No thank you. So much skill at turning love away had left me a novice when it came to holding on, weaving my way through it. Trouble, I said to myself, thinking about Larry. This will bring you grief and heartache, nothing more. But even when I said it, I could not believe it, some wishing hopeful thing had come alive in me.

I closed my eyes. It was my birthday. I resurrected childhood rules. I told myself I was entitled to one wish.

Edmund

AT EDMUND'S SUGGESTION, Currie meets him at the building which houses the occupational-therapy department. There have been many hospital activities in which Edmund has refused to participate—group therapy, the seasonal parties, the humiliating group sorties into the community for baseball games, shopping trips, and movies. But OT, or Shop, as it is so disparagingly referred to by the other inmates, is an activity that Edmund has found to be a useful, time-filling diversion. He has made a belt for Max, Naugahyde covers for several of his binders, the bookshelves that grace his room, and, of course, he has been inestimably helpful to his fellow patients in their fumbling efforts with the dull, crude tools that the OT department supplies for working with wood.

Edmund, so careful tidying up after himself, so ordered as he prepares to leave. He has cleared the area in which he worked, wiped it with a sponge, folded the apron that everyone is required to wear. Now he approaches Dr. Currie, who has been waiting patiently. Come, says Edmund as he holds open the door. We'll walk together across the lawn. There's time for talk before the lunch bell sounds.

By the time Anne went to Texas, Edmund had begun his seventh year of interviewing for the Fire Department. (The significance of the number 7 should not be overlooked, says Edmund in an aside to Currie. It is a numeral fraught with significance.) He continued to see Lucy twice a week, and she was generous in her encouragement of all his studies. Edmund missed Anne sorely, but he found that he'd grown rather used to her absences during the time she was in college; and although this most recent move of hers seemed more profound and permanent, it wasn't as life-altering as he feared it would be. The biggest change, the change that seemed most fabulous, that hardest to believe, was that Paul was writing, that in this small way Paul had been returned to him.

Dear Dad, Paul wrote. *The rainy season here in Ethiopia never came to much this year, and because of that we've had a terrible drought. The crops, the cattle, everything is dying. People drop on the road on their way to our infirmary. Yesterday, I baptized a baby dying in my arms. I spit on her head in lieu of wasting water. She was from a Hindu family, and I knew they didn't want my blessing for her, so I was careful, whispered salvation in her ear. "Do you renounce Satan? And all his evil works?" How well I remember how that ritual goes. I can still see the pictures in my first-grade prayer book of tiny winged souls. That baby was a dark-eyed beauty. God help me. I would have given anything to save her.*

Edmund kept Paul's letters in a box he'd built for just that purpose—austere and simple as the life Paul had chosen. He placed it on his dresser next to the box he'd made for Anne's missives, written weekly, on stationery of the palest blue. Her box was more ornate and showy, and each time he put a letter in either of them, he felt as if he was hoarding treasure, collecting from his distant children little shards of love.

Edmund thought that it was his new link to Paul that intensified his interest in St. Albertus Magnus. That, and the fact that St. Albert's spell had brought Paul back to him. Because, increasingly, St. Albert became one of Edmund's most important fire-tending inspirations.

Think of St. Albert, in his classroom, in his small monastic cell—his celibate life, the hours he spent alone, in prayer and contemplation. Think how easily the thought of transforma-

tion could take hold in a priestly mind, when transubstanti-
ation was what he did each day in the sacrifice of the Mass.
When Edmund was at work, he thought with envy of all the
free time a monk like St. Albert would have had to read and
study. Sometimes his mind drifted during interviews, and he
found himself back with St. Albert in thirteenth-century Germany, scouring the recesses of the monastery for a damp-
walled empty room, earthenware vessels, an unused bellows.
Souffleurs, the alchemists were called, and Edmund thought of
that word each winter when he lit his fireplace, when he
puffed his own soft breath over a waning flame.

And think, too, Dr. Currie, Edmund continues, of all there
was for Albert to study. There was the twenty-eight-volume
encyclopedia on alchemy that Zosimus of Panopolis wrote in
A.D. 300. The ancient Chinese writings on the "pill of im-
mortality." The dialogues of Morienus, Hermit of Jerusalem,
and Khalid ibn Yazid, an Arab prince, marvels of erudition.
And Albert's own *Little Book of Alchemy*, in which he listed
eight simple rules to be used as guideposts, equipment
needed, recipes to follow.

Impossible, whispered Edmund to his carved figurine of
Albertus Magnus. He'd moved it to a place of prominence on
Jeffers Street, to the parlor, or what had, by this time, become
his library, where it stood next to the gooseneck lamp on his
crowded rolltop desk. A cluttered room. Piles of books, Schumann II (the first bird died) in his cage next to a window.
Edmund had also moved some of the other saints into the
parlor, the ones he'd carved, a few of those made by his father,
and sometimes, absentmindedly, he spoke to them as well. He
knew their histories as thoroughly as he knew his own; he'd
shaped their hands, their backs, their faces to reflect their
suffering, or the ecstatic, beatific joy they'd known. He placed
Thomas Aquinas next to Albert. How wise it had been of the
Dominicans, he thought, to send shy Thomas to Albert, silent

bulky Thomas, known when he first came to Cologne to study as the "dumb Sicilian ox." Albert, scientist and theologian of renown, saw the genius hidden beneath his new student's rough exterior. So he encouraged Thomas, loved him, made him his disciple. They became like son and father, and it pleased Edmund to be able, in the small world of his parlor, to place them side by side again, to reunite them.

Some nights when he was reading, a feverishness came over Edmund; he lost all sense of time and place. On one such night he thought he heard the cries of the burnt woman he'd read about years earlier. On another, instead of words on the pages of his open book, he saw her crouched and kneeling, her hair ablaze, her arms stretched toward him, begging. And it made him wish he were miraculous again, like the boy he'd been, the one God saved from fever, the answer to a prayer.

Dear Dad, Paul wrote. *I'm worried that when you write you say so little of yourself. You never mention work, for instance. Do you like this interviewing that you do? I can just picture you looking deeply into the eyes of some young interviewee, that stony scrutiny of yours that made me fidget in my chair when I was small. I'd say that if your applicants survive the interview and your close questioning, they're ready to face anything.*

Yes, I got your letter, and I know you're lonely, but I'm not sure what to do about that, what to say. It's hard, from here, to know how to answer you. At times like this I wish I knew you better. I wish that we'd had more time together before I left, that we had talked more.

Did anyone produce gold? There are claims—some true, some, no doubt apocryphal. An Augustinian monk named Wenzel Seiler found a mysterious red powder in his monastery, and with it, in the presence of Emperor Leopold I, transmuted tin into gold. Nicolas Flamel, an illustrator of manuscripts, and his wife, Pernelle, who worked in 1382, studied a text they found for ten years before they finally succeeded in making gold. But most Adepts were inclined to keep success a secret, fearing they'd be badly used by greedy opportunists. Therefore, secrecy was central to the practice of The Art. Secret cells and secret laboratories. It was also believed that only one who had undergone a spiritual transformation could be successful with the physical experiment. So that the gold-making was a kind of test. Two men might follow the same formula for making gold, but only the Adept (or Magus or Initiate) would be successful. Greater alchemy must take place in the soul of a man before he can have success in the laboratory.

Formulas? asks Currie. They're difficult to find, Edmund admits, although after years of research he found several. The problem is that in most written instructions some crucial step is missing—another test. In the lore of alchemy it is assumed that a true Adept will intuit what that missing step might be. Thus, any formula requires extensive testing. So many alchemists were monks because monastic life was so well suited to alchemic experiments. It took months to complete them, the fires required constant tending. It meant commitment to a life of loneliness and meditation. The work is called the Magnum Opus.

There's a basic framework, stages that a substance goes through on its way to transformation. He made a list: solution, filtration, evaporation, distillation, separation, rectification, calcination, commixtion, purification, inhibition, fermentation, fixation, multiplication, projection. How to translate this into a transformation of himself he did not know. Endless study is required, said *Transcendental Magic*. All right, he answered. There will be many false starts, failure just when you think you're close. Patience is my middle name, he said aloud, undaunted. He kept a notebook by his bed in case some inspiration came to him at night. He slept with a pencil underneath his pillow.

Did you know, Dr. Currie, that Goethe's *Faust* was a product of his youthful alchemic interests? And that the Song of Solomon might be a veiled alchemic treatise? In every book he read he unearthed new treasures. And the book of spells—incredible, the things it offered. And they were things that Edmund needed. Because how to effect a transformation of himself seemed like a stumbling block. A problem. Aspiring adepts of old had mentors, someone to teach them. In many cases the formulas were never written down at all, but were passed on by word of mouth, so as not to be stolen or misused. There was no one to whisper secrets into Edmund's ear, he had no instruction manual. What there was, however, was the book of spells, and the rituals and incantations it described. So Edmund adopted St. Albert as his mentor, and used his book of spells as a kind of primer, a guide to help him train for the more arduous work which lay ahead. He copied spells into a notebook.

To Make Oneself Invisible
You must obtain the ear of a black cat, boil it in the milk of a black cow, then make a thumb cover of it and wear it on the thumb, and no one will be able to see you.

How to Be Able to See in the Darkest Night
Grease the eyes with the blood of a bat.

To Make a Mirror in Which Everything Can Be Discerned
Procure a looking-glass, such as are commonly sold. Inscribe the characters noted below upon it. Inter it on the crossing of two pathways, during an uneven hour, and take it out: but you must not be the first person to look into the glass.

How to Make Yourself Bold and Amiable
The stone called Actorius is to be found in the craw of any old capon. He who wears such a stone on his neck will always remain bold and beloved by all mankind.

That last spell ran through Edmund's mind for several days. Friendship, respect, and collegiality had formed the basis of his long relationship with Lucy, but from the outset he'd wanted more. His lustful dreams about her had continued unabated; guilt and misery about his past could not keep him from wanting her, but he kept waiting for a hint from her, some sign that she shared his feelings.

He had taken to running errands on his way home after he saw Lucy. Out of his house, roaming. A good time for library stops, the search for more books, hours of reading. He could have read at home and did, but he craved company, the sound of human breath and coughs and skidding chairs around him. The librarian must have thought he was some gray-haired old professor, she saved things for him, sent him postcards when she found a book she thought he should see, had a key made for the rare-book room. (Against the rules, a giant risk; he kissed her hand in gratitude.)

During one of his library stops, Edmund read of a white powder that Paracelsus always carried with him in the pummel of his sword. Azoth was its secret name, a mysterious life-principle, invisible eternal fire. Paracelsus believed that a man could do anything, even walk on water, if he used this life-principle, if he cultivated sufficient inner force. Fear robs men of power, he warned.

Edmund decided he'd let caution rule his life too much once he'd stopped fighting fire, especially when it came to working something out with Lucy. So he adopted boldness as his modus operandi. He consulted the last spell he had transcribed, got a capon, cut it up, took the stone out of its craw, put it on a string around his neck. Then he washed his hands before he picked up the phone in his front hallway and placed a call to Lucy.

"I want to take you out to dinner," he said in a rush, and even as he spoke, he realized that he hadn't eaten out in years, and had no idea where to go.

"Not a good plan," Lucy answered, sounding surprised and flustered. "Against my stated policy, no outside interaction with my clients."

"So you've told me, but it's time that things were different." His voice was firm, but his heart was pounding. "Get dressed," he said. "Be ready."

There was a long moment of silence, and Edmund feared that boldness was about to work against him. He closed his eyes and touched the amulet strung round his neck, imagined her ringed fingers cupping the phone, her long earrings dangling lightly at the angle of her jaw.

At last, her lovely, low voice broke the silence. "All right, Edmund," she said. "Perhaps you're right. I'll change. And I'll be waiting."

Anne

LANGUAGE IS THE TOOL of psychiatry. The patient's story, the therapist's responses. My interest in it has grown steadily since I began to spend so much of my time with infants. Because they don't communicate with language, I am required in my work with them to watch for other things—the slightest shift of gaze, the tilt of a head away. Sometimes I place my hand on a baby hand or rest my fingers on the back of a baby head, waiting for a bit of tension in the neck. No quickening is too slight, no movement too subtle for me to consider it a sign. Like the telling of a secret. There are times when I am awed by it, the prospect of listening with my hands.

I learned a lot about the way to be with kids in pediatrics. Up to then I'd been quite stupid about children, and I didn't really like them very much, but in peds I knew I'd have to figure out a way to be with them. So I worked at it, taught myself. I laughed at their dumb jokes, learned to make dumb jokes myself. "Rabbits," I'd say to a small boy with his hands over his ears, resisting my advances with my otoscope. "I've got to check for rabbits." Laughter, acquiescence. My voice, counting. "One, two. Can you believe there are six in there?"

But even as I became more skilled in pediatrics, I never learned to like it. There was too much sadness to it. We were the medical center, the specialists, we got the real sick kids, frantic, haggard parents. The waiting areas all had cartoon characters painted on the walls. Bugs Bunny with Elmer Fudd in hot pursuit.

A little girl named Maryanne was admitted to our service five weeks before I finished peds. She was four years old, big eyes, her wrist so thin my thumb and forefinger fit easily around it in a circle. Hair the orange-red of carrots. Too weak to walk.

"Up you go," I said, and lifted her into my arms to weigh her. I'd wheeled the scale down to her room from the spot where it was usually kept just outside the nurses' station.

Maryanne liked swinging through the air in my arms. Lighting on the scale. "You're strong," she said. Frank admiration.

"Not so strong." I had her standing, holding her under the arm with one hand, sliding scale weights back and forth with the other. But when I let her go to see how much she weighed, she teetered, almost fell. So finally I put her back in bed, got on the scale myself, checked my weight, picked her up, and weighed again. Subtracted. "You're just a little mite," I said.

"Tall, though," she said proudly. "Of all my friends I'm tallest."

"I don't doubt it. Prettiest, too, I'll bet." I warmed the cup of my stethoscope between my hands, slipped it underneath her gown against her chest, and listened. Her lungs seemed clear, in spite of a hacking cough. But her pulse was rapid, her blood pressure too high, and I'd noticed, when I checked her eyes, areas of focal spasm in the retinal arterioles.

"Were you prettiest, when you were little?" she wondered.

I almost laughed at her use of the past tense. Was I pretty? ever? once? at all? "Well, probably never as beautiful as you."

She winced. Docile as could be up to that point, she suddenly pulled her knees up to her chest, away from me, when I found a tender spot while palpating her abdomen.

"I'm sorry," I said. "I didn't mean to hurt you. Here, relax now. I'll be gentle as I can down there, but I've got to take a look. Come on now. There we go."

She uncurled herself, put her hands on mine to guide them. "Right there," she said. I felt the outline of a large mass on her left side. "Sometimes I cry, it hurts so much. Sometimes my tummy aches and aches."

"I'll bet it does." I straightened her gown.

"Maybe it's ice cream." She was chipper then, thinking that the worst of it was over. "Sometimes I eat too much ice cream, even when my mama says don't do it. Maybe it's a lump of ice cream stuck down there."

I sat beside her on the bed. "Hard to say." I smiled what Larry called my rare smile. "But I'll bet we can find out what it is, and when we do I think you'll feel a whole lot better." I produced a specimen cup from the cabinet beneath her bedside table. "Tell me. Do you think you could go pee-pee into this cup?"

"Into a *cup*?" She laughed.

"Yes," I said. "Into a cup. I'll give you a ride to the bathroom"—I made a scooping motion with my arms—"and show you what to do. And if your aim is good, you get a prize."

"Good," she said. "I love prizes."

I reached down and touched my white coat pocket, feeling past the stethoscope to the little troll dolls that I carried there for just such moments.

I turned her covers down. She put her arm around my neck. "I'll bet I know why you want my pee-pee," she said wisely.

I had her in my arms. She smelled like alcohol and talcum, like the just-washed cotton of her gown. "Oh really," I said. "Why?"

"Because it's beautiful and red, not yellow like other people's. I'll bet you just want it 'cause it's special."

Halfway to the bathroom, I stopped and shifted, rearranged my grip.

"That's right," I said. "That's why I want it."

"The old man wants a presentation, you've got the patient with the problem." My resident, Jim Grady, stopped me on the first floor of the hospital, told me Dr. Schmidt, our attending, needed someone to present at grand rounds about Wilms' tumors.

"But I've just got three weeks here, I've got finals, case reports to do. Besides, third-year students don't present at grand rounds."

He nodded, sympathetic, but glad, I could see, that he didn't have to do it. He shrugged. "It's the luck of the draw. The intern will be working on it, too. Look, the library should be full of stuff about this. It won't be so bad."

"Great," I said, trying to keep the sarcasm from my voice. "Terrific." I went quickly in my mind through all my patients. His pager beeped; he flicked it off, then turned to go.

"Hey," I called to him. "None of my kids have Wilms' tumor."

"Oh yes, one does. We just made the diagnosis late this afternoon." He looked tired when he told me. "The redhead. Maryanne."

Wilms' tumor. Most common organ cancer in children under ten. Most frequently arising between the ages of one and four. Large expansive spherical masses that totally dwarf the kidney. Sometimes weighing as much as the child. Myxomatous, fish-fleshed, solid gray . . . areas of hemorrhagic necrosis. Aggressive neoplasms, rupturing through renal capsules, metastasizing often to the lung. Microscopic views, abortive glomeruli in a loose fibrous stroma. Outlook poor, but changing with advances in treatment. Pictures of post-mortem kidneys, dwarfed malignantly. Small children, some just infants, abdomens like basketballs. Oddly, sadly pregnant babies. Hypertension, retinal changes, hematuria. Maryanne's bloody urine swam before my eyes.

She became sicker every day.

"I won't let you do it." Curled up in her bed, her back to me. (Talk to her, my resident said, she likes you. We've got to do these tests now, see how badly this has compromised her kidney function.)

"I know you've had it. All these tests, the IV in your arm."

"And my bottom hurts so much," she sobbed. Peeing into cups had lost its charm for her. We'd had to attach a urine bag with an adhesive edge to her perineum and let it fill, a bright red bubble there between her legs, a poor arrangement, the best we had. It leaked and stank and burned the tender flesh.

"I know it hurts. But we've got to do these other things, we really have to."

She pressed her face deep into her pillow, pulled away when I reached to touch her carrot-colored hair.

Maryanne's parents came from Hebronville on weekends. They were rice farmers, worked the land themselves and couldn't come to stay with her in Houston. "We'd come if we could," her mother said to me the first time I met her. One hand twisted the fingers of the other as she talked. She paused sometimes in a search for words, waiting for her husband to pick up sentences, to fill in for her. They were surprisingly young; they could have been teenagers dating. I felt old in their presence.

"The doctors say we ought to come more. That she needs

us. That she withers when we're gone. And I say, 'We're working people, Doctor, we can't walk away like that from what we do.' " Her fingers strayed to the nape of her neck in search of wandering strands of hair. Her husband sat beside her in the waiting room, his chair against the wall in such a way that Bugs Bunny's ears seemed to be his. "Still, I wonder," said the mother, "am I doing right? You're a woman, do you think I should be here with her?"

"She's such a little thing and she's so sick," I said. "How could you stay away?"

"Got no choice," said her husband, standing. "You need to be with me. Besides, she's dying, ain't nothing we can do." He used the calmest voice. I waited for the mother to cry out or deny it. Instead, she twisted her wedding band, focused on her hands. He stood at the window, looking out. The signal light on Fannin Street blinked red, then green then yellow. His face looked best in red light, hidden.

"She's been sick a year now," he said. "Seems in some ways like she never was well, sickly as a baby, weak and spindly all along. I'm a farmer. I know all about faith and blind hope, but I'm no fool. She's dying. They say radiation, medicine, we'll treat her. What do they know? She gets thinner every time we come here." He gestured to his wife. "Why should she watch that, I ask you? That baby knows we love her. I just can't sit there with her watching."

Maryanne in the procedure room. On the table. Me at her head. "It's all right. It won't take long. I'm here." A radiologist, two nurses; the tourniquet and needle on the table. The dye.

I'd thought Jim, the resident, would do the IVP, but a fellow in urology was sent instead. Hurried, pressured, chewing out the nurse who followed close behind him. "I told that fucker what I wanted, and I expect to get it."

Maryanne stiffened when she heard him.

"O.K.?" He looked over Maryanne at the others. "We all set here?"

"This is Maryanne," I said, hinting. Say hello, tell her what you're going to do.

"Who are you?" He narrowed his eyes to read my name tag. "Mueller. What are you, Mueller? Third year?"

I nodded.

"O.K., Mueller. Pay attention." He nodded to the nurse to hold Maryanne's arm down. She gave a little baby wail and tried to pull away.

"Just a prick," I whispered to her.

He went in steady with the needle, but missed the vein and began to probe from left to right, trying to find it. Maryanne, crying, dug her little nails into my hand. "She's got tough veins, they roll," I offered. Fool. Take it out, go in again. Don't poke around that way.

"When I need your advice, I'll ask you," he said. "The problem here is the kid is moving. Hold her down, for Christ's sake. Hold her!"

He went in two more times that way—the jab, the miss, the probing. Maryanne's moans had turned to high-pitched screaming. She choked on her own tears. "No more, no more," she begged us. The young nurse cringed and closed her eyes. The radiologist frowned and looked down at the floor.

"Shit." The urologist wiped his sweaty forehead on the arm of his green scrubs. I breathed, thinking that he'd give up now, call somebody from peds to do it, someone with a feel for children, a genius with small veins. But instead he picked the needle up to try again.

"Give it up!" My voice. The nurse's eyes came open, the doctor with the needle stopped mid-motion.

"What did you say, Mueller?"

"I said, give it up. If you can't find the vein, call somebody else. What do you have to prove anyway? Get the pediatric resident in here," I said. "She's just a baby. She can't take much more."

His eyes went black with rage. He pushed a shaking finger in my face. "Who do you think you are, trying to tell me what to do? I'll have your ass for this."

"Shh," I said. A final word for Maryanne as I watched him storm out of the room.

A visit to the dean, a reprimand. "But he was wrong," I said. "Do I have to stand and watch someone abuse a child?"

The dean raised a hand to silence me. "Your version, Miss Mueller. This child needed the IVP. Dr. Gorsky is a fine urologist, one of our best. Missing a vein is not a crime, Miss Mueller, you'll miss plenty in your career. Having a student call you on it won't improve your aim. You were there to observe and pacify the child, not give instructions in technique or bedside manner."

I looked down at my left shoe, angry, knowing if I looked at him I'd give myself away.

"You have quite a nice record here. Respectable grades, good comments so far on your clinical rotations. Next year you'll be applying for a residency. You'll need good recommendations. Watch your step. It won't help if you get a reputation for causing trouble."

It was late by the time I left the building. The sun was setting as I've since found out it only does in south Texas, with no hills or mountains blocking the view, the whole sky visible, the sun a bronze ball, the edge of the horizon the silver-blue of sage. I stood at the bike rack for a long time, my hands shaking, a bad taste forming in my mouth. I wondered if this is how it went in medicine, if silence, complicity was what would be expected of me. I'm not that kind of girl, I thought. If this is what they want I'll never make it. I took my bike lock from my backpack, then put it in again, thinking it would do me good to walk, to think, to take the long way home.

Maryanne was drugged against the pain. Legs drawn up as far as they could be around the hump of her abdomen. Asleep and breathing slow, but awake to my touch, my fingers on her bird wrists, her pulse rapid, thready.

"When is Easter?" The smallest voice.

"Five more days."

"Does the Easter bunny know that I'm in the hospital? Can he find me?"

"This is his first stop every year."

"Good." Drugged sleep, eyes closed again. I moved toward the door.

"Can't you stay?" Pat, pat. Her hand made a spot on the bed beside her. Grand Rounds in one more week, my grade in pediatrics, my damaged reputation on the line.

"Sure I can. Just close your eyes. I'll stay." I, who never had liked children.

The IV dripped. A siren sounded in the street below. I put my hand on Maryanne's, dimmed the lights and waited.

"You ready?"

Two days before my Grand Rounds presentation. My resident was checking on my progress.

"As ready as I can be." I was sitting in the room behind the nurses' station where we dictated notes, checking over reprints one last time. While I was reading, I was twining strands of hair around one finger.

"Why don't you go to the library?" Jim sat on the edge of the desk. "It's a lot more quiet. You'll be interrupted a hundred times tonight if you stay here."

I looked up from my book, my head and shoulders aching.

"I just wanted to stick around," I told Jim. "I thought I'd check in on my baby one more time before I go." I'd meant it to sound flip. My baby. Like we talk in medical school, "my guy in 402, my lady with the oozing aneurysm up in ICU." It didn't come out sounding that way.

"Careful, Anne," Jim said. "Getting close like that won't help you." He stood up to go. " 'Your baby' is a real sick cookie. All the test results are back now. The tumor's ruptured through the renal capsule, seeded in her abdomen. There's a shadow on her lung that looks like a metastasis. One kidney's shot, there's involvement with the other. Now she's got pneumonia. If we can clear up the pneumonia, we'll pull out the big guns, set up a protocol of radiation, chemo. But I don't think she'll ever get out of here. It looks bad, Anne."

I let the hair untangle from my finger, kept looking at the book as if I was reading.

"In this case, the prognosis is quite poor," I said. The auditorium was almost full. A swarm of faces, rows of white coats, green name tags. I'd spoken first about Wilms' tumor in the abstract, incidence, morphology, clinical manifestations. I had charts, I used a pointer. I spoke only at the end about the specific case that we were treating. Calmly, carefully. "This patient presents as a four-year-old Caucasian female . . ." Never saying Maryanne. Not "my baby." There were questions, then some comments, discussion of advances we were making in the treatment of Wilms' tumor. What we didn't know was that in a few years great strides would be made, miracle-like cures reported, even pulmonary metastases melting away as if by magic when managed with the proper protocol. Years later I read about that, stumbled upon the article while leafing through the JAMA, and I felt the swift sharp pain of recollection in my throat and chest.

The presentation was a great success. High praise and murmured compliments.

It was my afternoon for pediatric clinic, and we ran late, flu season, runny noses, fevers, mothers shushing softly in a misspent effort to stem the ebb and flow of children crying. It was early evening, my final coming up, I had studying to do. Before I left for the day, I went upstairs to write a discharge summary, one less thing to do tomorrow, and I thought I'd check on Maryanne while I was there. But her chart was gone, and her things were gone, and when I went out into the corridor, I could see the head nurse coming toward me, crying. Then I saw the cleaning crew on its way into her room with their cart of fresh supplies and disinfectant. Not the people who swing mops and dust halfheartedly. It was the crew that comes when a patient leaves, the crew that readies rooms for someone new, disinfecting beds and walls and windows. Scrubbing, scrubbing. Working late to remove all traces of the child who'd been there.

When I got home that night there was a letter in my box from Paul. I read it slowly, then, for comfort, took it to bed with me.

Dear Anne, It seems likely that I'm going to be transferred to India or maybe Sri Lanka. Who knows which? Communications are really rotten here, so I'll no doubt be the last to know if I'm going to be moved and where. The priest I replaced discovered he was leaving when I knocked on his parish-house door.

Since I knew from the beginning that I wouldn't stay long in any place, I'm surprised at how much I've let myself become attached to people here. I guess I hoped that by choosing missionary work, by moving frequently, I'd be spared the lure of closeness. Not so, I find. Too late. It's a lesson I would rather not have learned.

The end of my third year, summer. Rains came in late July in torrents. With hurricane season soon to follow. Abbey, Alex, Amy, Bess. August, September. Infectious disease elective. Trypanosoma cruzii, schistosoma mansonii, hepatitis,

TB, one Rocky Mountain spotted fever, a woman with malaria, a man who'd come home from safari with a jungle fever. I was sent to work him up. "Tell me about Africa," I said.

"Strange and beautiful," he said, sighing, while I palpated his liver. Then he showed me photographs he'd taken of the sunset on the Kalahari, a place known as Deception Valley in the harsh Botswana plains. Prides of lions, groups of native dancers, a missionary priest, young and tall just like my brother, with white and consecrating hands, holding high the Host.

It was time to begin thinking about residencies, time to decide what kind of doctor I would be. My friends, my classmates all seemed certain, crystal-clear; I was the only one who woke up, sweating, in the middle of the night without a clue as to what I wanted. I never liked the blood and guts of surgery; the idea of delivering babies every day had no appeal to me. Medicine seemed a possibility. I liked the detail, the piecing together of histories and lab results and symptoms. But there was something about psychiatry and those who practiced it. When I did my rotation early in my third year, I was struck by all the time they spent listening. So much patient contact, so much interest. All the talk there was about *feelings*, the unconscious, the dark secrets of the soul. Larry called it voodoo; his contempt was limitless. But to me it seemed like some vast impossible enterprise, just the challenge for a girl like me. It required things that I had always, secretly, wanted for myself. Some softness. Some quality of understanding. I talked tough, I acted tough. But it was wearing thin. I didn't know it until that rainy summer, but I was fraying. Things were about to come apart for me.

The worst storm came early in September: the sky never even lightened in the morning. Dark clouds heaved in the rolling sky. The wind broke branches and uprooted trees. And then the rains came. In sheets, in torrents, two inches in an hour, flooding. In the Methodist Hospital cafeteria at noontime I ran into Larry.

"I'll give you a ride," he told me. "Don't try to bike in this. I should be finished pretty early. Meet me in the lobby at about five."

So I waited for him. Me, leaning against the plate-glass window, looking out. A slice of sky had cleared off in the distance near my house. The rain had turned to a drizzle; the rising water had subsided. A Volvo pulled out of a parking space with headlights on, and then, as if the driver saw the clearing sky when I did, he turned the lights off, optimistic even after so much rain.

Five-fifteen. Five-thirty.

I imagined Larry kept late in his pulmonary elective, check-ing X-rays with his chief, scanning films in the viewing room, his lab coat fluorescent in white light. Larry, learning how to use a bronchoscope, invading hidden places, peering at some enemy disease.

Five-fifty.

I blew my breath onto the plate-glass window, fogged it, wrote my name in cursive, as I'd done when I was a kid. Egged on by Paul until I'd fogged every window in the parlor. Scrawled our names on every pane. Paul and Anne. Alone together, waiting.

Six-ten.

The rain stopped. The clear spot in the sky had widened. The guard who manned the desk for nighttime hours came in, went down the hall to find the after-hours sign in book. I pulled myself out of my reverie, shook my head to clear it, and I thought, there isn't any point in waiting anymore. The weather's clearing, you don't need him. I'd noticed new dark clouds forming in the west and I knew if I was going to make it home I'd better hurry. I stuffed my books and folding umbrella into my backpack, tied my hair back with a scarf. My bike was the only one in the bike rack, easy to find, hard to manage in the rising wind.

So much rain so suddenly. The old man said he never saw my bike or me. Maybe I skidded, veered into his path, maybe the rain had blinded me, maybe a certain carelessness about my life caught up with me. He said it was the thud that let him know he hit me. Bending over me, rain dripping from his face down onto mine like tears. On my back, in the street, my bike in a tangled heap beside me. I remembered putting my leg out to break my fall, my head hitting pavement. Looking up, my vision blurred. My backpack strap was cutting into my arm and shoulder. I moved to straighten myself, push the bike away, but couldn't. My leg felt angled away from me, as if it belonged to someone else. I reached down to touch it. Felt the warm ooze, recognized the familiar smell of blood. I scratched my finger on the bony sharp protrusion where the tibia ripped through my skin. The scream of a siren came to me as if through water. I was losing blood and consciousness. I heard the voices of a small crowd gathering, umbrellas like a multicolored awning, gathered in the air above me. Then there was a sharper voice, a paramedic. "Move aside, we're coming through."

One of the paramedics started an IV as soon as I was in the ambulance. "I'm a medical student," I said, as if that were more important than my name. "My leg is broken." No kidding? Bone stuck out, blood everywhere, what was I trying to prove? I kept giving orders, playing doctor, I wouldn't trust them to take care of a thing. I stayed tense and watchful, fought drowsiness and double vision, as I tried to read the label on the IV bottle. I bit the inside of my cheek until it bled—anything to avoid crying out against the fiery pain. Through the window, I saw the blur of streetlights, felt the swaying of the ambulance as we cut and weaved, sloshed through flooded streets. It wasn't something I was used to, all that motion, all that trust, my life in someone else's hands. Even when I finally closed my eyes, I couldn't let the rocking soothe me.

The leg was badly shattered; I had eight stitches in my head and a concussion. I floated in a blur of medicine and lights and worried talk about infection. I was in the OR fast, in record time. Open reduction, external fixation of the compound fracture. I made myself remember how the treatment went. A week in the hospital, five more in a cast, on crutches. Too long, I thought just before the anesthesia took effect. I don't have time.

I tried to be a model patient, but I wasn't good at it. I wasn't used to dependency and it brought out the worst in me. I'd never been sick before, not even mumps or chicken pox. It was as if I knew as a kid that there'd be no point, no volunteers to mop my fevered brow. Now I needed care, I should have been grateful for it, but I only found things to complain about—the food, the bedpan, my incapacity. The nurses kept the side rails up so that I wouldn't fall or bear weight on my leg too soon. I cursed them for it. I snapped at everyone, got a reputation for being the crank, the nag, the bitch in room 412 who ought to be avoided. The nursing supervisor came to lecture me. "You are a pain in the ass," she said.

Everyone who'd ever taken care of me seemed weighed down and burdened by it, and I'd sworn I'd die before I let myself become burdensome again. For the sake of peace, I made myself keep quiet, let everyone believe I'd acquiesced. But all the while I burned inside. The pain was easier to stand than the humiliation of asking for medication. I spent my days in a dark, sick fury, and lay awake most nights, my side rails up, confining me. As if I were a baby in a crib again.

Larry came to see me every day of my hospital stay. "I'm in the building all the time," he'd said. "It isn't any problem." Then he added, "Besides, if I'd picked you up when I said I would, you wouldn't be here."

On the day I was to be discharged, he came to take me home, a kind and helpful gesture, but he seemed rushed when he got there.

"You O.K.?" Larry asked. I was sitting in a wheelchair when he came, waiting for the ritual ride downstairs. It was raining again, but it was a gentle, soaking rain. I was looking out the window at it, hypnotized.

"Anne?" He had my crutches in his hand, my backpack slung over his shoulder. "The nurse is on her way to push you downstairs. It's time to go."

Larry had a ten-year-old VW bug. My leg, casted, unbendable, clearly wasn't going to fit. "We'll just put the seat back all the way," he said, but it wouldn't move. Old and rusted, fixed in its middle position, where it had spent the last five years. Larry tried to coax it, yank it, force it. He even brought some KY jelly out of his pocket (he was doing OB then) to see if it would help to lubricate the metal tracks. It wouldn't budge.

"Maybe I could climb in the back," I offered. Not easy in a two-door car even without a cast, but I thought that I might back in, somehow, stretch my leg out across the seat. Larry shook his head no, stubborn then, in combat with the stuck front seat. Sweat stood in pearls across his forehead. He tried KY jelly on the seat-release lever as well as the track, then accidentally wiped a smear of it across the leg of his khaki pants.

"Oh shit," he said. "I've got to wear these pants all afternoon."

I started to say "Cab." I was wobbling, waiting on my crutches, mad at him for being so damned stubborn, at myself for being at his mercy. All I wanted was to be alone in my apartment, this whole stupid scene forgotten, when suddenly, with a violence I'd never seen in him before, Larry kicked the seat, and it sprang back like some alive and frightened animal. Making just enough room for my damaged leg and me.

Mr. Landry had fixed my missing step while I was in the hospital. Replacing it with new wood, a red bow wrapped around it as if it were a gift. He'd installed an outside light as well, nothing much, a bare bulb in a socket, but it would make it easier to see at night, and safer.

"That's very nice," I said, looking up, admiring the step and bow. Larry looked at his watch, impatiently. The struggle with the car had made us late, traffic had been bad, he had to be in OB clinic. His reasons for impatience all were sound, but his eagerness to rush off chafed at me the way the edge of my cast rubbed my tender skin. I turned to small talk as protection, how very nice that Mr. Landry fixed the step, how kind.

"Very nice?" he said. "Dammit, Anne, he should have fixed that years ago. You pay him rent. He's supposed to fix things. It's a wonder you didn't fracture your leg here instead of on your bike."

"Oh, shut up, Larry." It was out of my mouth before I knew it. "He does the best he can, he's an old man, give him a break." There it was, my sharp tongue, the bitch I had become.

Larry turned to me. "What's with you, anyway? You've been scowling since I came to get you. I just think he should have fixed the step three years ago, that's all. I'm trying to be a nice guy, right? I drive you home, I want to help, and do I get a 'Nice of you to be so concerned'? A thank you? No. All you can do is jump down my throat. What's the deal?"

A fight. It seemed like just the thing to me.

"Oh, excuse me for my oversight. Thank you, Larry. Thank you. You're *so* kind." A bleating, ugly voice. I scorned him, I bowed to him in the mocking way I had that first day in anatomy. "I *have* thanked you, Larry. Three times in the car. Every time you came to see me. Thank you, thank you, thank you. For help in biochem, for showing me the light in anatomy, for dinner twice a week or when it suits you." Hating him, reaching back through time for old hurts, blaming him, finding someone, finally, to blame. "Oh, and while we're at it, thanks for humiliating me in front of the whole class our first year, and thanks for not showing up to take me home the day of the accident, and thanks for telling me so much about your love life and Elana, and how much you miss her, and how great she is, and how you can't wait to get out of here and back to her. My great privilege to listen to all that crap."

"Shut up," he said. But I was only getting started.

"So now, when do you thank me, Larry? For being such a pal, for being the girl that you have here, Elana to screw, me to have around, to get through hard times with. Me to help you get out of your gunner mode. 'Don't go to bed with Sam, don't settle.' " I lowered my voice, an ugly imitation of his. "Settling has nothing to do with this. You just want me for yourself, but not quite, just till school's over and we're out of here. Well, no more, Larry. *No more.*" I'd been screaming. I saw the next-door neighbor peering through her Levolor blinds.

"Are you finished?"

"Yes, I am."

"Good. Because I won't listen to this shit for one more minute." He grabbed my arm. "I'll just help you get upstairs and then I'll go. I've got better things to do."

I yanked my arm away. "I don't need your help," I shouted. "I can manage by myself." I hadn't yet decided how to navigate the stairs, but inspiration seized me. I sat down on the bottom step, thinking I could scoot up on my backside, step by step, my crutches in my left hand, my broken leg dragging along behind me.

"Come on." Larry reached for me again. "Don't be stupid. The steps are soaked. Stand up and put your arm around me."

"No!"

"Damn you," he said. "*Damn* you!"

But I was well on my way up the stairs already, moving right along. I stopped to rest a minute on the new step Mr. Landry had made. Then I took the bow he'd used for decoration and placed it over my head, like a necklace, or a prize. Tired, but not about to show it. Looking down at Larry with just two more steps to go.

I heard the footfalls first. The two steps across my tiny landing. The hesitation. The knock. It was my first night home, and my leg was stretched across the bed, my flowered terry bathrobe wrapped around me. I'd fallen into a light sleep. I thought the knock came from a dream until I heard it again, and then heard Larry's voice, a hoarse, projecting whisper.

"Anne, it's me. Larry."

I took up my crutches, hobbled to the door.

"What a surprise," I said. A lie. Somehow I'd been expecting him. The bare bulb that Mr. Landry installed on the landing cast a harsh white light. I thought I'd never seen Larry's face so clearly. I maneuvered to one side to let him in.

"It's late for drop-in visits, don't you think?" It sounded harsher than I meant it to. There was no reason to be cruel to him now. Everything between us had been said. His hands were in the pockets of his slacks. Blue shirt, his khaki jacket. No, I thought. There really is no reason to be cruel.

He closed the door. "You had a lot to say today."

"Yes. I guess I did."

"So, tell me, when did you figure all this out about me?"

"Look, Larry. I'm sorry. It really doesn't matter anyway, what I've figured out. Let's just forget it."

"Hard to forget," he said. "Especially when it seems so true." He hesitated when he took his hand out of his pocket, as if he was still trying to decide how far to go with this. Then he touched my cheek. "How did you get to be so smart?"

I looked down at the floor.

"And when did you get to be so pretty? All this time, and I never realized how pretty you are." He stepped toward me. His fingers drew a line down to the place between my breasts where the lapels of my robe met.

I shook my head no. But his hand was gliding past the border of the robe, across my breast. With his other hand he took the crutches from me. I leaned against him, ready for him, three years of foreplay already to our credit, mating rites performed day after day. He moved me toward the bed, but my leg made him think better of it. We eased down to the floor.

Larry, slighter than I might have thought without his clothes, the hair on his chest the color of white sand. Kisses for my calf and thigh, my cast, the only obstacle to his hand's roving.

"Sorry," I said when his knuckles hit against the plaster.

Kisses for my hair, my eyes. His fingers circling my nipple, his sweet tongue moistening me. He smelled of beer and, could it be, formaldehyde? Two years later? Still? Were we so marked by what we'd done together?

"I'll never leave you," he whispered. An amazing promise, how I loved him for it. "I want you," he said, and it made some simple, perfect sense. I moved my cast aside to ease his entry.

For weeks we let ourselves believe that love makes all things possible. Larry left each morning to deliver babies, I labored all day in my apartment over a paper I had to write to finish my elective. We filled our days with work, then spent our evenings together. He packed a small bag, moved right in. He cooked for me; he propped my casted leg on several pillows as if I were fragile, precious. He entered me from every angle; it was as if he hoped to probe the darkest parts of me, to ferret out some hidden secret girl and claim her. I'd never been so still, so calm, believed so much. He brought mezuzahs, placed them over every door. He said he only wanted me, and all I wanted was to believe him.

"Of course," I said. It makes you smug and certain when you think you're loved that much. It makes you foolish.

It was late October before Elana's name came up. He'd have to go back home, he said. He'd have to tell her. My cast was off, I didn't have the limp the orthopedist feared I might, everything about my life now seemed a miracle to me. It was only when I saw Larry's face the night he came back from Boston, when I met him at the airport, that I realized he'd be Elana's in the end. Only then did I begin to prepare myself for the day he'd have to leave me. I was well rehearsed in this; I knew how it went. So that even as we made love in my bed that night and the next, and I listened to his promises, I forced myself to think about the time when he'd go back East for good. I required myself to focus, to imagine it, even when such imagining made me weak inside and sick. I concentrated, until I could see it plainly—the day he'd leave, five years from now, my future without him. The accidental meeting—how we'd run into each other at some medical symposium in a tropical resort; how we'd recall good times and old affections in brief notes and cards at holidays. Short, remote, communiqués like the letters from my brother. Or the static-ridden late-night phone calls—so much noise and distance between the dad I loved and me.

Three weeks after the cast came off, I learned I was pregnant.

At first I wouldn't let myself believe it. I'd taken the pill in college, then used a diaphragm when the side effects of the pill began to worry me. No problem. There had never been a problem. After that first surprising night with Larry, we'd been careful every time.

"So. Big surprise, eh?" My gynecologist motioned me into her office after the exam.

"Yes."

"Well, what's the plan? Is this somebody you could marry?"

I folded my hands in my lap. "No. I don't think so."

"We can do a routine D&C. If you do it in the next few weeks, there'll be nothing to it."

I looked across her desk. There was a picture of her husband and kids (two boys, a girl) in a mother-of-pearl frame, a boat in a bottle, and a plastic model of the birth canal with a plastic baby head wedged in it.

"Or you could leave school, have the baby, let it be adopted. I mean, if that's what you'd prefer."

No response from me. She shifted in her chair. I could see that she wanted to get this settled.

"You forgot one other option." I looked at her. "I could have this baby by myself and keep it." I hadn't even thought of it until then.

She frowned. "Well, yes, you could do that. But let's face it, Anne, it wouldn't be easy. You're not even finished with school. You still have years of training. It would be really tough to be alone and have a baby. I'd think that over carefully if I were you."

But I was hardly listening. The baby would be a girl, I thought; she'd look like me.

I got up to leave.

"Anne?" She stopped me at the door and touched my arm.

"Plan one gets my vote. I could put you first on the schedule day after tomorrow. A day or two of rest, a little cramping. Really, Anne, there's nothing to it, you'll hardly feel a thing."

But I would, I thought. I would. I don't know how I knew that, but I did.

I was young then, I hadn't given much thought to the way instincts guide you. I just knew I'd have that baby. It flew in the face of every plan I'd made, it was nothing that I'd longed for, but there it was, baby cells dividing in my belly, making arms and face, lungs and a brain, a crazed extravagant production that my pumping heart supported. If I had come to myself for advice, I would have said abortion is the only choice here, but that advice seemed suddenly for someone else, too late for me. My face had rounded, my freckles darkened, my wide mouth grown soft and full. Each night, I spread my fingers in a fan across my still-flat abdomen.

"We need to have a talk," Larry said. A mid-November Sunday at the zoo. An unexpected day off for each of us, together. Walking would be good for my leg, he'd said. So we went to see wildebeests, giraffes, and kangaroos. We were in the mood for hot dogs, so we had them—warm sun, lots of time. A talk. He was going to marry Elana. In defiance of a sign that said: "Don't Feed the Animals," I threw a peanut to an elephant.

"Do you love me?" I asked.

His face was flushed. "That's not the point."

I shook my head. "Apparently it isn't. Still. I'd like to know."

"Of course I do. But it doesn't matter. This can't work. It would be too hard if we tried to stay together. We're too different, you're not Jewish; if I stay with you it would kill my parents. I've made plans. Everything about my life is set. I've got to go ahead."

"I see."

"Is that all you're going to say?"

Already I could feel the buttons of my jeans dig into my thickening waist.

"Should I say more? How about goodbye, good luck? How about I'm pregnant?"

"What?"

"I said, I'm going to have a baby."

"Oh, Anne." He reached for me, tried to draw me to him, but I pulled away, took a breath, then told him what I'd decided.

"What do you mean, keep the baby? I'm saying I can't marry you, Anne. I'll help you, I'll arrange everything for an abortion. I'll take you there and stay with you—whatever you need. But I can't marry you."

"I didn't say anything about getting married."

"Well, what are you saying? That you're going to raise a baby by yourself?"

"That's right."

"That's crazy."

There was a spot of mustard on his chin. "I know it sounds crazy, but I've thought it through. I've set up interviews for residencies in the next few weeks before I'm showing. I'm applying for a year from this July, so I can work part-time somewhere, make some money, be with the baby this next year. None of the places I'm interviewing need to know a thing about this until the letters of acceptance go out in March. The baby's due in late May. I'll work and finish my last elective in the fall."

We kept walking. Larry pleaded with me, reasoned with me; he ticked off on his fingers all the ways my plan would fail. He gestured with his arms, his hands sliced the air. I watched him, studied him, gathered pieces of him for my memory, things I could retrieve one day when my baby asked about his father. I heard Larry out. But I didn't let anything he said move me.

Larry sat down on a bench next to the gorilla cage. He put his elbows on his knees and pressed his face into his hands. "Please," he said. "Don't have a baby that I'll have to leave. If you love me, don't do this to me."

If I loved him. I felt some unfamiliar stirring underneath my heart. When I realized what it was, without thinking, I reached out for Larry's hand and placed it on my abdomen. "It moved. Can you feel it? Just the slightest little flutter. Here." Then I pushed his slender fingers hard into me.

Larry came for Christmas dinner. It was the first I'd seen him since our visit to the zoo. He'd moved his few things out of my apartment on an afternoon when I was gone, at my suggestion. Once or twice he called, thinking we should get together, "talk things through," but I knew that all he wanted was to try to change my mind, and I didn't want to hear it. I only relented about Christmas because I missed him so much that I couldn't eat or sleep; I was growing sick from longing for him. I said yes to Christmas as a kind of test—I would be nonchalant, I would be casual, I would show him that I didn't want him anyway, I didn't care.

Candles, turkey, pecan pie, a small tree with the string of lights I'd bought three years before. I wore the shamma that my brother sent me, loosely draped; I wore the beads. I wanted to be nonchalant and beautiful.

Larry had just gotten back from Boston.

"So. How were your interviews?" I asked.

He said they'd gone fine. Extremely well. One of the interviewers had done everything but offer him a place.

"Lawrence Klein, M.D. Thoracic surgery." I tried to smile.

He told me how one interviewer had had a twitch, a facial grimace, how hard he'd had to struggle not to stare. While he ate dinner he leaned back in his chair. We managed something approaching ease, a strained politeness during dinner. Then, when we were finished, he pulled back my chair for me. He'd wash, I'd dry. We'd do the dishes.

But sometime between the eating and the clearing of silverware and glasses the strain of all that effort began to show. Larry said that he'd choose Harvard over all the others if they offered him a place.

"That's great," I said with false good cheer. "Terrific. Just what you wanted, right? Just where you want to be."

"Right." Larry got an S.O.S. pad from under the sink and started working on the roasting pan. "Just what I wanted."

We'd set records for cold temperatures that winter. Now they were predicting snow. The wind rattled the windowpanes. Bare tree branches scraped against the roof.

Larry's shirt cuff dipped into the greasy water. He held both arms up so that I could roll up his sleeves. The soft hair of his forearm brushed against my wrist. I blushed, he looked away. By the time he'd turned back to the sink, the ease we'd struggled for had disappeared.

"So," said Larry, frowning. "How are you feeling?"

I put my dish towel down. "Don't use that tone of voice with me."

"What *tone.*"

"That tone of labored patience. Your shoulders sink like some damned beast of burden when you ask me how I feel. And I just hate it. So please. Don't drag us both down this way. I'm fine. Go ahead and let yourself be excited. It sounds like things are set for you in Boston. Time to be happy. Everything is going to be all right."

He scrubbed harder at the pan. "We should get married. Face it. That's what we should be doing."

I took his arm to make him face me.

"All right," I said. "Do you want to ask me to get married, Larry? Go ahead. Ask me. And do you know what I'll say?

I'll say no. Nice offer, but it isn't what I want. Not now. Not anymore. I just want to get through this year and have this baby. Please. You're off the hook about this."

One week later, New Year's Eve, he called me. Long distance from his parents' home in Boston. "Married," he said, sounding slightly drunk and happy. "We just went ahead and did it. We decided it would be better not to wait."

"Good for you," I said. Then I winced because the baby kicked me.

Elana stayed in Boston to finish school; Larry came back to finish school with me. By that time I was showing. On my rotations and in the lecture halls. Miss Mueller still. My love affair with Larry had been brief and secret; no one guessed the baby was his. But when anyone was bold enough to ask me outright who the father was, I fell back quickly on Catholic rhetoric. "It's a miracle," I said. "Another virgin birth."

On an April afternoon, I wrote to Edmund. Telling him about the baby, about dreams that had been troubling my sleep. Once when I was ten he'd gone to fight a two-alarm at the home of an old man who'd been a hunter, eighteen guns in a gun rack in his front hall, loaded still. Edmund told me how the old man stood there by the fire trucks, watching, as everything he owned went up in flames. All quiet, but for the spitting sound of fire and the gush of water pulsing from the hoses. Then all at once, Edmund said, he heard the sound of guns, the whiz of bullets flying by. The ammunition, reached by fire, exploded like the attack in late-night movies of a cavalry brigade. My dad was the last to realize, the last to hit the ground. One bullet struck his fire helmet, the hard-pressed leather rim. The bullet was deflected by it, but made a slice across his skull that needed twenty stitches. A half inch lower and that bullet would have killed him.

He laughed when he told the story of the guns, using it then as he would through the years as proof of his good luck.

For me, it held another message. That while I lost my mother only once in a great while, I ran the risk each day of losing him. An awful thing for kids, I said in my letter. So much fear and losing.

My baby's due next month, I told him. No wedding, no husband, just me. Already I am trying to think of ways to fend off sorrow for her. I am accepting all suggestions, especially from you, the grandpa. The person I know most experienced in sorrow.

Three weeks later a crate came UPS. About as tall as me and twice as wide. A hand-made wooden cradle packed in Styrofoam and cotton batting. I knew his woodwork like I knew his voice. Finely made and big enough for a good-sized baby for a good long while. When I pushed its side to rock it, there was a creaking sound, a murmur.

My labor started two weeks early. The small light waves of tightness first in the early hours of evening. Larry came just minutes after I called him, there beside me, one last time, just as he'd promised. With what he picked up in OB and learned about Lamaze from reading, he sat beside me, coaching. We'd decided to go outside the medical center for the birth, to a Catholic hospital nearby. Nuns in starched white habits, a crucifix on the wall of every labor room. And how we labored. He used the softest voice to coach me, even when I cried out, hurting. Soothing me. Holding up his fingers with the number of short breaths I should take between each blow. Wiping my hair back, placing his hand on my forehead, urging me to rest between contractions. His breaths almost matching mine. An old nun kept coming in to check us, then skidded off with whispered promises of prayers to Mary, patron saint of mothers. "Oh, goddamn, it hurts!" I cried once and she poked her head inside the door to scold me.

"Just leave us, Sister. We're doing fine." Larry pushed her out the door.

Hours, hours. Each pain building on the last, and cresting, easing off and starting up again.

"Don't push, don't push," he said. The sudden unexpected pressure made me cry out. "Transition," Larry said reminding me, my cervix open, the baby passing through. "Hang on, Anne, hang on. After this you'll get to push some, they say that feels better. Just hang on." But the baby had another plan, ready to be born faster than anyone had thought it would be. No time to take me to delivery. I could feel the baby's head between my legs. Larry left my side to look, opened the door and shouted down the hall. "We've got a baby coming here. *Nurse!* She's ready, past ready, damn it, let's go . . ." Too late. I was heaving, pushing, even though I knew I shouldn't. Baby coming, baby coming, baby almost there. I could see Larry's head framed in the V my legs made, see his sweaty forehead glisten in the light. He used his forearm to push his glasses up his nose. "Ohhhh," I cried out with that last contraction, tired from fifteen hours of labor, giving my all to the final push.

"A boy," Larry said. There was no bulb syringe in the labor room, nothing to be used for suction. So Larry put his own mouth to the baby's and sucked in hard to clear the mucus. Better than syringes, I thought as I lay watching. Like some life-giving kiss. I heard a whimper, then a howl. Then Larry held our baby up for me to see, molded head and little blood-streaked body. Larry placed the baby on my stomach, took my hand and placed it on the baby's back, as if it was a gift. Then the nun came in and saw us, and the doctor rushed in shouting orders, with sterile gloves and sterile sheets, trying to make a clean and ordered thing of the work we'd already done.

I'd been planning on a girl. Someone who would grow as I had to have long hair and skinny legs, breasts and periods in adolescence, who would do the things that I had done, and have the kinds of feelings I remembered. What would I know about having a boy? When he was two hours old, they brought him to me wrapped tight in a blue receiving blanket, wide awake but quiet. The nurse began firing off instructions. "Five minutes on the left breast, then five on the right. No more. Unless you want cracked and bleeding nipples, no fun, I assure you." I looked at her dull, plain face, then down at the perfect beauty in my arms. What did cracked and bleeding have to do with anything? She wanted me to bare my breasts and start up while she stood there to instruct me, but I dismissed her. When she was gone I rearranged him in his blanket, pulled him close to me.

"O.K., Max, here we go," I said. Larry's father's name. It was as if I'd always known what I would call him. I said it again, and it seemed right, I thought it suited him. A simple strong name. A handy thing, I thought, to take into a complicated life.

From the beginning he was a baby with his own agenda. He wanted to nurse almost constantly; he hadn't read the books that talk about schedules and routine. At night, in the cradle Edmund had sent him, I could hear him shifting, waking, sucking on his fist for seconds, whimpering, then wailing, his sweet mouth in a perfect O. No grimaces or purple rages, that simple round-mouthed wail. More like a song than crying. When I nursed him, he turned his face and pressed it into me, rooting, mouthing the fabric of my cotton gown, willing to do anything to cut through barriers and get to me. In those early weeks, he cried, I nursed him, we rocked, I sang. Movement always seemed to soothe him, so I, who'd learned to give up dancing, took up dancing once again, little swaying motions that made Max stretch and sigh and press his little body hard against me. On days when exhaustion overtook me, I'd often sit drowsily beside him, or doze in a rocker while I held him in my arms. More than once I woke up thinking I'd heard a voice or felt some presence near me. "Ghosts in the nursery," Selma Fraiberg called them. Mothers dead and living. Absent but evoked companions, shadows on the nursery ceiling, whispers in the walls.

A letter came when Max was three weeks old; Paul didn't know about the baby yet. My last four letters to him had come back to me unopened; I guessed he was in transit, on his way to his next assignment. So I'd been waiting for word from him, and while I waited I kept writing, even though I couldn't mail the letters, figuring I'd send the whole stack of them when I finally got his new address. I felt untethered when we were out of touch, and there were even days when I imagined he'd be lost to me again, the way he had been for a while right after he ran away to the seminary. During those first few weeks of nursing Max, I remembered how I'd tried to get him to promise he'd baptize my first baby, and either that or some postpartum hormonal rush made me cry long and hard when his letter finally came.

Dear Anne, Paul wrote. *Poverty is the biggest problem in Sri Lanka. So much hunger, I feel ashamed to eat. The children clamor for their First Communion because they want the chance to eat the Host. The things that pleased me in the early days in Ethiopia are all gone here—no basketball, no camaraderie between the other priest and me. He drinks himself into a drunken stupor every night, and the longer I'm here, the less I blame him.*

I dreamed last night about the time you came to see me when you were just a kid and I was still in the seminary—the way I kept myself from you. In my dream I do it differently. I forgive you for the simple sin of needing my care when I was too young to give it.

We grow tea here. And spices. And rubber trees that grow tall quickly.

Edmund

B Y T H E T I M E Anne's baby was born, Edmund was seeing Lucy three times a week. Most often he would stay
two hours; a double session was required for all they had to
do. She was teaching him the things he needed to know about
celestial bodies, Jupiter and Venus. What to look for in the
night sky when. Sex first, then theory, stars and tarot cards,
her voice as she read aloud to him from the works of Paracelsus.

Or, some days, theory first, then slow seduction. ("Variety
is everything," she claimed.)

"The soul is male, active, fiery, most frequently equated
with the sun," she told him one day, helping with his zipper.
"The moon is spirit, cool and female, the receptacle of the
sun's rays." (This in bed, with her beneath him, her bowl-
like pelvis swaying.) Once he asked her, "My mind shuts
down, pure lust takes over, how can I remember what I
learned in passion?" She wrapped her legs around him, moved
her fingers slowly up his chest. "Don't worry. My lessons will
be etched forever in your heart."

For a while he thought he'd find a way to marry her, but
she said, Our bad luck, again the stars were wrong. "There's
no one else," she said, and he believed her. But her principles
and skills were everything to her; her charts and theories her
religion. She turned her back on love the only other time it
found her, in deference to the stars. He knew she meant it
when she said she would again. Disappointment cut him
deeply, but even when they caused her to resist him, he stood

in awe of her beliefs. Still, admiration not withstanding, twice
a year he begged her, Check the stars just one more time, you
might have been wrong when you worked it out before, and
twice a year she told him that stars never lie.

Edmund pauses, looks down at his broad-palmed hands. Oh,
Dr. Currie, Dr. Currie, the mind drifts when you're alone.

There was so little in his life of value then. When he walked
through the fire station, to his windowless office every day,
he had to avert his gaze when he passed the trucks. To see
them waiting to be filled by other men was to have the breath
pulled from him. Whenever he heard the sirens sound he had
to grip the edges of his chair to keep from rising up, from
running. Every fire he didn't go to felt like a lapse to him.
Every death or injury he read about seemed like his fault. He
felt as if his hands were stained with blood. At home, he
carved a figure of the kneeling, pleading woman, and she became, for him, the patron saint of Death by Fire. He prayed
for her forgiveness.

He forced himself to go to work. The wearing of his uniform was a travesty, he felt unworthy of it, and the candidates
he saw seemed unworthy to him, too.

"What makes you think you're brave enough for this? Have
you ever *been* to a fire? Do you know how shaky those exten-
sion ladders feel when you're up hundreds of feet above the
ground on one of them?"

Some of them looked at Edmund as if he was a crazed old
fool. Others turned away, embarrassed by his zeal. Young
men, some dull and lazy-looking, some like Edmund was
once—eager, anxious, willing. Lots of them just wanted jobs;
they had no sense of fighting fire as vocation, as a thing worth
dying for. Once Edmund started shouting. He took a young
buck by his collar and screamed into his cocky little face. He'd
been slouched in his chair, looking tired and bored, as if Ed-

mund was there to please him and was failing. "You little piece of shit," Edmund shouted. With one hand he pulled the kid up out of his chair. *"Don't you know that men have died for this?"* A slip from proper procedure, the beginning of the end of his career as an interviewer. Just as well. It had gotten harder for him. He was getting more and more distracted during interviews, his mind wandered. He knew his fireman life was over, so he wrote his resignation letter, beat them to it. "I'll miss you all," it said. "Fire's been my life for forty-six years, hard to think it's over. I'll take the gold watch, my old Timex having perished in a blaze some time ago. I'm sorry that the tiller's been retired. It was a fine and useful thing, an honor for a man to steer it. A privilege younger men will never know."

Edmund stops to push a book across the table toward Currie.
"The Book of Mercy," says Edmund, "by Jābir ibn-Hayyān, a famous Persian alchemist who died in Tus in 815, with this, his final, uncompleted manuscript, under his pillow. His Magnum Opus left unfinished, mercy beyond his reach."
And beyond Edmund's as well, or so it seemed to him. After his retirement, he spent most of his time at home alone. And without the demands of daily employment—the getting up, the getting dressed, the brisk walk through the city thoroughfares—he felt that he was aging quickly. His knees ached, his hands began to bend arthritically; his vision, always perfect, had begun to dim as soon as the flush of fire was no longer reflected in his eyes. Now it dimmed even more. He wrote to Paul and Anne, but in spite of letters they seemed out of reach, a million miles away.
Paul had been moved to El Salvador that winter. He wrote about the warring factions there, and all about the priest who lived there with him.
A big man. A bastard, I thought when I first met him. He wore

jeans and a red Budweiser T-shirt, with a pack of Camels jammed into the pocket. He looked like one of the Salvadorian rebels I'd been told so much about. Coarse graying hair, a close-cut beard. Hair made damp by humidity curled on his lower arm, rose above the neckline of his T-shirt. Taller than me, about my age, with muscles rounding out his arms. I imagined he had been a wrestler in his former life, and I felt thin and insubstantial when he offered me his hand to shake. He called himself Jake Flynn. He didn't smile.

El Salvador was not the place I would have chosen. Soldiers with rifles roam the village streets. I can hear gunfire in the hills.

Monsignor Shaeffer, who'd brought me from the capital, stayed for dinner that first night. Jake cooked—squash and salad, lettuce from his garden, and a chicken. "We raise chickens," he said, and the "we" made my stomach turn, reminded me that I was here to stay. We drank the Scotch that Monsignor brought, and not-so-fine red wine that Jake pulled from a cabinet in the corner. With our plates pushed back, our stomachs full, the candles on the table burning down, we could have been three priests in a parish house anywhere. The gunfire in the hills could have been thunder—a warning of an un-expected, quickly moving storm.

I'd worn my Roman collar for the evening, as had Monsignor. As a gesture of propriety and grace. But grace seemed lost on Jake, who yielded just enough to change his T-shirt and brush the loose dirt from his jeans. I could see that there was no love lost between him and the Monsignor. He called Jake James, he criticized his cooking, he went on like that all evening, until he fell into a drunken sleep, leaving Jake and me the last of the Scotch. The edges of the native tablecloth stirred in a light breeze. Rain clattered on the metal roof, so noisy that it made talking impossible. A blessing. The Scotch, the breeze after a day of killing heat. I took my collar off. Jake filled my glass again.

Edmund placed the letter in Paul's box with all the others, and as he stood at his dresser, slipping this last letter into one of the string-tied bundles, he wondered what it was about himself that made everyone flee from him. How had he come to be deemed so unworthy?

Be merciful with me, he said under his breath to a God he no longer believed in. Give me the power to set things right again. I'll use the Elixir well, make every effort to be wise and careful. Just one more chance, he breathed. Just one more chance for me.

His loss became obsession, and he gave himself to it. For the next three years, he read volumes on perfection. He packed away woodworking tools to make room for fire and furnace, cleared shelves for charts and diagrams. He committed one end of the basement to the things he needed for his efforts with the spells—cats and bats and swallows, the fungus of a linden tree. He started to collect the eighty-odd pieces of apparatus he would need in his search for the Vital Essence. Furnaces, lamps, cucurbits, water baths, ash baths, dung beds, reverberatory furnaces, crucibles, mortars and pestles, sublimatories, to name just a few. He took bricks out of his back yard, planted herbs for potions. He told himself that all he had to lose was time, which he had plenty of. He made a list of what he'd need. Drew sketches, knowing he'd have to fashion some of the equipment himself, guessing that chemistry-supply stores didn't stock athanors and aludels, pelicans or Balneum vapori furnaces. He found a formula in an old manuscript.

A True Revelation of the Manual Operation for the Universal Medicine Commonly Called "The Philosopher's Stone" by the celebrated philosopher of Leyden as attested upon his deathbed with his own Blood, Anno Domini 1662.

The Process.

In the Name of God, take sea salt, brought by ship from Spain, let it be dried in a warm stove, grind it in a stone mortar, that it may be dissolved in Dew-water gathered in the month of May or

June, when the Moon is full, during an East or South-East wind. Drive sticks into the ground, one and one half feet high, lay four square plates of glass upon them, and as the dew collects on them, drain them into your waiting vessels.

Now, when you have enough dew, close your vessel, set it in a cool place where no warmth can come to it, or else the subtle spirit will rise and be gone. Close it with wax.

Now, in the Name of God, dissolve the salt in this Dew-water, then put this compounded water into a round vial with a short neck, lute it with a good lute, a cover and stopper that fit it well, that the living spirit of the dew may not fume away. Set it in the furnace of Balneum vapori to putrefy. Make a slow fire and let it digest for forty days or fifty, so that the fume of the water be continually round about it, and you will see your matter grow black, which is a token of its putrefaction.

Have your dry furnace ready. Set your glass in it, give it a slow degree of fire, continue it for twelve or fifteen days, and your matter will begin to coagulate and to fasten round about your glass like a gray salt. Then return to your putrefying furnace as before. Set your glass in it, and give the same degree of fire, and let it stand for twelve days. When you see it black, set your glass as before to co-agulate, and when it begins to be of a grayish color, set it in a third time to putrefy, and coagulate to the fifth time, until you see that your water in its dissolution is clean, pellucid and clear, and that it appears in its Calcination of a fine white like Snow. Wet it again in the furnace of putrefaction then let it cool, open your Glass and you will find your Matter lessened a third part, and it will be a fine and very penetrating water which the Philosophers have hid under very wonderful names—it is the Mercury of all true philosophers, the Water out of which come Gold and Silver, for they say its Father is Gold and its Mother is Silver.

With enormous care, Edmund distilled from the formula the crucial information, the necessary steps, made careful calculations of the time involved. Forty to fifty days for the first calcination. Twelve to fifteen days for coagulation. Times three more putrefactions, times five coagulations, plus several days for cooling, plus the time it took to gather enough dew to get started in the first place . . .

His head swam. He designed several different kinds of laboratory notebooks. With pen and ruler in his hand and calendar beside him, he made charts and tables, plugged in times. Double-checked all his figures. Scientific precision was his goal.

What did he think about Anne's baby? He thought it was fine. He took it as a sign that his life-generating experiments might work. He was far beyond his Old World scruples. He wasn't even curious about who the father was. He might have worried about how she'd manage, but he had magic on his mind, a great distraction. I would like to see that baby, bring him home, he wrote that spring, but with all his efforts to build his alchemic kitchen, with all the preparation he still had to do, he was just as glad when she said no. It would be hard now, she wrote, with the baby. Why don't you come here? She called him Thanksgiving evening, late. Saying, You missed my graduation, couldn't you come now, for Christmas, see this baby who looks a lot like you? And even though, in his heart, he wanted desperately to see her, he said no. Wondering even as he said it, what was happening to him, what kind of father was he? His chance to go there and it was easy to refuse. A hell of a thing, he thought, but he thought it as if from outside himself, an observer, watching a bent old man who wasn't him, a scene from someone else's life.

He sent away to Spain for salt, had the glazier cut the four square plates of glass he'd need for dew collecting. Got wax and corks, then built his still. He ordered firebrick for furnace building, knocked a hole in the basement wall, and designed a chimney. It was mid-winter when he started, perhaps he would be an Adept when the May dew came. He studied his formula. He knew to prepare himself for failure the first time or two, a galling thing for him, a failure for so long. He began talking to himself, reminding himself that if he failed once he had to keep at it. "You're a tough old bastard," he would say. "Remember that. If at first you don't succeed . . ." All that sort of thing. Brushing his teeth, baking ham, lectures to himself in his front hallway mirror.

Anne

LARRY LEFT for Boston late in June, in time to start his residency July 1. During the weeks after graduation, he came by to see Max and me. He brought baby pictures of himself and wondered, Does he look like me?

"Just like you," I said.

Elana was not told about the baby. A bad way to start a marriage, but the best I can do, Larry told me. He was sitting on the floor with Max, pumping Max's little legs bicycle-fashion. Addicted to all medical advancements, Larry had read a book on baby exercise. "He could be a tennis pro," Larry joked. "I mean, besides being a great cardiovascular surgeon."

"Or anything he wants to be," I said.

Larry had decided to cash in some savings bonds he'd had since high school and give me the money, so that I could have a few months before I had to find a job. He opened a joint account in Max's name and mine that he could add to every month from Boston and made a presentation of the checkbook to us. Anne Mueller, Max Paul Mueller. I kept one of those checks as a souvenir for Max, a reminder of how, when he was only three weeks old, his dad had imagined a future for him as a writing person, of how his dad loved him even though he couldn't stay.

He left his old car with me, too. "It would never survive the trip to Boston. Keep it. Besides, I'd worry too much, you without a car. Suppose he gets sick in the night or something." It was the day he left. Larry had come to my apartment early, spent the whole day with Max, playing games and singing. He wore Max out with so much fussing, then held him in the crook of his arm until he fell asleep. "I wanted him to be sleeping when the cab came," he said. "I don't want Max to see me leave."

For the first six months Larry called regularly to see how we were doing. He sent toys for Max, notes to me that said, Don't answer, Elana comes home first and gets the mail, letters from Houston in a woman's hand won't do. I felt sorry for her, beautiful Elana, knowing I'd had the best of Larry, that she'd been left with a furtive secret-keeping man she hardly knew.

Thanksgiving night, I called my father. Come for Christmas, I said, thinking that Max would somehow bring us back together. After all, once we'd been everything to each other. We'd cooked together, danced together. He was retired now and free to travel. Surely, I said to myself, after all this time he wants to see me.

But his no was as firm as his reasons were vague and insubstantial. Too busy, he said. I have great and time-consuming work to do.

I wrote to Paul, wondering if he could get a leave, come home. Don't missionaries get vacations? I asked, with three big question marks. Something's wrong with Dad, I pressed. I feel it in my bones. And, when you think about it, El Salvador is not much farther from Pittsburgh than Texas. I have a baby, and I'm starting work, and I don't have the money, but one of us should go, Paul, and, given that you've been gone twelve years, I think it should be you. Please, I wrote. Do this for me.

After Christmas, I started working in the anatomy lab three days a week. I took Max to Mothers' Day Out at a church nearby where he could stay from eight to two, a good arrangement at a small fee. But I still found it hard to leave him, maybe because I knew that soon enough I'd have to leave him plenty.

But the job was a good thing for me. An anatomy-lab instructor like Ms. Alvarez. Now it was my turn with first-year students, my name on their lips. My name tag pinned me as Dr. Mueller, the first time I'd had a chance to use my new name officially. Every time one of my students called me, I'd think yes, that's me. Then I'd leave at two to go fetch Max, see him open his arms to me and call me. Mama, Mama. And I'd think yes. That's me, too.

Sometimes I wondered about Larry. Sometimes I missed him.

Dear Anne, Paul wrote. *I got your letter and I'm doing everything I can to get away. But because I'm new here I'm last in line for a vacation, so strings will have to be pulled. It will take time.*

I'd be lying if I said I was eager to go see Dad. I know how awful that sounds, but I'm afraid I'm just not very good at reaching out, at helping. A real handicap, given my career choice. I struggle with it every day. Sometimes I feel as if I'm being mocked by God —punished for becoming a priest when I knew I never had a calling. All I wanted was to get away.

The year was over before I knew it, time to leave for New York for the residency I'd accepted. One year general medicine, then three more of psychiatry. By that time Max was walking. He had Larry's sandy hair, a stubborn little jaw, and eyes like blue stars.

Mr. Landry saw us off the day we said goodbye to Houston. He gave Max a farewell gift of cowboy boots. Everybody told me I was crazy, going to New York. Larry sent a card at Christmas. Why not stay in Houston, where you know your way. Or Pittsburgh—that terse message from Edmund. But I'd committed myself the year before, made up my mind, so

I sold my few pieces of furniture, packed what I could fit of Max's things and mine into our VW. (It took me ten months to stop calling that car Larry's.) Mine, I said to myself. I strapped Max into the car seat beside me, showed him how to blow a kiss for Mr. Landry. *Mine.* I'd had the engine tuned, it purred.

The residency had subsidized housing, cheap by New York standards, across the street from the hospital. My apartment had two tiny bedrooms, a bathroom so small you couldn't turn around in it. But the floors were hardwood, the ceilings high. The windows could be opened spring and fall to let in city sounds and cool Northeastern air. It was air not unlike that which I'd grown up in, and the familiar smell and crispness of it, after the heavy, hot humidity of Texas, made me feel like I'd come to the end of some long wanderings. As if I was almost home.

A second-year resident and his Greek wife lived two floors below me. The Greek wife's name was Themis and she babysat to earn extra money. I got her name from the residency chief. The day after I arrived, I called her.

She was tall and Maria Callas-beautiful, lush red lips, a mane of walnut-colored hair. Full of Mediterranean passion and high spirits. She rolled her eyes, she smacked her forehead, she cursed in Greek, she adored her shy husband and doted on her dark-eyed daughter, Faye, who was four months older than Max. The day after I called she invited us to tea, and she and I talked while the kids circled each other warily.

"Your husband," she asked. "Is he also a resident?"

"I'm not married."

"Divorced?"

"No."

"Widowed?" In sympathy she pressed her hand against her cheek. "A terrible thing! And you so young."

"I'm not a widow. I've never been married."

She looked at Max, then me. "Never married?"

Max stood up and handed her a half-chewed cookie. She smiled and took it, thanking him profusely as if he'd handed her a jewel. His chest swelled, a grin blossomed on his face, he basked in the bright effusion of her smile. I knew that this would be the perfect place for him, that everything depended on this woman's saying yes.

"No doubt this 'never-married' business is a long story, too long to tell right now." She grinned and winked at me. "Another time. When we know each other better."

Then she shook my hand and promised she'd take good care of Max.

A rotating internship the first year, every third night call. Because I'd taken a year off, I had to work hard to keep up with the other interns fresh from school. I went in at 5:45 to bone up before morning rounds, dropping Max in his PJs, still half asleep, at Themis's.

"I know it's early." That's how I greeted her most days.

She rolled her eyes. "It's too early to be up, you are a crazy person," she said. Then she opened one arm for Max and with her free hand poured me a cup of coffee.

I managed my first code alone and then my eighth and twelfth; faced the family of a man who'd died; got into trouble for countermanding an order of a third-year resident that I knew was wrong. When I wasn't on call, I picked Max up in the evenings as soon as I was through. I worried that I was gone too much, that I'd become a bad, neglectful mother.

When Themis saw me wearing down, she found a hundred little ways to help me.

"You do too much." I took her out to lunch on one of my rare days off, to a small Italian restaurant. Linen tablecloths, waiters in bow ties and long white aprons. A splurge for both of us. She ordered Pernod as her aperitif, then leaned across the table toward me and dropped her voice as if we were conspirators.

"I like helping you. All my life I've known it is a man's world. We women have to stick together." Then she rolled her eyes and laughed and raised her glass to women.

My colleagues tell me that I'm hard on medical students. Eager not to hurt my feelings, they try to ease the sting of what they say by reassuring me that I am known for my good work with patients, admired for my research. "But the students quake when they see you coming," my colleagues say.

But they learn from me, I'm sure of that. They come to psychiatry rotation thinking, Oh well, here we go, witch-doctor time; why, this will be a breeze. So I'm tough with them. I want to see to it that I have their attention. I'm hard on them now because I remember how it was for me when I began. How ignorant I was, how little I understood.

The first year of psychiatry was all in-patient work. Four residents to a unit, five patients each, we reported to our unit chief about how things were going. I had my own tiny office at the end of the hall, opposite the nurses' station, my first real office. I put a pot of dried pussy willow in the corner, hung a Zúñiga poster of a broad patient woman on my wall.

Everything I did required a different kind of thinking and I came to see psychiatry as more philosophy than science, a struggle after some hard-to-measure truth. And that sense of it appealed to me. There'd been something missing for me in the focus on the physical; I wanted to know more about the secrets of the soul. I imagined myself easing old pains. Miraculous because of all I knew. I studied with a missionary's zeal.

Linda was admitted to my service two weeks after the birth of her first baby, with a diagnosis of postpartum psychosis.

She wore a chapel veil when she first came to my office, knelt on the floor when I offered her a chair.

"It's Lent," she said.

It was the second week in August.

"I don't think so."

"Shh." Her finger to her lips. She was on her feet suddenly. Checking my pot of pussy willows, running her hand along the wall. "This place is bugged," she mouthed.

I shook my head no. "This is my office. I know it isn't. It's safe to talk in here."

"Don't tell me it's safe. My baby has been kidnapped. How can things be all right if my baby's gone?"

The head nurse had had a call that morning from the foreman of the construction crew across the street. Linda was steaming up the window of her room and printing messages, backward, in hope that the construction crew could read them. "I am being kept a prisoner here by Nazis," or "The CIA will kill me at dawn if I'm not freed."

Linda turned and stood with her back to me, her arms spread wide as if to protect me from an invisible intruder. Her chapel veil fell like a lace flower from her head into my lap. "It's O.K.," she said, cajoling, to the closed door of my office. "She's one of us."

Early in my residency my teachers talked a lot about the art of listening. Freud suggested that analysts use their own unconscious minds as they try to understand their patients; he wrote of "evenly suspended attention" as a way of trying to listen. Reik borrowed a term from Nietzsche—"listening with the third ear"—a way of hearing the meaning beneath the spoken word.

How kids are "heard" affects what kind of hearers they become. In her pioneering work with mothers and babies, Selma Fraiberg described the case of a mother who made no effort to console her screaming baby. It was as if the mother didn't even hear her, had grown deaf to the cries of her own child.

The Fraiberg case had a good outcome. The infant workers, the therapist, even the baby herself, "taught" the mother to hear. But hearing is a thing that's hard to learn. In psychiatry you need it badly, right away. Early in your training you do your best, but you can miss a lot. The third ear is undeveloped. The ability to suspend attention hasn't been acquired. You have to learn to use your very self, reach down inside and find the best you have to offer. Now I have those skills, but then I didn't. I tried, but especially early on, I missed things with my patients. I was better than the flip and careless girl I'd been. But still, I dug down inside myself and more than once found myself wanting.

Francis was my age, thirty-one, a plumber with his own small business. He cried nonstop during the in-take interview, then every day when I saw him in my office. I offered him encouragement and Kleenex, and open-ended questions. With Art Sawyer, my unit chief, to guide me, I prescribed one antidepressant; then, weeks later, another. But nothing worked. "I've spent my whole life with my head underneath somebody's sink, and I can't face it anymore," he said on the tenth day. He was overweight and acne scars had left ridges on his boyish face. Gloria, his girlfriend, came to see him. She brought him chewing gum and candy and tried to treat him like a person who'd just had an appendectomy, as if he'd be home in four days good as new. "Just do what the doctors tell you," I heard her say brightly one day as I passed the patient lounge. "These doctors here are real good, Francis. Do like they tell you, in a jiffy you'll be fine." Unlike some of my other patients, who had to be hunted down and almost dragged into my office, Francis came eagerly. The only time he smiled was when I opened my office door and asked him to come in.

When the construction crew did not come to save her, Linda went on a hunger strike. She got hold of several rolls of white adhesive tape and sealed her mouth closed so we wouldn't try to feed her. Crisscross strips of tape over her lips, an elaborate wrapping around and around her head. Her nurse found her taped like that, lying on her back on the floor in her room, her feet crossed at the ankles, her arms spread out above her head, like Christ crucified. The tape had to be cut off, and it left her face striped with long welts and red irritated tracings. Her husband, a stoic up until that time, broke down when he saw her. "This is not the girl I married," he said to me.

"The food is poison." Linda in my office, after she'd knocked a cup of coffee off my desk. "I've told you. What's the matter with you? Don't you listen?"

I wiped at the coffee on my blouse with Kleenex. "I promise you. The food is *not* poison. You've got to try to listen to me."

She smiled bitterly. "My breasts are full of milk, crying for relief. Why don't you make these motherfuckers give me back my baby?"

"All that trouble in her eyes," Francis said. "I can't stand to see it. She told me she was bored, I thought maybe chess would help her pass the time." He had taught a teenage patient named Irene how to play chess. It was his first effort to connect with anyone. I hoped it was a good sign, but it was still hard to be optimistic about him. There was a warning in his eyes each time I asked what he was feeling. Too close, too deep. It was as if sadness was at the center of him and he was not about to let it go.

I thought it might help if Linda saw her baby. We arranged for a conference room downstairs, a private place where she and her husband and the baby could spend some time alone. Her nurse helped her dress and fixed her hair. I saw them waiting at the elevator and smiled when Linda gave me the thumbs-up sign.

But things went badly. Her nurse said that the baby arched his back and screamed.

Later in the afternoon, I tried to talk to her.

"So, what happened?"

Her eyes flashed anger. After she was with the baby, she'd cut her hair in little tufts and patches, so that she looked like someone shorn.

"Who are you trying to kid?" she hissed. "That baby isn't mine."

Francis was decorations chairman for the Halloween dance. He used his free time to carve jack-o'-lanterns and cut out paper witches. On the day of the dance, he brought me a pot of mums when he came for his session.

"Transference," said Art Sawyer when he saw the flowers. "Sometimes you help someone, they think they love you. It happens. You'll need to be careful."

"I danced every dance," Francis told me the Monday after Halloween. "I taught Irene some of the steps we used to do —the stroll, the twist. I said, You are a lucky person, Irene, make no mistake about it. Your whole life ahead of you. Don't get tripped up now, I told her. Don't end up like me."

After Max and I left Houston, gifts and letters from Larry stopped coming. He sent a monthly check in a plain white envelope, nothing more.

But letters from Paul came more frequently. On the bench outside the hospital, I'd sit and read. This Jake was the first real friend he'd made. An alteration in his lonely life that pleased me. I sent photographs of Max and me, even though

Paul told me not to send him things in letters. *Letters are stolen if they look like they have something special in them,* he explained. *Sometimes they're even stolen for the stamps. That's how desperate people are for something wonderful.* But I sent the photos anyway. Max dressed like a bunch of grapes for Halloween, Max and me in Central Park, Max with my stethoscope in his ears, my white coat draped around him.

The parish house is one large room, wrote Paul, *with two bedrooms tacked onto one end. Half of the big room is the kitchen; the other half, a space for living. A vinyl sofa, two slatted wooden chairs. A crucifix on one wall, a picture of the Pontiff on the other. The Kelvinator icebox is the oldest one I've ever seen. My room has a bed and a sagging chair. A lamp with a fringe of tiny native dolls that dance when the oscillating fan blows past them.*

It's morning as I'm writing. Jake whistles while he cooks breakfast, he bangs pots and silverware around, a lot of noise, like a mother making breakfast on a schoolday. No matter when I get up, he's already out there, mixing Tang, cracking eggs from "our" chickens. We're without power now, it happens routinely, but Jake's learned to manage with candles and an ice chest and an old butane stove.

He's included me in his routines. Mass and sick calls. Pastoral visits to hamlets in the hills. We take our old jeep, bring the Eucharist, several just-killed hens. Jake speaks flawless Spanish with the accent of a native, and he even looks like one: tanned darkly, with patches on his jeans, sandals on his feet, helping men haul dirt or replant burnt-out fields.

We hear confessions on these hamlet visits. We hang a tea towel on the branch of a tree—the barrier between us and the sinners. And Jake says Mass. He brings altar cloths and a folding table, and a chasuble with a white cross emblazoned on it.

Our church is a reconverted chicken coop, twelve times vandalized by soldiers and rebels in Jake's two years here. Windows broken, the crucified Christ's loin cloth hacked off, his face destroyed. The window has been shattered three times by bullets, three times repaired, until

*Jake finally gave it up and left the shattered glass alone. When the
sunlight hits it in a certain way, it makes a rainbow on the wall
at Jesus' feet.*

*Two of our priests in other parts of the country have left here in
the last few weeks for medical reasons, so I doubt that I'll be given
a leave unless there's some dire emergency. My request is still in place,
and I haven't given up entirely. But I don't expect to get home any
time soon. Still, Jake is trying to help me speed things up, and when
I do come, Anne, I'll come to New York after I go to Pittsburgh.*

After six weeks I thought Francis was ready for a weekend
pass. He lived alone in a small apartment. He and I talked
about how he'd spend his time.

"I can come back if I need to?"

"Of course," I said. "This is a weekend pass, not a sentence.
There's nothing to prove."

He came back Monday morning in good spirits. He'd had
his hair cut and bought two new shirts. Good cotton. He put
his arm out, wanting me to feel the sleeve.

"And I didn't have to come back." He folded his arms
across his chest. "I had a couple of tough times, but I said to
myself, You can do this, Francis. Just hang in there."

I nodded. "Good for you."

"Yeah. Twice I got real scared, but both times I told myself, You've got to do this, it'll make Dr. Mueller proud."

I squirmed in my chair. "And it does, Francis," I said. "But
this is for *you*. *You* should be proud that you manage."

"Sure." But his look was blank and disappointed. "But I
thought you should know that I did it for you."

It was early November, three weeks until I moved to another
unit. The patients had known from the beginning that they'd
have to change doctors when the residents changed, but when
the time came, knowing didn't help much.

Francis cried when I told him. "You can't just go," he said.

"I'm doing better because of you. It's not the medicine, or this place, or me. It's you."

He paced the halls, he cried. He slipped notes under my door, raged against me. All the pain of being left, abandoned, began to choke him, and without warning, it choked me, too.

Day after day, Francis's crying took on a roaring, anguished quality. His scarred, contorted face; his needful, desperate begging. He fell on his knees in my office once, pleading, and even as I reached to help him to his feet, I felt myself flinching. I went to my unit chief. I said, Help me. This is torture, the way he begs me not to go. I arranged for a medication consult, I talked to my supervisor about transference, I *did* what I was supposed to do. But in my office, in Francis's presence, I reached into myself and came up empty-handed.

I arranged to introduce Francis to the resident who would take my place. In the hall, on the Tuesday before I was to leave, I told him, You must trust me about this, Francis. He's a good man, he'll take good care of you. Francis spat at me and walked away.

On my last day on the unit, Linda blessed me. "I am a priest," she said proudly. "The first woman ever, ordained today."

Francis refused to come for his last session. I walked down to his room, told him I was waiting, wouldn't it be better if we said goodbye. He was in bed, with his blinds drawn, covers up around his neck, his back to me.

No answer.

I went back to my office, wanting to be there if he changed his mind. I packed a few books, took my poster down. Waiting, hoping, cursing myself because things between us had ended badly.

It was late when I was finally leaving. I almost didn't answer when the phone rang, I was anxious to get home. Finally, on the sixth ring, I gave in and got it.

And heard the triage nurse from the nearby ER speaking. "We have one of your people here, he's got an ID from your place in his pocket, nothing else, we didn't know who else to call. He was DOA. Francis something. Stepped in front of a bus. The ambulance just brought him in. You people ought to keep these guys locked up, you know? I mean, if they're this crazy, somebody ought to lock the doors."

I'd learned early in life to keep myself going through hard times and I'd come to assume that skill would never leave me. But this seemed different, a leaden thing.

Not your fault, my supervisors told me. A fluke. No threats, no previous attempts. He'd dressed like a visitor, slipped into the elevator, gone out the front door like a man who knew his way. Not your fault.

Still. I wondered what I might have done to make it different, the word I might have said that could have saved him. I knew I'd shrunk from him, instead of standing firm to help him. I couldn't sleep. I began to fear that some flaw in me had crippled me, that someone else would need the best, least frightened part of me, and wouldn't find it.

"Eat." Max offered me the curled top of his ice-cream cone. We'd gone to Häagen-Dazs, dessert after a Sunday-night spaghetti dinner. He had pressed his back against the wall at the far end of the booth where we were sitting, but when I turned toward him, he moved closer. He placed his hand on mine to guide it as I took the cone. His tongue stuck out as mine slid around the surface of the ice cream.

I was rethinking psychiatry. I wasn't sure it was what I should be doing. My teachers said, Don't be foolish, but I could not be reassured. I moved onto my next unit, but my heart was missing. Cautious when I had been eager, frightened when I'd built a life on being brave. I panicked, refused to see patients. I'm dangerous, I said, I could do them harm. The head of the program called me in, suggested therapy. There were able people who would see a resident at a reduced fee. "This isn't the time to leave," he said. "It's the time to find out what's going on."

So I called, made an appointment, went to an office with venetian blinds and faded carpet, a soft-spoken, balding man. His fingertips together like the steeple of a church beneath his chin as he sat in a chair across from me.

"I thought I'd make people better," I tried to explain. "I thought I'd . . ." I searched for the right phrase. "I thought people would get well because of me." Every time he nodded understanding, it was easier, more words came. A flood of words. I feared for him. I thought I'd drown him.

Death is a way of life, Paul wrote in a letter I received that afternoon when I got home. *In bigger cities there are body dumps, piles of corpses, stacked and rotting, relatives of the disappeared digging around with handkerchiefs pressed to their faces.*

People are murdered randomly. We make rounds in our jeep and find dead people thrown by the roadside. It makes me sick, more than once I've had to step away to throw up while Jake wraps a body in a tarp we keep in the back of the jeep. He gives me his handkerchief to wipe my face when I finish puking. He and I are the only ones who claim these dead. Our parishioners are too afraid.

We bury them in our back yard, between the church and our house. Jake makes wooden crosses, small crude markers, and we go through the burial rites, taking turns, one of us as priest, one as respondent. "Lord, welcome into your presence your son, whom you have called from this life. Release him from all his sins, bless him with eternal light and peace, raise him up to live forever with all your saints in the glory of the resurrection. We ask this through Christ Our Lord.

"Amen."

Edmund

NEW YORK *is a lot closer than Texas. Come now?* Anne wrote.

Soon, Edmund answered, but "soon" had no real meaning. Time seemed to have stopped; it no longer existed for him. Sometimes he'd see the date on the top of the newspaper, and wonder where the days had gone, how weeks could have slipped by without his notice.

The newspaper was delivered every day, but Edmund never read it, except for the obituaries. His firemen friends were old, several had died; he was going to funerals more than he was doing any other thing. For those he shaved, he wore his only suit, he knelt and prayed before the catafalque like a believer. If asked, he led the rosary. Then went back to his solitary life, his haven. Sometimes he was lonely. But bored? Not once. He read as if his life depended on it, some days he didn't take the time to sleep. He read while he washed clothes, he read while cooking. Books propped open on the windowsill above the sink, places marked with strings of cooked spaghetti, sprigs of valerian he grew in his garden. He filled thirty-seven loose-leaf binders with notes and thoughts and sketches, trying every way he could to organize his mind.

He'd built his lab three years earlier, had gathered the May dew, tried the Magnum Opus each spring as the formula instructed. But he'd had no luck. He kept thinking about the warning he had read—a crucial step is always left out of any written formula—and, with that in mind, he varied his approach ever so slightly each time he tried it. At the same time he continued his search for other formulas, and continued as well his efforts to find the best part of himself so that he could be an Initiate and worthy of success.

In three years he found five more formulas to follow, new terminology with which to contend. "Pontic water," "Peacock's Tail," "Raven's head." Was the Philosopher's Stone indeed a stone, or was it, in fact, a red elixir? And what about the prima materia, first matter, the substance upon which the Magnum Opus must be worked? The descriptions of it were confusing—imperfect body, constant soul, a penetrating tincture. On one thing only did all scholars agree: it must be present before the Philosopher's Stone could be produced; a man must find it in himself before he can be an adept. "The child is the prima materia of the adult," one Magus wrote.

"You're losing weight," said Lucy. Wide strips of gray waved through her heavy hair. She pulled at his pants where he'd bunched them at the waist, adjusted his shirt collar, two inches too big, gaping at his neck. "In bed, on top of me, you're so light, I hardly know you're there. You need new clothes, your hair will be as long as mine if you don't get it cut soon. I fear for you," she said. "You need to rest."

But when he tried to rest, his books called out to him and woke him. Prima materia. You must find it now, the work of transformation may only be begun in spring under the sign of Aries. It is January, time is passing, those books hissed. When he dozed he dreamed of children, he dreamed of his. He went through photo albums, trying to remember. What had they been like when they were young, what about them had he missed?

Come home, he wrote to Paul. *We'll talk. I want to make things right between us.* But their letters crossed in the mail, some were lost, their correspondence felt strange and disconnected. If Edmund asked questions, it sometimes took Paul months to answer them, if he answered them at all. The day Edmund wrote asking Paul to come to him, a letter came instead.

Dear Dad, We have been without power for a week. The government forces hit the generator late last night as they have five times before.

You asked in your last letter what the fighting is about here. It started as a protest for land reform, better treatment for the poor. But the issues are muddied now, the fighting has taken on a life of its own. Jake is more sympathetic to the rebels. The government has death squads, they are responsible for the desaparecidos, people who have been "disappeared." He speaks out against the government in sermons from our pulpit. A dangerous thing. Churchmen have been killed before here. But he says it's important. If we become afraid to speak, he says, then we might as well not be here.

Please come home, Edmund wrote. *A leave, the shortest visit. Bring your friend Jake if you want, I'd like to meet him. We'll shoot baskets, I'll cook the things you love for you. Your room is ready. Come in winter, see the snow again.*

The clearer it became that Paul would not come home, the more Edmund thought of Max, his grandson. Anne sent pictures, she let Max talk into the phone each time she called Edmund. He began to wonder who Max looked like, who he was, what he'd see if he looked into his eyes. Anne wrote, *He is a splendid boy.* Even when she talked about his stubbornness, she spoke as if she loved it, as if she found something to admire in everything he did. A golden child, Edmund thought, and that thought made him want to see him. Spring was on its way, no time to lose.

I could come in February. Old age made him tremble. He wrote his message in a faltering hand.

Anne

IN FEBRUARY of the second year of my residency, Edmund came to see his grandson. We met him at La Guardia. I hadn't seen him since I'd left Pittsburgh for Texas. Seven years. I felt ashamed. He was an old man now, very different-looking from the dad I'd left behind. I lifted Max into my arms. "Look." I pointed. "Grandpa."

Max squealed. I smiled and waved and drew Max close so we could elbow through the crowd.

"Look at you." Edmund leaned to kiss my forehead. "And *you.*" He reached to take Max from me. "Now, aren't you something!"

Max was almost four and not very keen on strangers, but he smiled as if in recognition and fell into Edmund's arms.

He handed me a shopping bag. "I've got something for the boy." I reached in and found a worn stuffed tiger Paul had always loved. Max took it, kissed it, called it "cat." Edmund smiled congratulations.

"You hold Max," I said when we got down to the baggage claim. "Sit over here and visit while I get your bags." I stood at the conveyor belt, watching them instead of the stream of passing luggage. Patty-cake, and peekaboo, the itsy-bitsy spider up the water spout. I'd never seen Edmund play so many games; I didn't know he knew the words to nursery rhymes and songs.

"Jeez, lady, get your bags or get the hell out of the way," a man from the Bronx growled at me, and I snapped back,

"Take it easy, buddy," in my best imitation of a tough-guy New York voice.

I made spaghetti that first night. Max's favorite. Red sauce and ground beef covered him.

"It's been a long time since I had this." Edmund wiped his plate with Wonder bread I'd bought because I knew he liked it. Then after supper he sat cross-legged on the floor while Max played around him. He liked Grandpa's hair, the coarseness of it. He pushed his small hands through it, pressed his face into its just-washed whiteness.

After I put Max to bed I came back to the living room and found Edmund sitting on the sofa, reading. When I looked over his shoulder to see what the book was, he snapped it closed.

"Sorry. I was just curious. What are you reading?"

"Thomas Aquinas," he said.

"Oh." I was surprised. "Theology?"

He took his glasses off. "He was more than a theologian. He was a scholar. A student of Albertus Magnus. Everyone should study him. *You* should." He shook his finger at me.

"I've got a lot of other things I have to read now, Dad. Maybe, someday, I'll take up Aquinas."

"His mother didn't want him to be a Dominican. She had his brothers kidnap him and hold him hostage to try to keep him from it, did you know that?"

"No."

There was an unfamiliar ardor in his voice. "Well, she did. She was a vain, proud woman; she kept him in the family castle, sent harlots to him, trying to tempt him." He got to his feet, began to pace, launched into a rambling discourse— the story of Aquinas, his brave escape from Monte San Giovanni, the years of study with Albertus Magnus.

"Albertus Magnus built a robot, an automaton," he said.

"He worked thirty years to make it, used metals he chose according to the planets. When he finished, it was a magic thing, it spoke and thought."

Talking robots, magic—did he believe what he was saying? Curious, I moved forward in my chair. "What did the automaton think and speak about?"

"The Android. It was called an Android."

"What did the Android think and do?"

"It knew magic formulas and invocations."

"Magic?"

"Yes. And then Aquinas destroyed it."

"Why did he do that?"

"Because he thought it was an instrument of the devil."

"You say it took St. Albert thirty years to make it. Sounds like a lot for him to lose."

"Absolutely. Thirty years' work. Gone." He snapped his fingers. "Just like that."

"What did St. Albert do to Thomas?" I pushed my hair behind my ears.

"Nothing."

"What?"

"Nothing. He forgave Aquinas. The way you would a lover or a son. Which gives you some indication of how fine a man he was. A better man than me." He slapped his book against his thigh. "Me. I'm afraid I would have killed him."

I took three vacation days so that we could spend time together. We did what tourists do—rode the Staten Island Ferry, saw the Statue of Liberty, ate lunch in Chinatown. I filled him in about the details of my life; he stayed pretty closemouthed about his. There was a cautiousness about the way we dealt with each other that colored everything we did and said. We spoke briefly about Paul, although I didn't say he might be coming. No use raising hopes, I thought. But neither of us mentioned Fanny. I thought I was deferring to him in this; maybe he thought he was protecting me, but in those three days we never spoke her name. I made no reference to the dashed-off, pointless postcards ("Greetings!" "Cheers!" "Wish you were here!") that she had continued to send sporadically to me. I didn't know how she'd found my address and didn't care. I'd gotten her out of my system, finally, or so I thought, and when Edmund didn't bring her up, I hoped it meant that he had, too.

More than once he told me he was sorry, and I thought we'd begin to *really* talk then. But when I pressed him—"Why are you so sorry?"—he wouldn't tell me. He had clipped death notices from the Pittsburgh paper, taped them in a scrapbook; he showed them to me. Men he'd worked with, Mike Jankovich, John Schlusser. "It's wrong," he said. "We're old, I know, but I'm not finished with my life, I don't want to die."

You're not so old, I said. We walked in Central Park, I showed him the carousel. He reminisced about his tiller-driving days. When I asked if he'd made any furniture, he lectured me impatiently about having more important things to do. With every conversation, I worried more. I knew that years had passed, that he'd aged; of course I understood that people change. But this was more than change, more than a heightening of eccentricities. The dapper, tiller-driving fireman seemed to have been replaced by a brooding, pacing stranger. He didn't even sound the same, he talked about Goethe and Robert Browning, used an entirely new vocabulary. His wire-rimmed glasses were smudged and bent, he wore a squashed bow tie and an old rumpled jacket, clothes he used to mock when he admired himself in his dress uniform in front of the mirror in our entry hall. As I walked with him, I looked at him and wondered what was going on, how this change had taken place. I thought I ought to have him checked out while he was with me. A physical. A check of his mental status. A careful evaluation by somebody besides me.

On the fourth day of his visit, I had to go back to work. Max wanted to stay with his grandpa instead of going to Themis, but I thought that would be too much; Edmund seemed too lost in his own thoughts to manage Max. I didn't want to leave them for the whole long day together. So I got up early, took Max to Themis, but by the time we got there Max was crying. He wanted Grandpa.

"Look," said Themis. "Why don't you just leave them at your place today? They'll have a great time together."

I should have said he's old, confused, maybe even a little crazy. But old habits are hard to break. Lies about the way things were at home just tripped off my tongue.

"The day would be too long," I said. "He doesn't know his way around New York. He needs some rest."

That night, when I came to get Max at six-thirty, Themis looked surprised to see me. "Your dad came by at about eight-fifteen this morning and got him, Anne. He looked fine, and Max just ran to him. They were so glad to see each other. Your dad said not to worry, the two of them were going to spend the day exploring. Have lunch. 'Do Manhattan,'" she said, quoting.

It was eight, then eight-thirty, dark and getting colder. Standing at the window, I realized I'd never been alone in my apartment. Max had always been with me.

They got lost, I told myself. They're having dinner. He's probably hailing a cab right now, I'll bet they're having fun. But my heart was racing. I made a sandwich for myself, but couldn't eat it. I called Anthony at the desk downstairs to ask him if he'd seen an old man and my baby, was there any message for me. He scanned the message pad, he asked

around, he came back to the phone and told me no. No. I
forced myself to make tea, I willed my shaking hand to hold
the cup. He's a grown man, I told myself. He's lived a long
time in the world, a hard life. What could happen? But then
it was ten and then eleven, twelve hours, no nap for Max, my
dad a failing old man, a stranger to the city, where in God's
name could they be? My stomach cramped, I started sweating,
I put my coat on to go out searching, then realized that was
crazy, where would I start? When I called the police they said
that "the parties" needed to be gone longer to be missing,
call back in the morning. I almost said, But I'll be crazy in
another minute, maybe dead, I will *die* if something happens
to my baby. That awful thought. It made me realize how
alone, how insular and cut off Max and I were. I riffled
through my phone book, for one crazy moment I thought I'd
call Larry in Boston. Instead, I called Themis. The line was
busy. I talked to myself. "Breathe, it's going to be all right."
I leaned my head against the cool glass of the window and
closed my eyes, and when I did I saw them mugged and
murdered, drowned. "Oh, Max," I cried. I said his name, and
when I did I felt it in my womb, the place he'd lived. I started
bleeding. "Oh, please!" I begged the walls, curtains, God.

Midnight. Twelve-fifteen.

" 'Fire! Fire!' said Mrs. Dyer." It was almost one when I
heard them in the hall.

" 'Where? Where?' said Mrs. Dare. 'Down the town,' said
Mrs. Brown."

Max's baby laughter. Edmund's deep voice, rhythmic and
rhyming.

" 'Any damage?' said Mrs. Gamage."

I opened the door. Max reached out his arms to me.

" 'None at all,' said Mrs. Hall."

I almost slapped Edmund, I wanted to pound his chest and
scream.

"Where in God's name have you been?" I could barely manage a whisper.

"Out," Edmund said. "We've been exploring." He had a shopping bag in one hand. A red plastic fireman's helmet poked out of it. He looked at my face and frowned. "I'm sorry," he said. "I guess I should have called, but I forgot to write down the number." He mussed Max's hair. "He's pretty tired, but we had a good time. We went to the library. And to the park down the street. And we tried to get to the museum I've read so much about—the Metropolitan. But we took the wrong bus, ended up way downtown in some God-forsaken place called TriBeCa, before I figured out that we were going in the wrong direction."

Max pulled on Edmund's arm. "And fire trucks. Tell Mama."

"I thought the boy should see a fire station. I knew I'd be welcome, that a fireman is never a stranger in a city, and I was right. Station 16. Fine men, they let Max see everything, they even let me slide down the pole for him."

Max rubbed his sleepy eyes. I held him tight.

"And, our good luck, one of the fellows had a camera, one of those Polaroids. Right beneath his bunk, so we put Max up there behind the wheel, with a fire hat and a grin, me right there beside him, so he wouldn't fall." Edmund looked at Max, adoring, then took his hand and kissed it. "And I swear, he looked so much like Paul up there. He could have been Paul in that hat." He fumbled in the pocket of his old brown overcoat until he found the photos. Max and Edmund, Max and the captain, Max and the Dalmatian, who looked just like the Eugene I remembered. Max grinning, the fire helmet almost covering his eyes. Max the initiate. Like Paul, I thought. Like me. A fireman's kid, a child of fire.

I took Edmund to the physical exam I'd scheduled early the next morning. I'd filled Dr. Stewart in about my worries.

At the last minute, Edmund resisted going. "Not only am I fine, things are improving. I can feel it. I'm feeling better every day," he said stubbornly.

But I would not take no for an answer. That afternoon, Dr. Stewart asked me to stop by his office before I left for the day.

"Well, you're right," he said. "There's something up. His mental status is all right, short- and long-term memory pretty good. If he's hearing voices, he denies it. He's quite cagey, though; he knew I wasn't just listening to his lungs. He was very careful when he answered all my questions. Guarded."

"So?"

"Well, he certainly doesn't seem to be organic. His thinking is too clear for that. And he's not actively psychotic, at least not as far as I can tell. He may be somewhat depressed, maybe a little paranoid. He has a lot of regrets about his life. About mistakes he thinks he made. And he kept referring to some big plan he has, something he's working on that he thinks will change his life. Based on what you told me, I asked him if it had anything to do with magic. He became quite coy then, asked me what I meant. So I said I was just curious about whether or not he believed in magic." Dr. Stewart smiled. "So he looked straight at me and said, 'Look, Doc. I'm just an ordinary fellow, a fireman. You're the one who thinks he can unlock the secrets of the soul. It looks to me like you're the guy who thinks he's a magician.' "

"So, what do I do?"

"Nothing much. Keep an eye on him. If something's really troubling him, I think the burden of it might very well break him down."

"He lives in Pittsburgh," I said. "I can't keep much of an eye on him from here."

"No relatives? No friends?"

"Some neighbors. But I don't think he sees them much. I think since he retired he spends most of his time alone."

"Well, call a neighbor. See if you can get someone to check

in on him. Or you could call him every few days. See if he sounds O.K."

I nodded.

"I don't think he'd take medicine, even if I gave it to him. He's pretty suspicious. Also, I don't think he needs it yet. I know some people in Pittsburgh who could treat him, but good luck getting him to go. I'd like to be some kind of help, Anne, but I don't think there's a thing to do now. Just keep an eye on him. Wait to see what happens."

That night I dreamed I was split in half, two watchful eyes, one hovering in New York over Max, my patients, and my life there; one in Pittsburgh, in the house on Jeffers Street, peeking out from a hidden place to watch my dad in a star-studded robe and pointed hat: a wizard.

Max wore the plastic fireman's hat when we drove to the airport. He sang fire songs, recited fire poems, a perfect little mimic. "Lady bug, lady bug, fly away home . . ." Edmund hovered at the airport, holding Max's hand. He told me things that I should teach Max in a frantic way, as if this was good-bye forever. "He should be an honest, good man, teach him to value simple things. Teach him to speak his mind. It never works to keep old grudges deep inside you. Tell him."

I nodded.

"And see to it he meets nice girls, steady girls, girls who are serious and sweet."

I touched his arm to reassure him.

"You were good to have me come here," he said finally, his attention drawn for a minute from Max to me. "I got a chance to do some things I should have done when you and Paul were kids. I got to be a good guy with my pal Max."

"Well," I said. "It was past time, don't you think? I wanted to see you. Besides, I love you." I had not been sure I'd be able to say it. In our life together, we'd never talked about such things. He looked at me, but didn't answer. Then he dropped quickly to one knee and wrapped Max in his arms. "I love you," he said. To Max. But they were words he'd used so seldom that they had some great expansive quality; they took in everything around him, they took in me.

Outpatient work the third year. Work with children. A long course in development. Anna Freud and Spitz and Brody. Theories of cognition, what babies know and when they know it. It was during that time that I changed my area of training to child psychiatry, and began my life of work with infants.

I imagined when I started in psychiatry that I would treat adults, find some talent in myself for administering the talking cure, healing by listening. And I did. But during my first two years of training, the more I saw adult patients, the more discouraging it seemed. Full of hope about what I could do when I began, I came to understand that I would need more modest goals. That what I had to offer couldn't ennoble souls or alter characters, could not make straight what Kant called the crooked wood of man. I began to think that adults came for therapy too late, with characters and selves already forged. A shift in attitude, better skills for "coping"—these things were the most I had to offer.

When I started studying babies, everything seemed possible. Brand-new, no damage done. I saw it first in Max, how much he mirrored what I gave him. Now every day I see it in the babies I observe. Treat the needs and wishes of a baby with respect, he feels respected when he moves through the world; attach to him, he learns the pleasures of attachment. Even young infants collect experiences and memories; from the very first a self is being formed. I've come to believe that if the self is poorly made, it's hard to remake later on, in life or in therapy. I see it in the adults I treat; the facts of my own life add to the evidence. In my own therapy, more than once I said, There is a hole in me. Something missing. I have patched it, Max has helped patch it—my work, my therapy. I am "better." The pain of something missing can be eased, lived with, survived. I've had to settle for that in my own life, but surely it's all right to wish for something better in my work than eased pain, lives lived in a residue of sorrow. I want to go back to the beginning—to understand how infants experience the world and are shaped by it, how the self develops.

Some of my colleagues fault me for being reluctant to do patchwork, for saying that patchwork isn't good enough for me. Others accuse me of trying to remake the world. But the more I see, the more I believe in my work with babies.

Max wants to fill the world with music. I want to fill the world with sturdy children, magically endowed.

The magician child of my magician father.

Spring now, Paul wrote. *We're seeing sprouts already in our garden.*

People try to leave El Salvador, but it's not easy. There are troubles with Honduras, not much hope for a better life in Guatemala. So there are many refugees, camps set up to try to help them. Twice a month we go to one about thirty miles away to help nuns distribute food and medicine. Jake is better at it than I am. He has a certain charm.

But charm leaves him on the drive home. He takes turns too fast, curses at the road, yanks at the gearshift as if he'll pull it from its mounting. I have to hang on to the seat and roll bar. On those rides I know he hates it here as much as I do. That the only difference between us is that he is cursed with the wish to believe that what he does can make a difference.

I think it's time to see both you and Dad, so I'm reapplying for a leave. It will come through soon, I hope. Don't lose heart, Annie. Wait for me.

Max, almost five, in need of glasses, tortoiseshell frames, a contrast to his light curly hair. The glasses made him look

more like his father, and he was like Larry, too, in his aloof-
ness, his quick mind. Independent, stubborn. Asking all the
time about his father. "Everybody has one, why don't I?"

Then, in April, Larry sent a letter with his check. He said
he'd like to talk to me. He wanted to see Max. At the park,
while Faye and Max played, I showed Themis the letter.

"He's left Elana. He says a life built on a lie is nothing."

Themis raised her eyebrows, pursed her lips. "And you?"

"Max and I don't need him. It isn't fair of him to want to
come back now, just when we're both doing fine."

"Not so fine, if you ask me. Men ask you out, you never
go. Don't try to deny it, the other wives and I talk about you
all the time. And don't look so startled, it isn't gossip, Anne,
it's worry. This isn't good, the way you live. And what about
Max? He asks all the time about his father. What about that?"

I shook my head stubbornly. "I don't want to see him."

Themis shrugged. "Well, of course, it's not any of my business. But aren't you even curious? Don't you want to talk to
him?"

"No."

"Maybe he's changed."

I shot her a sidelong glance. "Whose side are you on?"

Faye and Max were swinging on the jungle gym. Max slung
his legs over a bar and hung upside down, waving at me.

Themis looked at me wisely. Then she placed her hand over
her heart. "Call me a romantic, but once you thought you
loved him. He is *inquiring.* He wants to *talk* to you. Maybe
he'd be good for Max."

Max. A big boy suddenly, in Catholic Montessori school.
Half day at the beginning—a morning child—then after
just six months "invited" to stay all day. Tall and ready. For
afternoon-child status, and overnights at friends, songs and
number rods and early reading.

On Max's fifth birthday, a letter came from Paul.

The rainy season. The jeep's four-wheel drive could manage the

road for the first few days, and we went about our business in ponchos
and boots. Mud caked on our boots and pants legs, we dragged it
into the house, where it made a dust so fine, so penetrating that it
turned the dark hairs in our nostrils, on our lashes, gray. When the
mud threatened to suck the chickens into it we brought them inside.
Then we had chicken shit as well as dust to deal with. The noise of
rain against the tin roof made my head ache. We shouted to be heard
above it, and then, too hoarse to keep that up, we wrote instead, or
made complicated signals with our hands.

The rain and mud began to wear away our graveyard. Three days
ago I looked out the kitchen window and saw our crude cross markers
floating past. The mounds that we had made gave way, the ground
beneath them sank, and I feared that the corpses would be unearthed,
that we would be swept away by the dead we'd buried. As I stood
there, Jake came up beside me, looked out too. And I knew he had
the same fear, that in the absence of talk we had taken up the business
of reading what was on the other's mind.

The graves held. The rains subsided. We resumed our work. Jake
preached one of his "subversive" sermons and was shot at the next
day as he was driving in the jeep. The bullet missed him but hit a
tire. My life is charmed, he said.

"Anne?" Larry's voice. As soon as I heard it, I could see him.
I wondered if his hair was thinner, did he have new glasses,
were his feet propped on his desk, or was he leaning on his
elbows.

"Yes," I said.

"I waited until it was late to call so that Max wouldn't
answer."

Silence.

"Anne?"

"Yes. I'm here."

"How are you?"

"All right. Fine."

"You got my letter?"

"Yes." He would be halfway through his residency. Maybe he was at the hospital, just finished in surgery. Maybe he was tired from all-night call. He rubbed his neck when he was tired, he moved his shoulders back and forth to ease the tension there. Maybe he'd saved a life that night. Maybe he had lost one.

"So you know why I'm calling. I want to talk to you. I want to see Max."

"I know."

He cleared his throat. "You're not going to make this easy, are you." I could see him take his glasses off, rub the sides of his nose with his fingertips.

"Should I make it easy?"

"No. Of course not. Look, I know I've mucked things up, I know I've done everything wrong that there is to do. But I'm different now, I'm five years older. Smarter. I'm not calling to make a mess of your life. I want to help. I want to be a father to Max. I want a chance to love him. Nothing has been right without you two. I can understand if *you* don't want me, Anne. Really, I understand that, but I know I could be good for Max."

I wondered if he knew how to play baseball, if he knew the words to lullabies, if he knew how to be patient with a kid who can't seem to learn to tie his shoes. Things I'd never known about Larry. Things I'd never asked.

"This is hard for me, Larry." I'd said that to him a hundred times when we were in school. It's hard, it's hard. He'd shrug, and smile and try to reassure me.

"I know it's hard. And I don't want to press you. Just start thinking about it. You'd know better than I would how to go about this, how to talk to him, how to bring me back into his life. Please. Just say you'll think about it."

I didn't answer.

"Please. I need your help."

I thought about Amelia. All the help he'd given me. "Give me a little time," I said.

"Sure, fine. But you'll think about it?"

"Yes."

"And you'll call me?"

"Yes."

"Soon?"

"Yes," I said. "I promise."

Edmund

CURRIE, arriving late in the afternoon, finds Edmund sitting, staring out of his west-facing window at the slowly descending sun. Lately, their sessions have seemed to be more tiring for Edmund, and Currie, worried, has made them shorter, has let his patient set the pace. But he can tell that Edmund is less and less eager to see him when he comes, that he is reluctant to end this story, that the ending is, by far, the hardest part.

On this day, Edmund doesn't even turn in his chair to greet him when he enters. His gaze is fixed on the cloud-laced red-orange sky. And when he finally begins to speak, it is as if he were continuing a thought already started, a reverie in which he was completely and utterly absorbed.

There is something about fighting fire that makes you think you can live forever. That death is a thing for other men, for victims. Once a wall collapsed and barely missed Edmund. Once a floor gave way under another firefighter standing beside him, and he fell, screaming, to an awful death below. For years after that, each time they went out Edmund thought of it. *Suppose I die this night. Suppose they have to send the chief to wake my kids and tell them.* Then, as time passed, he began to think that nothing could harm him, that he would always beat the odds. Once when Anne and Paul were little, he said that to them, bragging, and Anne put her fingers on his lips to shush him. Now he knows he married Fanny with that same damned smugness, with the sure sense he'd defied death and drabness.

But on Jeffers Street, when he returned from seeing Anne in New York, death-defying feats seemed quite beyond him. The Elixir of Life, just out of reach. Twice he tried the Magnum Opus, twice he failed. He let the fire get too hot the first spring; his reverberatory furnace cracked. During his next attempt he dozed and let the ash bed beneath his athanor grow cool. Still, he believed that he was making progress. He'd made structural changes in his Balneum vapori furnace, increased the surface area of charcoal under his three-armed still. And he'd found a description of the Universal Medicine which seemed clearer to him than any he had read before.

> *The solution in the alchemical retort will turn into a red elixir, the Universal Medicine. Fiery water, luminous in the dark. If the augmentations of its power be carried too far the test tube will explode and vanish as dust, or it will seep through the glass, for there is no physical container sufficiently strong to hold it because it is no longer a substance, but a divine essence. Liquid fire.*

He wrote his commentary in his laboratory notebook.
Note #1. Red elixir, luminous in the dark, like liquid fire.
Note #2. Watch the stars. The spirit of the earth is fed by them.
From another book he learned when to expect what color changes and to be especially careful of the fire during the transition of the solution from white to red. Too much heat could make the color change too quickly, which was one of the warning signs that the experiment would fail. His fire-tending skills were more refined than ever; forty, fifty, sometimes sixty watchful days over a low flame had made his eyes and senses keen again. In his efforts to speed his internal transformation, he wrote almost every day to Anne and Paul, trying to be the kind of father he had never been. But even with so much working in his favor, when he began, once more, his efforts at the Magnum Opus, he was consumed with worry

that he'd fail again. His strength was waning. The hauling of coal and gathering of supplies was hard work, and he was getting too old for it. When he began his preparation for the gathering of May dew that spring, he knew that this might be his last chance. That he didn't have another year to lose.

As days passed and Edmund made his plan, he tried to find a specific test to prove that the end result of his experiment was indeed the Elixir he was seeking. Vague descriptions of the Vital Essence (fiery water, pellucid stone) could no longer suffice, he thought. He needed evidence, some clear sign. When the time came he wanted to know at once that he'd succeeded.

With spring approaching, his poring through his texts and documents became more frantic. Then finally, late one cold March night, he found what he was searching for in the cracked and brittle pages of an old manuscript. *Take seven pieces of metal chosen according to the planets. (Mercury/Mercury, copper/ Venus, silver/Moon, gold/Sun, iron/Mars, tin/Jupiter, and lead/Saturn.) Arrange them in your darkened chamber in the order in which they stand in the heavens. Then place on each, one drop of your Red Elixir. If it is the Blessed Stone, forthwith a flame of fire will spread itself over the whole chamber, and shine more brightly than the sun and moon. And over your head you will behold the whole firmament as it is in the starry heavens above, and the planets shall hold to their appointed courses, as in the sky. Let the fire cease of itself, and in a quarter of an hour, everything will be in its own place.*

Imagine, Dr. Currie, the glory of such a moment. The wonder of fire filling your chamber, the heavens opening above you. Edmund collected the necessary metals so that when his potion appeared to be ready he could drip some of it on his metal strips, perform this test, and in this way know that the Tincture had at last been found.

Edmund's voice drops to a whisper. It's late, he is exhausted. Currie knows that he should leave, but it seems impossible to go now, he must press forward, he needs to know.

"And what if the heavens opened up?" asks Currie. "What exactly were you planning to do with the Philosopher's Stone once you found it?"

Edmund, looking out his window all this time, turns finally to look at Currie, his lined face half lit by the sunset, half obscured by the darkness of the room.

"I wanted a miracle," he says. His voice, so unfaltering for all these weeks, through all this telling, breaks; his own words choke him. "I was ready to trade everything for a hopeless dream."

And so, on Jeffers Street, he had locked his doors, pulled down the blinds, made his house secure. He made plans to move down to the basement, eat there, sleep there, be alert and vigilant. He took his notebooks, matches, books, quilts and a pillow, a stash of plain canned food. Before God he swore he'd manage that last fire perfectly. He blessed himself, declared himself to be an Adept.

Anne

O N   T H E   D A Y I finished my residency, a letter came from Paul.

I'll be in Pittsburgh July 15th. Could you and Max come and meet me? It would be easier, I think, if you were there. But don't tell Dad until the day before. Everything is set, and there shouldn't be any hitches, but this is El Salvador, after all. Anything can happen.

If you get there the fourteenth, I'll call that night. Then you can tell him that I'll be there in the morning.

That letter came six years ago, but I remember all the details of it clearly. No need for a swallow's heart for me.

I can see myself stepping off the elevator into the hallway leading to my apartment. I'd gotten the letter from our mailbox in the lobby, then read it on the slow ride up. Paul's coming home. I tried to imagine the look on Edmund's face when he saw Paul in the vestibule. It would be just the thing, I said to myself, to stop his downward slide. The sight of Paul would save him. I'd been calling Edmund once a week since he'd come to New York to see me, and every time we talked he was pleasant enough and unfailingly polite. But I was pretty certain things hadn't improved with him. Why would they? Alone in that old house, nothing left to him but remembering and brooding. Dr. Stewart's words came back to me every time I talked to Edmund. "Pretty depressed, a little paranoid." Perhaps the sight of Paul would snap him out of it. Not very realistic of me, to be sure, not very astute psychologically. But my therapy, besides saving my life, had turned me into something of an optimist, and in the hallway I indulged in optimistic fantasies. Paul and I were older, more resilient. The specter of Fanny couldn't harm us any more. It's not too late for the three of us plus Max to find a way to be a family, I said to myself. We'll get it right this time.

I guess I stood in the hallway longer than I realized, because suddenly I heard a door open, the sound of sneakers padding down the hall. Max had come looking for me, left his job hanging paper streamers for the party we were having that night.

"What's that?" he asked, and he moved as if to take the letter from my hand. He was six years old, toothless in the front and lisping. "A congratulations telegram? A message from the President?" He laughed, liking to think of himself as smart and funny, big enough to tease me.

"None of the above." I smiled, folded the letter, and put it in the back pocket of my jeans. "Just a letter. News about Grandpa."

"Good news or bad?" he asked me, craning his neck, eyeing the letter sticking like a flag out of my pocket.

I didn't answer. "How'd you get confetti in your hair?" I asked instead. I reached to brush the glittered snips of paper from his head, thinking to myself, yes. Of course we'll go. I'll show Max Pittsburgh. He'll get to see the house on Jeffers Street.

"Back to work," I said brightly. I took Max by his shoulders, turned him toward the apartment, and popped him softly on his bottom to urge him down the hall. Then I popped him again, until he was giggling and running, confetti dropping from his hair and leaving a trail on the wood floors, like the bread crumbs Hansel left on his way into the dark woods, into the hands of the witch.

Max and I had six weeks before we had to be in Philadelphia for the job I'd taken—part-time teaching, part-time private practice. Until Paul's letter came, I'd imagined a leisurely car trip—Gettysburg, the Baseball Hall of Fame, a weekend on the beach in Erie, a few days' stop in Pittsburgh. Now plans had changed, we'd spend the whole time on Jeffers Street.

On the day we were to leave New York, Max helped me pack the car. He handed me his Garfield bag for the road, full of things to do in the car—crayons, an Etch-A-Sketch, and thirteen plastic Adventure people, with career-specific plastic vehicles and gear. The ambulance brigade. "In case anything goes wrong," he said.

His school class had a farewell party for him the day before. He'd been fine there, shaking hands with his teachers, sharing Hawaiian Punch and chocolate cupcakes with his buddies. It was only when we got back to the apartment full of packing boxes that he'd cried, told me he didn't want to leave, that if I wanted to go to Philadelphia so much I could go alone. Then he stormed off to his room and slammed the door, spent almost an hour there, while I put the last few things in boxes—the coffee pot, his favorite mug. When I was finished, he came out with red, swollen eyes and said he was hungry, would it be all right if we ordered pizza in. His way of letting me know that he was O.K., that he was with me again.

We sang on the way to Pittsburgh, rounds and Sesame Street songs that Max remembered. A picture of the house I'd rented in Philadelphia was taped to the sun visor on Max's side of the car, the plastic fireman's hat his grandpa gave him three years earlier was on the back seat behind us. Max was glad we were going to Pittsburgh. He kept the Polaroids from his fire-station visit with Edmund on his desk, pleased to have a past, a grandpa, a family he could talk about.

"Mares eat oats and does eat oats and little lambs eat ivy." Max opened his window. His little-boy voice streamed out the open window.

———

It was dark when we drove into the city. Most of the steel mills had been closed years before; their dark hulls clustered bleakly on the banks of the Monongahela River. Streetcar tracks had been paved over, the park where Paul and I had played had been beautified with benches; but the basketball court, what had been the center of Paul's life once, had been let go to ruin. A black boy stood alone in the bright artificial light, sweat-soaked, panting, shooting from the line. Down North Taylor Avenue. The neon Iron City Beer sign flashing in Nick Brennan's window.

On Jeffers Street, there was no porch light, no candle in the window. I pressed my nose against the beveled glass square that was the top half of the front door, peered inside, seeing nothing in the inky darkness. How odd, I thought. I'd talked twice to him in the last week. He knew that we were coming. I tried my key; it didn't work, so I rapped my knuckles hard against the wood.

"Where is he?" Max stood next to me, on tiptoe, peering with me through the glass. "Doesn't he know we're coming?"

"Of course he does," I said, then knocked again. And again. Using my fist when my knuckles got too tender. Finally through the glass I saw a strip of light across the far end of the hall, the edge of the basement door as it swung open. My dad's shadow, then the details of him as he came nearer—squared shoulders, his signature long stride, the mist of white hair bushing up around his head, like an aura or a halo, a pale blur in the blue-black darkness.

"Anne?" He fumbled on the wall beside him for the porch light switch as he opened the door, but the light was burnt out—a sharp click. Nothing.

"Yes," I said. "It's me."

He tried another switch. The vestibule looked dingy in the light cast by a low-watt, dusty bulb.

He was thinner than he'd been when he came to New York.

The collar of his shirt, so neatly buttoned, was too big for his neck. His smile was wan, not very welcoming. I reached up to kiss his cheek.

"Did you forget that we were coming?" I asked, trying to sound cheerful, looking over his shoulder, beyond the vestibule, into the dark house.

"I guess I did," he said. He stuffed his hands into his pants pockets, shook his head regretfully. "It isn't time," he said. "You should have waited."

"Waited for what?" I asked.

But Max couldn't, wouldn't. He stepped between us, ready to be recognized, remembered.

"Grandpa, it's me. Max. I'm big now, but you remember me, don't you?" Max had his plastic fire hat gripped in his fist behind his back. With a toothless grin he sang "Ta da!" then swung the hat around, and put it on.

Edmund's face softened. He bent toward Max, then slowly reached out to shake his little hand. "Well, of course. There's always a place here for firemen," he said. Then he stepped aside and let us in.

It was like entering a museum, a place where relics of a long-forgotten life were on display. I left Max and Edmund in the parlor talking while I walked through the first floor, room to room, as if I'd left something of myself in every corner and was going back, retrieving. The couch where Edmund napped on his days off. The china cabinet and sideboard, the dining-room table he had made, with two leaves for expansion, big enough for seating twenty people, a monument to his pre-nuptial fantasy of a life with friends and food, good conversation. The mirror in the entry hall where Edmund had always checked the tilt of his hat before he went to work each day. Everything the same. But when I went into the kitchen I saw that, in fact, many things were different. China, pots and pans, all evidence of kitchen life had been cleared away to make room for books. Books on countertops, in glass-fronted cupboards, underneath the sink, on the stovetop. *The Manifestations of Karma*, *The Hidden Way Across the Threshhold*, *Metamorphosis of the Soul*. *The Four Great Initiations* so old the edge of the book spine crumbled in my hand.

"So, what else can he sing?" Max's voice from the parlor. The sound of a canary tweeting.

"Schumann IV," Edmund explained when I joined them. "Every time one dies, I think, enough, they're too much trouble, but then I decide the house seems empty without him." Schumann cocked his head and hopped across his perch, then chirped out a tuneful little three-tweet run. Max clapped his hands and begged for more, and Edmund reached his hand into the cage to stroke Schumann's soft head with his index finger.

I closed my eyes and listened to the old familiar sound of Edmund whistling, and Schumann's plaintive answering song.

We put Max's things in Paul's room, mine across the hall in what had been my nursery. In the refrigerator I found eggs for omelettes; I cut mold off the edges of a chunk of cheese, retrieved butter from the freezer. The green Formica table with the matching vinyl-covered chairs was gone, so I took the old card table from the pantry, went through kitchen drawers until I found a tablecloth to cover it. Bright-colored plastic with a Christmas motif, Santa and his reindeer, a string of decorated trees around the border. I brought two candles in wooden holders from the windowsill and lit them.

Edmund ate his omelette greedily. His stacks of books cast long shadows on the walls and ceilings. He kept looking toward the basement door all during dinner and each time he did I wondered what was down there. Max showed his grandpa how good he was at passing his finger quickly through a candle's flame. He filled the silence with his conversation—how his baseball team lost all ten games last season. Everything about his best friend, Daniel, the fact that Daniel's father had a glass eye. Edmund dozed, his chin resting heavily on his chest, and I sat back and let Max talk until all his excess energy was spent and he was sleepy, too.

It was past midnight when I woke Edmund, and got Max and him moving, out of the kitchen toward the stairs. A step behind them, prodding them. Saying, "Up you go, up you go." Thinking I'd get them to bed, then get the flashlight from the car.

There had never been a padlock on the basement door, though there was now. But since it wasn't locked, I told myself I was meant to enter. The stairs opened like a dark well below me. Two steps down, I reached for the simple wooden stair rail. As I did, my arm brushed against the cool damp wall.

The basement had once been an ordered place. Wringer washer and clothesline at one end, woodworking bench and power saws at the other, tools hung precisely from a pegboard nailed to the wall. Now makeshift shelves rose from floor to ceiling, flasks and peanut-butter jars lined every surface, some stuffed with leaves and roots and herbs, some filled with iridescent liquids that glowed jewel-like in the light. There were shoe boxes on some of the shelves, others were stacked in corners, each labeled with Magic Marker—cantharides, assafoetida, essence of the Tonquin bean. Two workbenches, pockmarked, nicked, tainted darkly with what looked like the stain of blood. A dissecting kit was laid out neatly on the Formica table that was missing from the kitchen. Crates and cages filled the basement's narrow end. I heard the sound of birds' wings flapping against bars, small animals scudding about. I aimed my flashlight toward a cage and saw the spread wings of a bat.

I reached for a dangling string and turned on the bare-bulb light that hung from the ceiling, then moved toward the far end of the basement, toward the door that led up to the yard. There I found a small brick oven with a low fire in it, a chimney reaching up and through the ground, a worn-out lawn chair with a poker propped against it. A metal apparatus stood beside the chimney, with still-warm ashes in the bottom, a glass dish suspended just above them, a clear lid arched across the top. A multi-armed contraption looked like a makeshift still.

"You should be asleep. Not wandering around down here."

I jumped and whirled around, dropping the flashlight at Edmund's feet.

"What is all this?" I said, my hand on my chest, my heart pounding.

"Tools for my experiments," he said.

"What kind of experiments? I mean . . . what are all those animals for? And the scalpel and retractor? What is this?"

He was as calm as I was flustered. "An alchemic laboratory," he replied. "A hobby. An occupation for my old age."

"A hobby?" I tucked my hair behind my ears, willed the quiver from my voice. "Woodworking is a hobby, reading is a hobby, *this*"—I gestured around the basement—"is *not* a hobby."

He bent to pick up the flashlight, and there was a coldness about him when he handed it to me—his eyes, his voice, his absolutely steady hand. "Well, in any case," he said, "it's not your business. This is my house, I can do as I like here."

"Look," I said. I could feel a wedge of fear rise in my throat. "I know it's your house. Your business. But I want to understand. What's the point of all this? What are you trying to do?"

"I am trying to achieve the Magnum Opus," he said patiently. "I'm in search of the Philosopher's Stone. The Elixir of Life. I'm going to make myself young again, and then I'm going to bring your mother back to you."

"You're not making sense," I said as calmly as I could. "What in God's name does this have to do with Fanny?"

"She's dead, I know, but with the Red Elixir I can bring her back. I can be a Magus, Anne, and raise her from the ashes."

"Daddy. Please." I reached for his arm. "You don't know what you're saying. Fanny isn't dead. I got a postcard from her just a week ago."

He yanked his arm away. "Of course she's dead," he said urgently. "Don't you remember? Don't you read the paper, Anne? The winter of the snow? The second year you were away? It was your mother, kneeling, waiting for me, begging me to save her. I should have been there, don't you see? Fire was my life, and I let it get away from me. I *let* it destroy her. But I've atoned, I've labored years at this, my penance. And now I'm going to raise your mother from the ashes. She'll be the girl I loved again. Things will be as they were meant to be."

"What?" I whispered hoarsely.

He stepped toward me and dropped his voice as if we were conspirators. "I'll tell you what I know, but you must keep it a secret. All wisdom of this kind is meant to be passed on by word of mouth alone. I've settled on a formula that dates back to 1662. The only problem is, each time you do it, it takes months. And if the fire goes out you have to start again." He shook his head. "It's happened to me twice now. So much disappointment. It's tempered me. This time I've moved down here, that's why I've made that pallet for sleeping. It's also why I practice other magic on the side." He pointed to the birds, the bats, the jars of roots. "To keep my mind alert. To pass the time."

He moved over to what had been his woodworking bench,

rooted around until he found a flask with a cloudy, oily liquid in it. Turning, he offered it to me.

"What's this?"

"This potion will make your freckles go away. You never liked your freckles."

"Dad . . ."

"Also, I know the spell for making someone love you. What to do to understand the song of birds. How to remember everything, how to see what no one else can."

I put my hand out. "Stop."

But he was only getting started. He wanted to show me the book of spells, guide me through the intricacies of his equipment. The more he talked, the more insistent he became. He took me by my shoulders and held me tight, taller by a foot than me, and strong. He wanted me to look at him, to understand.

"Let's go upstairs. Let's talk." A doctor's trick, a distancing defensive thing to say. How stupid I was. He was laying his heart, his hopes, his desperate plans before me, and all I had to offer was a dumb cliché. Ashamed, I heard a tone of labored patience in my voice.

He must have heard it, too, because he slammed his fist down on the workbench. "Don't treat me like some crazed old fool. *I am not mad!* Your mother was the one who was crazy, the one who left."

All that had been seething in him came rising to the surface. It spewed from him. His eyes were wide with it. It flew from his mouth like venom—his spittle in a thin white spray.

He paused, searching for the words to reach me. "Remember me? *I* stayed. *I* waited. First she went off, then Paul went off, then you."

He had me by the shoulders and each time he said "you," he shook me. "You who promised. You who crossed your heart when Paul left. You who swore." I made no effort to resist. I let him scream and shake me. I couldn't think of a single word to say in my defense. It had gone too far for that. He'd lost too much in that old house. "I'm sorry," I finally whispered. Again and again. "I'm so sorry."

When he let me go, he saw that his fingers had left red marks on my arms. Frightened, he brushed his hand across his eyes, as if to clear a cobweb or a troubling thought away. "I don't want to hurt you. But you must leave me alone," he begged.

He reached to a shelf above his furnace for a jar filled with an amber powder flecked with sparkling dust that caught the light. He took some between his fingers, then closed his eyes and mumbled over it before he threw it into the open mouth of his furnace, onto the low flame. There was a sound like thunder, a small explosion of bright light.

"You see." He made a fist and raised his arm. His dark eyes blazed triumphantly. His voice dropped to a low vibrato. "I can do anything. *I am magic.*"

I left him whistling "Scenes from Childhood," stoking his furnace. I moved slowly up the stairs, flipped on the kitchen light, and was about to sit down at the card table when I thought of Max asleep in Paul's room; and in a moment beyond reason I was on my feet, halfway up the stairs, ready to wake him up and run, throw our things into a suitcase, disappear. But on the landing I stopped, trembling, and with an awful clarity realized that that was what Paul and I had done before. This time, I knew, I'd have to do it differently.

I sat down on the top stair, tried to think things through. Did the word "psychotic" occur to me? It did, but I closed my mind against it. This was my father, after all. I'll find a doctor, he'll be given medication, a few days in a hospital and he'll be fine again. Besides, I said to myself, Paul's on his way home now. Everything will be all right when Paul comes home to help me.

———————

Days, even months later, I wondered about the moment when it happened. Was it when Max and I were hanging streamers, preparing for our party in New York? The morning that we left? Or at the moment when my dad called his life what it had been, a sacrifice? I wondered if Edmund felt it like a stab wound to his chest, the way I've heard parents do sometimes. I wondered, Was Paul finally happy, was he in a state of grace? Did it frighten him? The dark-eyed men, the storming of the church, the guns?

I'd gone back to the kitchen, sat there most of the night. The sun had barely risen when the news came in the early morning. First by phone, then by confirming telegram. Father Paul Mueller killed by unknown assailants in El Salvador. Stop. Letter to follow. Stop. Yours in Christ . . .

Stop.

Oh, Paul, I thought. Oh, baby boy. Please, *please* come home to me. Be walking through the park now, be crossing North Avenue, be almost at the door. I'll wait on the stoop for you. Kathleen's gone, I'll have my best stew cooking. Be wounded only, be paralyzed, be in a coma—I'll spend my whole life taking care of you. But don't leave me now, not now, sweet brother. Don't leave me again to manage all the trouble here alone.

I closed my eyes tight, keeping tears back, thinking if I didn't cry someone would call, would take it back, it would turn out not to be true. But when I opened my eyes the telegram was in my hand, and sorrow bore down on me. I stretched my arms out across the table, put my head on them, and gave way to the weeping, to the pain of my breaking heart.

Jake came later that morning, as I had imagined Paul would come, when, as a girl, I stood at the window watching. In priestly black, the white square of his Roman collar at his neck. I knew him from Paul's letters. The beard, the burliness. A battered duffel was on the stoop beside him.

Max had gotten up to find me crying, and for the longest time he stood there mutely, helplessly beside me, patting me awkwardly, on my arm and on my head. Calling me Mommy, wanting me to be myself again, thinking it would happen if he called me by my name. So finally, for him, for his sake, I picked my head up, wiped my eyes. Poured dried cereal into the one chipped bowl I found. Gave Max breakfast, reminded him to brush his teeth, asked him not to go down to the basement. I wasn't sure how or what to tell him, where to begin, so I'd told him nothing. He was playing in the back yard when the doorbell rang. He must have heard it, because before I had a chance to speak to Jake, Max was standing beside me, smiling. I'd told him when I tucked him in the night before that his Uncle Paul was coming.

"What do I call you?" he asked, looking up at Jake. "Uncle? Paul?"

"Father," I said. "Call him Father."

Jake put his hand on Max's head. "My name is Jake," he said. "And you can help me make some tea."

Jake followed me into the kitchen and moved about it easily. "I came because I thought your father was here alone. I didn't think this news should come to a man alone."

Max sat with his elbows on the card table, his chin resting on his hands. Relieved to have another grownup on the scene. His worried eyes fixed anxiously on me. "I like my tea with lots of milk," he offered.

I reached behind a row of books into a cupboard to get mugs. "You don't like tea at all," I reminded gently.

"I want to try it." He watched Jake get out three tea bags. I'd found the top part of an old TV tray and was preparing it to take to Edmund. Toast with melted cheese. Hot tea with sugar. Another mug for Jake and one for me. "All the men are having tea," Max insisted, counting cups. "I want some, too."

Jake pulled out another tea bag.

"Where's Grandpa?" Max asked when I put his mug in front of him. "You said he was sleeping, but I checked, he isn't in his room."

"He's in the basement," I explained. "He and I need to have a talk. You can see him later."

I picked up the tray and moved toward the basement door. Jake stopped me. "I'll tell him," he said. He placed his cup of tea next to Edmund's on the tray. I opened my mouth to say that I should be the one, but something about the firmness of his voice, his lack of hesitation, stopped me.

"Mr. Mueller?" he called out as he started down the stairs. I heard him introduce himself. I heard my father call him "Father." Jake's voice saying, "Yes, of course, I'll bless you."

I closed the basement door and went to Max. I took his tea and blew across it. Then I told him what I knew. About Paul and my dad and the basement. In simple terms a boy could understand. I let him climb into my lap, a thing he rarely wanted anymore. He leaned into me, one ear against my chest, and when I finished I pulled him even closer and pressed my hand against his other ear, wanting to protect him from the wounded wailing cries of an old man cursing God.

Jake stayed a long time in the basement. When he came up, I started down the stairs.

"It's my guess he wants to be alone," Jake offered.

"What did he say?"

"He said he should have started sooner. Then he explained a little to me about alchemy."

"What did you do?"

"Listened."

"What do you think?"

Jake shook his head. "I think that's one hell of a lab he's got down there."

The brown package Jake brought had Paul's things in it. The duffel had his. Both were small, not much in either one.

"It's not much of a life," Jake said by way of explanation.

A breviary, a deflated basketball, two pairs of gym shorts, a Mont Blanc fountain pen. Two hundred dollars cash.

"This is it?"

Jake and I were sitting in the parlor. Jake had picked up the statuette of St. Anselm and was fingering it distractedly.

"There's a small trunk coming. Pictures, letters, clothes."

I spread the flattened basketball across my knee. "What happened? How did this happen?"

Jake lit a cigarette, leaned back in his armchair, spread his long legs out in front of him.

"Paul offered to say Mass that morning. It was my turn, but I'd been sick the night before—fever, chills, and stomach cramps. So he insisted. 'Shut up and go back to sleep,' he said, when I tried to get out of bed. So I did. God help me. I did. The next thing I heard was the gunfire." His voice caught. "There'd been threats," he went on. "But there were always threats. I just never thought . . ." He looked down at the floor. "I couldn't even bear to walk back into that house after I buried him. So I got into the jeep and drove like hell—four hours, straight to the airport. Called the bishop, got on a plane." He leaned his head against the chair's high back and closed his eyes. "He'd told me he was coming here, and that you were going to meet him. I just didn't want you and your dad to be alone."

"I can't believe this," I said, brushing tears away. "It seems impossible to me."

Jake nodded. "I know."

I put Paul's things back in the envelope. "Paul wrote a lot about you in his letters."

"Yeah?" He brightened a little. "I don't think he liked me much at first."

"He liked you fine. I think you just took some getting used to."

He smiled. "A common problem. Or so I've been told."

I heard the murmur of voices. Max talking to Edmund in the basement.

"Max shouldn't be down there." I wiped my face with my hands as I stood up, about to go retrieve him. "It's not safe. He's got chemicals and bats and God knows what."

"If you're worried, I'll go check on them," Jake offered.

"I should go. He's *my* child," I said, defensive, proprietary, half sick with sorrow, claiming the only thing I had left to me.

Jake looked surprised. "Sure he is. But you've had a hell of a day. I'm pretty good with kids. You should go upstairs and get some rest." His dark eyes looked closely at me. He reached out to touch my arm.

My throat tightened. "All right." I nodded thanks, and for the second time that day I let Jake go underground without me.

Even though I thought I couldn't, when I lay across the bed I did sleep, deeply, for a long time. Waking up abruptly when I heard the front door slam. Jake had taken Max to get some groceries.

"I got everything I think you'll need," Jake said when I went down to the kitchen. He was putting tomatoes and lettuce in the refrigerator. Max was stacking canned soup and saltines in the pantry.

"Thanks." I rubbed sleep from my eyes.

Jake had changed clothes and was wearing jeans and a

T-shirt. He was folding the grocery bags he'd emptied. "If I were you, I wouldn't expect your dad to come upstairs tonight. Or anytime soon. He's got his fire going and he means to sit there with it."

Max had gone upstairs to get one of Paul's model airplanes to show Jake.

"What are you going to do about him?" Jake gestured toward the basement door.

"I don't quite know. He needs to see a doctor, but I'm not sure he'll go." I shook my head as if to clear it. My mind was muddled. No coherent thought would take shape in it. "I really don't know," I said again.

Jake scratched his chin. "Look. There's no place I have to be. I'll check into a motel, stay in Pittsburgh for a while. It looks like you could use some help here."

Max was in the doorway with the model plane. "You can stay here," he said. "We've got lots of space."

Jake muttered something about trouble, inconvenience, but I interrupted him before he could finish his sentence. "Yes." I nodded. It would be a new thing for me. Somebody steady. All that help. "That's a good idea. Please. Stay here."

At first I thought Jake would tire fast of the mess he'd stumbled into—the worn-down, damaged house, the quirky people in it. Instead, he made the house a challenge, took care of things that hadn't been tended to in years. He put batteries in clocks and bulbs in lamps, oiled door hinges, cleaned leaves from gutters, patched places in the roof that had leaked mottled stains onto the walls. He weeded Edmund's strange little garden, figured out what were weeds and what were magical herbs, while Max, with a trowel and rusted shovel, dug in the dirt beside him.

Jake's voice echoed in the rooms, more sound than those rooms had heard for a long while. He said hard work took

him out of himself, made him almost happy. He even relieved
Edmund the alchemist, watched the fire for him so that he
could rest, for a short time, on his quilt-covered basement
nest, since no amount of coaxing could make him leave his
fires to come upstairs. Jake was careful and respectful, listened
to him, treated him as if he were someone old and wise.
"Which he is," Jake said. "In his own way."

While we worked on the house, we let Edmund have his
basement life. I knew what I was doing, I knew its name—
avoidance. It was obvious that I couldn't let him stay down
there forever, but I couldn't bring myself to stop him, especially once I talked to him and knew how long he'd planned,
how much this magic meant to him. So I washed his clothes,
took him meals on trays, and sat with him while he ate. Jake
trimmed his hair and helped him shave. I let days go by. The
men spent time together, in the basement, without me; Max
spoke of it importantly. My dad showed Max and Jake his
book of spells; together they tried different potions. Max
spread some of the freckle oil on his cheek and that night he
swore three freckles disappeared. He wanted to try to make
himself invisible, but that required the ear of a black cat, and
he and Jake agreed that they couldn't bear to think of mutilation.

Each day I thought, I'll find a doctor, make a plan tomorrow, and when tomorrow came, I postponed it again.

The first night Jake was there, I couldn't sleep, I supposed
because I had slept so soundly when I napped. So I went to
the kitchen for warm milk and found him sitting at the table,
no lights on.

"Sorry," he said. "My bad habit. Too quiet in the dark."

I turned on the stove light, then held a pan up, offering
him milk. He nodded yes. "So," I said as I lit the burner.
"Tell me about Paul."

"What would you like to know?"

"Everything. What kind of man he was. If he was happy."

Jake leaned forward onto his arms. "Happier lately, I think. But never *really* happy. He tried, God knows. But it was so hard for him. He didn't want to be a priest; he had no natural talent for taking care of people. And really, when you think about it, the fact that it was so damned hard for him makes his efforts that much more moving. More touching. I'm a back-slapping enthusiast—scooping people up; caring for poor souls and sinners comes naturally to me. When Paul cared, he gave pieces of himself away, and he was using himself up. He was too fragile, too finely made for any world, let alone the world of El Salvador. The politics, the intrigue, all that killing. He hated it, he called it the land that God forgot. He lost faith there." He rubbed his hands together. "I don't think I helped him much with that. I'd more or less lost faith myself."

The surface of the milk began to tremble, on the verge of simmering. I rinsed out two of the mugs we'd used for tea that morning, and filled them to their brims. Steam rose from them to mist my face.

I sat in the chair across from him. "It's been so long since I talked to him." I looked down at my milk. "Isn't that awful? My own brother. My own life. And I feel that I just let it slip away from me."

I was wearing cotton pajamas, a matching robe, terry-cloth slippers. The familiar softness of worn cotton, the sweet smell of warm milk. Sometimes when I was a kid Paul and I used to meet in the kitchen this way. An unplanned midnight rendezvous for hot milk and oatmeal cookies. He'd heat the milk, and warn me not to burn my tongue; once, when I begged him, he stood behind my chair and tried to braid my hair for me.

"Now all I have of him are letters." With my fingertip I

traced Santa's profile on the tablecloth. "I want to think that he had friends," I said, "that people loved him. Can you tell me that? Did people love him?"

Jake frowned and hesitated. "I thought you knew," he said. "*I* loved him. We were lovers."

I was bringing my cup up to my lips, and when he spoke, I stopped mid-motion. "No," I said. "I didn't know. He never told me."

"Well, I think he was planning to. When he saw you. He was just getting used to it himself." Jake was watching me carefully, checking my reaction. He reached into his T-shirt pocket for his cigarettes. "That kind of love, *my* love, came as a surprise to him."

I went to the stove to get the pan, refilled our mugs, then sat back down.

"I'm sorry. This whole day I've only been thinking about myself and my dad and—I never thought—about how hard this is for you."

"It is. It was, for both of us. We were in the middle of deciding what to do."

"Do?" I asked.

"Well, after all, we were both priests. We'd taken vows. There were choices to be made. Would we give up God, or each other? How far were we willing to go for love?"

I tucked my slippered feet up under me. "And did you decide?"

Jake lit his cigarette. "Not really." He cleared his throat. "But three days ago the decision was taken out of my hands. Decision by default." He shook his head. "A solution, Annie, that I don't recommend."

Paul's name for me. In spite of everything, it made me smile to hear it.

"And now it's your turn."

"What?" I asked.

"Are *you* happy? Do *you* have a lover."

"I have a child," I said. "I think it's safe to assume that I had a lover."

"Were you in love?"

I hesitated. "Yes."

"Well then?"

"Well then, what?"

"Well then, where is this guy?"

I laughed. "Larry. His name is Larry."

"So?"

"He's in Boston."

"That's a damned fool place to be when you and Max are going to Philadelphia."

"I'm sure Paul told you. In this family, we're not very good at—" I paused. "We fumble a lot, I mean."

Jake raised his mug and finished off his milk. The last of it left a white film on his upper lip, which he wiped off with his hand. "Fumbling doesn't make it bad," he said. "It just makes it complicated."

So we began late-evening talks. Some nights we drank wine; other nights, tea. We never spoke about it or arranged it, but each evening we met there, interrupting ourselves as the hours wore on, to check either on Max or on my dad, coming back to sit longer, to talk into the night.

Jake said he had no family. His mother was dead, his father lived with a topless dancer in L.A. and didn't stay in touch. He said family was something he didn't know that much about. Sometimes he yearned for it. He envied Paul. Letters, pictures, cards from home. I told him everything I knew about Paul. I searched my past, dredged up long-forgotten memories, of cross old nuns, and St. Bart's basketball, and the thick elastic bands festooned with plastic daisies that Paul gave me on my eighth birthday, something pretty for my not-so-pretty hair.

And in those hours while we were talking, the kitchen

seemed to shed some of its shabbiness. The plastic Christmas tablecloth began to look almost festive, the stacks of books on every surface began to seem less menacing, comforting even.

Max wanted to explore the neighborhood. I took him to Lou Lazarra's store only to find that Lou had died, that a man named Barney Klemer owned it now. He gave Max a pickle, just as, years earlier, Lou Lazarra had given one to me. He introduced Max to his son, Dominic, and over ice cream they became new best friends.

We went to the park, the Aviary. I talked about my kid life, shared it. I told him stories about his grandpa, about having a big brother. We played hopscotch on the playground at St. Bartholomew's. The more I talked, the more I told him: how I'd come to leave, about the skies in Texas, the way I met his father, the way his father pushed his glasses up his nose, the fact that he, Max, looked so much like him. Up to then I'd kept my whole life, *his* life, a secret from him. A secret from myself. On those walks, I passed it on. Long walks. We could be gone for hours, because Jake was with Edmund.

"It's a good place," Max said about the city. His grip on my hand tightened. "Did you like it, living here?"

Lucy called in the middle of the second week. The phone had not rung at all up until then, and when it did ring it seemed like a sound from another lifetime—foreign, vulgar, loud. Lucy identified herself as Edmund's "spiritual advisor," but wouldn't offer any more. She deflected my first few questions, and a firmness in her voice kept me from asking more. She had only called, she said, to leave Edmund a message. "Tell him the stars and planets are perfectly aligned. The heavens are in order this time. Tell him."

Edmund smiled and nodded when I gave him Lucy's message, but he kept his eyes fixed on his fire.

"I'm sorry my success will come too late for Paul," he said.

"I'm sorry about Paul, too. But it's not your fault."

"Well, you can say that," he muttered, rubbing his eyes with his hands. "But I think Paul is my fault."

"He was a good man. Jake admired him." I put my hand on his knee. I wanted to choose my words carefully. "Daddy, you must know you can't just stay down here forever."

He reached down, took my hand from his trouser leg, and placed it coldly back into my lap. "I know no such thing," he said. "And as for Jake, I like him fine, but I wonder, why is he staying here? He must have other things to do. Don't they need him back in the missions?"

"I don't think he'll stay much longer. Does his being here bother you?"

"I just don't want him to interfere. He's big, I'll bet he's strong. But I don't want you thinking that he can stop me. As God is my witness, I will not be stopped."

"I see." I reached out again, to take his hand, to touch him. But he was rising from his chair. "How much longer?" I asked softly.

He didn't hear me. He was opening the door to the furnace, looking in. The fire shone with a pale orange light, made his face seem warmer, more alive. Younger. His movements were quicker, his eyes more alert. And as I was there with him, for just a short while I let myself imagine that his experiment was working. That, even as I watched him, he was becoming young again. Young Edmund Mueller, tending fire.

Three weeks turned into four on Jeffers Street. Jake put up screens, sorted through Edmund's woodpile, got rid of what was wet or rotting. And like a castle in a fairy tale after a hundred years of sleep, the house began to come to life again.

Max's toys, laundry drying on the line. Two days of rain followed by sunshine made Edmund's garden grow. Jake showed me how to change the washer on a faucet, how to weatherproof doors and windows, how to make repairs.

"Paul was good at fixing things. I'm surprised he never showed you. You need to know this," he said repeatedly. "Nothing's perfect. Knowing how to mend things is the key."

At the end of the fourth week, Jake suggested that we paint the parlor, something we'd always talked about when I was young. He had opened all the windows and a summer breeze blew in. We could paint the house, he said, as if we were going to stay.

It was Paul's favorite dream when he was growing up, on the days when he let bright hope fill him. He'd stand in the middle of the parlor, hands on his hips, making daring, elaborate plans that mercifully, sweetly included me. He'd pick up paint chips on the way home from school, then fan them, like a riverboat gambler, across the parlor's hardwood floor. We could have any color we wanted, he'd say boldly. "How about ruby red?" he'd ask, and I'd nod happily. "Or a stark and simple white, or eggshell blue." We'll dismantle "The Shrine," he'd say; we'll fling the doors open, invite the neighbors in. We'll have dancing and a party. Or, in our wildest dream, we'd plan escape. We'd run away together. He'd make a boat with his own hands; I'd learn to sew, and make the sail.

"We could paint the walls," Jake said.

Edmund in his basement hideaway. His children upstairs, dreaming.

"What color should we choose?" I asked Jake, pretending. "Stark white? No. How about pale and shimmering gray?"

"Sounds lovely," I said.

"With a slightly darker trim."

"Perfection." Then it was time to break the spell. "He

won't leave here willingly. I can't leave him here like this, and I can't stay indefinitely. I've spoken to a lawyer and two doctors," I said. "I've made arrangements." I felt hot tears on my cheeks.

Jake nodded, his smile disappeared.

"It's just a thirty-day commitment, but they'll start him on medication, he'll get treatment. I can stay here, too, see him every day. He'll get better, maybe he'll be able to come back home again." Such familiar words, spoken so often in this house before. Words fraught with hope. The kind of hope we'd clung to for so long about my mother.

The next day I arranged for Max to spend the night with Dominic. Dominic's mother had said she'd keep Max through lunchtime. That way he wouldn't have to be at home, he wouldn't have to see. Edmund was to be picked up in the morning—an ambulance, three attendants, one of the doctors who agreed to sign the papers. There was no way to tell Max what was going to happen; I'd have to try to tell him later, find a way to help him understand.

Then Jake and I were left to face that final evening in the house. In my parents' bedroom, I packed Edmund's bag. Put fresh paper on the floor of Schumann's cage. In Paul's room, I gave Jake Paul's St. Bart's scrapbooks, trophies from his winning seasons, his letter jacket.

"We should go out for a while," Jake said. Half an hour, fresh air and a walk. "It would be good for you." Edmund was composed and quiet, sure that success was imminent, completely focused on his furnace and his fire. For a short time he'll be fine, Jake said to me.

When I took Edmund his dinner tray, I sat beside him for a minute, looked with him into the belly of the furnace. A large crucible was resting on a nest of bright coals, the oven's floor was thick with hot embers and ashes. His cheeks were flushed, his eyes alive with hope. I knelt in front of him as I spoke, placed my hand on his cheek. "We're going out for just a little walk, some air. We won't be long." It was hot outside but cool in the basement. I put a blanket on his lap and kissed his forehead.

I should have believed him when he said he had magic powers. That he could see what others cannot see. I hadn't said a word to him, but of course he knew. What options had he, really, once he understood what I was planning? To sleep and let himself be led off in the morning? The consistency of the elixir was wrong, the color change occurred too quickly, but it was his last chance, he had to try it. Of course he had to test the seething potion then, that night, to reach into his furnace with his metal tongs for the hot crucible, to pour, with shaking hands, the bubbling red corrosive liquid. In my mind's eye I can see it. Base-metal strips arranged around him, the reflection of the red elixir, red flecks in his dark eyes. And I picture, too, the unexpected stumble over the poker he'd left propped dangerously against the wall. The reaching out to right himself, the hiss of spilling liquid, the coursing of it toward the embers, the whoosh, the flash, the fire's sudden roar.

The night-piercing wail of sirens, the staccato flash of spinning lights. The fire trucks turned onto Jeffers Street as we did, and I looked up as they passed to see the yellow-slickered men lean forward as they rode, strain forward, willing the red steed beneath them to move faster, faster, faster toward the burning house, toward the smoke billowing from doors and windows, oozing through the walls.

Nick Brennan had seen the fiery flash, had made the call. And when they heard Edmund's name, they rose up like avenging angels, this next generation, these men of his engine house. His rescuers, his brothers. A threat to one of theirs?

Vain threat. One of them leaped from the still-moving truck, hooked hose to hydrant; three others broke through the door and disappeared into the house, into the smoke, with hose nozzles and hatchets raised, as I watched, breathless, restrained by Jake from running with them. Calling for him, screaming out his name, begging him to stay with me, pleading, until at last two of the young firemen took shape in the swirling smoke, rose up from it, coming toward me, soot-streaked, panting, bent, but with one of Edmund's arms around each of their necks. Edmund caught up triumphantly between them.

His arms were burned. Your father will be scarred, the doctors said, but not too badly. The whole first floor had smoke and water damage, and while the fire had been confined to the basement, the ruin there was total, his laboratory completely destroyed. When I went to the hospital and told him, he recited to me from the Browning poem "Paracelsus."

> I give the fight up: let there be an end,
> A privacy, an obscure nook for me.
> I want to be forgotten even by God.

"Oh no you don't," I said, taking his face between my hands, forcing him to look at me. "No more pulling back, no more disappearing. We're it now, Daddy. You and me and Max. We've got to do better."

And so we started. I called Philadelphia, said family emergency, I'll need a few more weeks. I stayed in Pittsburgh, went to see him every day, first on the burn unit (where I could take Max with me), then on the psychiatric unit of the hospital. And during those weeks we did do better. Some implicit understanding grew between us. Not so much because of what was said, but because of what was acknowledged, realized, between us. And as a result of that, as he improved, I wanted to take him home, to Philadelphia, with me. But his doctors advised against it, and Edmund, surprisingly, agreed. He liked me fine, he said gruffly, but he thought it would be unwise to drop himself into the center of my life. "We hardly know each other," he pointed out, taking my hand.

He was right, of course. We needed to find a way to talk. So we began. Tentatively, at first, but we kept working at it, even touching finally on the hard things; on the fact that Paul was dead and Fanny gone. But he never, until recently, would share with me the details of his magic.

"Some secrets are best kept," he said.

I nodded. I had secrets of my own.

Before he left, Jake helped me clear away the damage in the house. We freed the bat that had survived the fire, at night, so the neighbors wouldn't see; packed what were left of Edmund's texts and notebooks into boxes. I hired a man with a truck to come to clear away debris, but beyond that, I did nothing to the house. When I left in late September, I put Schumann's cage into the car, pulled the blinds and locked the door behind me. Max pressed his nose to the car window as we crossed the bridge to leave the city.

"Does Grandpa know," he asked, "how much I'm going to miss him?"

From the beginning I went back to Pittsburgh fairly often, visiting Edmund, who after four months was moved from the hospital to a kind of nursing home. ("He needs care," the doctors told me. "Someone to see to it that he takes his medication.") But, for all my Pittsburgh visits, it took two years to go back to the house on Jeffers Street, to sell it, to make decisions about what was worth keeping. Edmund's fire hat and boots, the photo albums, the saints and furniture he'd made. His books on magic. I gathered some things I thought Lucy might like to have, tracked her down and took them to her. Glad to meet her, glad to hear that she went to see Edmund. "We reminisce about the past," she said. She read my tea leaves, did a tracing of my skull.

Philadelphia turned out to be a good place for Max and me. Our house has skylights and tall windows, the most extraordinary light. Jake wrote long letters to us from El Salvador, and each time I wrote back, Max drew a crayon-colored picture to mail with it. Jake waited until a replacement for him could be found, then arranged to take a leave of absence from the priesthood, which eventually turned into a full-blown defection. He took some time, traveled—Italy, Bombay, Bangkok. At first alone, and then, after eight months, with a lover, a man he'd met at a café in San Juan. He promised that he'd bring him home to us, that we could meet him. We were his family now, he wrote. We taped his postcards to our refrigerator. Max learned the word "exotic" to describe the mysteries of distant lands, tacked a giant world map to the wall of his new room.

Our life was good, but I could see that, especially for Max, something was missing. He'd liked the time we'd spent on Jeffers Street with Jake and Edmund. We'd had a kind of family life, a life of tending and repair. I'd learned to share Max. I'd let him join the world of men and magic, a world apart from me. I knew it would be wrong to call him back.

On Columbus Day I wrote to Larry.

Philadelphia is nothing like New York or Boston, not a bit like Texas. But the air is clear, the leaves are turning, it promises to be a lovely fall. It's time for you to come to see your son. And me.

We go to see my father once a month. In between, Max writes long letters to him, and when we're there Edmund introduces Max to all his friends. "This is my boy," he says, and Max allows it. They walk the grounds of the nursing home together, side by side. I fall behind them, listen to the murmur of their man talk. Sometimes Edmund makes rough sketches for my son, of aludels and pelicans, and other tools of magic. Max listens to him carefully; he keeps a notebook full of sketches, spells, and formulas.

My dad and I know each other better now. Sometimes when I visit he takes my arm, sometimes I take his. We walk the grounds. Noon is his favorite time of day, he likes the blazing, warming sun. "We play a lot of checkers here," he says. "I like that. It reminds me of the fire station, it's a little like it was then, men together, passing time. Waiting to be called."

BOOKS IN THE HARVEST AMERICAN WRITING SERIES

Diana Abu-Jaber
Arabian Jazz

Daniel Akst
St. Burl's Obituary

Tina McElroy Ansa
Baby of the Family
Ugly Ways

Kathleen Cambor
The Book of Mercy

Carolyn Chute
The Beans of Egypt, Maine
Letourneau's Used Auto Parts
Merry Men

Harriet Doerr
Consider This, Señora

Laurie Foos
Ex Utero

Barry Gifford
Baby Cat-Face

Diane Glancy
Pushing the Bear

Donald Harington
Butterfly Weed
The Choiring of the Trees
Ekaterina

David Haynes
Live at Five
Somebody Else's Mama

Randall Kenan
Let the Dead Bury Their Dead

Julius Lester
And All Our Wounds Forgiven

Sara Lewis
But I Love You Anyway
Heart Conditions
Trying to Smile
and Other Stories

Lawrence Naumoff
The Night of the Weeping Women
Rootie Kazootie
Silk Hope, NC
Taller Women

Karen Osborn
Patchwork

Mary Lee Settle
Choices

Jim Shepard
Kiss of the Wolf

Brooke Stevens
The Circus of the Earth
and the Air

Sandra Tyler
Blue Glass

Lois-Ann Yamanaka
Wild Meat
and the Bully Burgers